OUR SECRETS DIE WITH HER

OUR SECRETS DIE WITH HER

SIMBI FEYISARA

ISBN: 978-1-917217-03-3

For Randi and Robbi

ONE

A wail of sirens pierced the room. Flashes of red and blue illuminated the walls, casting shadows across the pale, lifeless figure slumped on the bed opposite me. Sunken eyes bore into the ceiling, unmoving. Then they blinked—because Dani wasn't dead. I just wished she was.

The walls pulsed; music and jeers clashed with the sirens. The dorm room filled with the scent of a house party—traces of sweat and vomit. I had planned to be out of The Bells before the party started, but there was one thing I couldn't leave without—my cell phone. I turned my back to Dani to lift my pillows and pull back the duvet. I didn't think it would miraculously appear, but I had already checked the bathroom and every corner of our dorm room. Well, I hadn't looked through Dani's side, but there weren't many hiding places. In fact, there were fewer than usual. Gone were Dani's photos, candles, and fairy lights. She had no study books. I doubted if she had opened a book or done an assignment herself. She had people to do them for her. Only her gold swimming trophies and medals remained, bundled under her desk, along with a few hair products scattered on top. And although the bruise was fading, looking at the chipped wood on the white matte finish, I still felt the soreness on my hip from my latest attempt to take back the clothes she had stolen. Today, I'd been forced to wear a mocha-colored dress a few shades lighter than my skin.

I dropped my bedding and took a sharp breath as my eyes roamed to Dani's closet. A bathrobe hung off the door, obscuring the contents, my clothes likely among them. I could picture my cell phone there. I stepped toward it.

Dani turned to face me, smiling as smooth brown hair fell on her face, the strands almost instinctively avoiding her eyes. Green irises trailed me around the room, as they always did, wide-eyed and looking for secrets. It was how Dani knew my cell's four-digit PIN and how she'd managed to go through my messages, contacts, and photos. She had never admitted to it, but it was the only way she could know the things she did.

I had a clear recollection of placing my cell phone on the bed. I lifted the sheets once more, and Dani's gaze followed. I bit down on my lip, accepting that I would have to leave without my cell phone. I made my bed, angling pillows and tucking in sheets. I had no intention of coming back if things went well tonight. I picked up my jacket folded over my desk chair.

The sirens stopped. Screams and laughter grew louder, and the smell of smoke mixed in the stagnant air. Dani leaped up and stepped onto my bed, ruffling my freshly made sheets and toppling my carefully stacked pillows to the floor. She climbed onto my desk and rested a knee and dirty sneaker on my study notes. She leaned out the window, and I fought the urge to shove her out of it. I scoffed, gesturing to the perfectly functional window on her side of the room, but she didn't notice. She didn't even open it, coughing heavily into the crook of her elbow before her deep-set eyes tracked movement below, neck craned, and shoulders hunched.

I took the chance. My body was drawn to Dani's side of the room. I moved cautiously, making sure Dani was still perched on the windowsill. I pulled back her cover, exposing wrinkled sheets that didn't quite reach the edge of the mattress. A slip of paper peeked out from beneath the corner of her pillow. *Sherwood Station* was written in bold for two out-of-state tickets tonight. No return. My hands instinctively reached for the tickets. Then the silver case of my cell phone caught my eye.

Heat surged through my body. Dani had watched me search for half an hour while leaning on the very thing I needed. I tapped the screen awake. Blocked, with one minute remaining. At least she hadn't worked out the new passcode, but now her smile had a new meaning.

"Dani," I called, a sharp edge in my voice.

She didn't move, her lips a thin line. Her skin was tinged red. Her glazed eyes were focused on something outside. I stepped toward her, my cell phone clutched in my hand.

She started. In a swift motion, she jumped down from the desk, pulling the blue tartan curtain closed. The room darkened. Her cheeks were flushed, and sweat lined her forehead. She looked at the cell phone and smiled, her teeth gleaming. Dani cocked her head. "You changed your passcode."

Rage brewed in the pit of my stomach. She wanted a reaction. Every part of me screamed to give her one.

"Sienna, you should know better than to leave things lying around." Dani's eyes were wide with amusement. She stepped slowly toward me as she returned to her side of the room. She wiped her forehead and leaned back on her bed.

I ignored her. My head was pounding from the heat. I walked to the window and reached for the curtain.

"Leave it closed." Dani was propped up on her elbow, an unusual note of panic in her voice. "Please."

I wanted to rip open the curtains to spite her, but I held my arm there. "What's gotten into you?"

"Nausea." She settled back into the bed, massaging two fingers against her temple, and forced a lazy smile. "I'm sure it'll pass once you leave." She pulled her pillow forward, obscuring the tickets.

"Looks like you're the one going somewhere."

She leaned back against the pillow. "You know, I've always admired your wishful thinking."

I dropped my hand, took my jacket, and angled my cell phone out of view as I typed in my passcode, earning a smile from Dani.

The screen flashed with a message from Tyrell: *Am I supposed to believe it's only a coincidence you're late when I pick the movie?*

I couldn't contain the smile that spread as I clicked to respond.

"So, that's still going on," Dani remarked. "That explains where you were last night."

I slid the cell phone into my pocket. "I don't know what you're talking about."

Dani didn't bite. She pulled a blue gym bag from under her bed. "Oh yeah. You can have back those clothes you lent me."

I looked at the ceiling, taking a deep breath, before walking over to retrieve the pile of clothes Dani had stolen. I inspected them, threw mine into a bag, and folded the rest over my desk chair. I would find their owners later. There was another bag under Dani's bed. Half open, it held bundles of sweaters, dresses, and skirts. Some were rolled and tucked in neatly; others looked as though they had been thrown in. Dani followed my gaze and kicked the bag farther beneath her bed.

"Don't worry. None of it's yours." She squinted, her eyes lit with a twinkle of mischief. The door rattled, and the look of amusement quickly disappeared from her face.

"What's up with the door?" I asked, moving toward it.

Dani wiped at the sweat on her forehead. "I locked it."

As my biggest threat was already living in the room with me, I had never taken to locking the door, and neither had Dani, until today.

"Dani, I know you're in there."

I rolled my eyes at the familiar shrill voice, unlocked the door, and let it swing open.

Our housemate, Ainsley, stood there with a hand on her hip, her thick braids cascading over one shoulder, her dark skin covered in shimmering gold makeup. The air was thicker. In the dim haze behind her, bodies packed the hallway, singing loudly.

Ainsley wedged a foot in the gap. "Where are you going?" She scanned my outfit with disgust.

"The choices were between this party and Dani, so I've found something better to do."

Dani scoffed, a newfound confidence in her tone. "I still think you could aim higher, Monroe."

My body stiffened, the way it always did when I heard that name. I swallowed quickly, lowering my head and stepping back to let Ainsley in. The weight of two pairs of eyes on me was heavy. Ainsley's sparkled with recognition. She knew Dani was playing with a secret.

There was a sudden roar from the party—the guests were seemingly impressed with the DJ's latest offering—but the silence here was deafening.

Ainsley still stood by the threshold, impatience etched on her face. She stepped aside. "Get out."

I took my bag with my clothes. "Only since you asked so nicely," I muttered and passed. If it was strange that Ainsley was kicking me out of my own room, I didn't care. In the stuffy air of the hall, I glanced back at Dani. Something haunting was in her expression. Shoulders back, chest out, she held that familiar playful grin. Then Ainsley kicked the door shut, rattling the bronzed number four.

The four dorm rooms of The Bells were confined to a single rectangular hallway, with one room on each side of the walls. The common room was on the left, and the kitchen was on the right. People I had never seen before flowed between the rooms, dancing and singing. At the back, next to my dorm room, was a small utility room. I opened the door and dropped my clothes inside before weaving through bodies in the hall. I had never been to a party at Stedmond, and it didn't fill me with confidence that Ainsley had shared the entrance key code to The Bells with half the campus.

I made it to the lobby, where the air was lighter because the door was propped open by a fire extinguisher. Its contents had been fired over an unsuspecting victim, who was passed out on one of the plush chairs.

I stepped into the cold and shrugged on my jacket. The police car was gone. The police had been regular visitors at The Bells since the death of Alex, a student from Stedmond, had forced the college to at least look as though they were taking the war on drugs seriously.

"Hey, Sienna." Bianca, one of my roommates, was climbing the steps to the entrance. She was still in her gym clothes. Her deep-brown curls were damp, and the faint smell of chlorine lingered on her. Even if she wasn't just coming from swim practice, something told me she would have looked out of place at this party. "Have you seen Ainsley?" She folded her arms across her chest. "I wanted her to do something about the noise."

"Good luck." I held back a laugh and hoped for her sake the music couldn't get any louder. "She's in my room with Dani."

"Dani?" She blinked, arms tightening around her. "Is she feeling better? She said she was too ill to go practice."

Dani was the best on the swim team. But talent didn't equal likability. Her flu was probably the best thing that had happened to the team in a while.

"Don't worry, you still have a bit longer without her."

Bianca blushed. "No, I didn't mean—" She shook her head. "Are you staying?"

"As tempting as that sounds... I have already made plans."

Bianca swallowed. "Okay, then I'll see you later."

Stedmond College was once a prestigious institution, but now it was plagued with drugs, cheating, and death. Pathways connected the various facilities, main buildings, and residential areas. The Bells was on the edge of campus.

I walked down the steps and through the parking lot. Streetlights towered the usually deserted parking lot. Crushed soda cans and cigarette butts lined the ground. As I waded through the narrow rows, I heard the thunk of a car door hitting another, then an alarm filled the air. At the edge of the parking lot, there were two routes. One pathway led farther into campus, and the second followed a dimly lit alley to Stedmond Park.

It was the light that pulled me in that direction—casting one shadow along the cracked sidewalk. I recognized the straw-like hair as belonging to Jamie, Dani's ex-boyfriend. His hands jerked, and he leaned through the open window of a silver sports car. The headlights were too bright for me to see the driver. Jamie was shouting, his jaw tense, and veins pulsed in his neck. I couldn't make out any words above the muffled noise of the party. He moved back, pulling at his hair, looking frantic. The car jerked forward, and Jamie lunged. He banged on the hood then clasped at the door handle, trying to force it open. When that didn't work, he put his arm through the window.

"Let go," I called. I was moving now, my breath hitching as my feet hit the ground.

Jamie was trying to grab something. I opened my mouth to shout to him, but I wasn't fast enough. The window flew up, trapping Jamie's arm. The car sped up, dragging him. His face reddened from the effort as he fought to free himself.

He did and smacked to the ground then tumbled. The car tires screeched, and the engine roared as it sped off. I felt the rush of wind as it passed me in a blur.

"Are you okay?" I called, crossing the street.

Jamie threw a fist on the ground. "Do I look okay?" He propped himself onto his elbow and groaned. Small scratches were carved into his reddened skin.

I paused in the middle of the darkened road. "Do you want me to call someone?"

He shook his head. I didn't know exactly who I was offering to call. Jamie didn't have friends. It was always him and Dani. They'd been inseparable... until she left him for Michael.

"What about the police?"

Irritation flashed on his face. "I fell," he said through gritted teeth, wincing as he pushed himself up. He brushed at his clothes. Blood seeped from his split lip.

"That's an interesting way of putting things."

"We both know you don't care."

"Who was in the car?"

"A friend."

"Seemed like it."

He inhaled sharply. "People fight when they care about each other. Speaking of which, how's Dani?"

"Still with Michael."

"Ouch." He threw a hand to his chest. He masked it well, but the slight clench of his jaw revealed what everyone knew. He wanted her back. "It won't last," he said confidently, looking over his shoulder at the iron gates and greenery of Stedmond Park. "I'm going to stay here. Don't let me stop you from your date."

"It's not a date." Heat rushed to my cheeks.

He laughed as I turned and walked away, the sound becoming strained as he broke into a cough.

Tyrell and I were acquaintances. I wasn't built for relationships. Tyrell was convenient for the only thing I needed —an excuse to escape The Bells. Screams and music quietened as I moved against the flow of people heading away from the center of campus. The library and main buildings were empty, with only a few lights on. The presence of security increased as I got closer to Platinum. I'd begged Mom to stay somewhere like this. Everyone had their own room, and there was a reception desk and an indoor cafeteria. Mom insisted it was important not to be isolated and to make as many friends as possible after all the unfortunate things that happened. That was how she described all my friends turning their backs on me and our neighborhood hating us. Not that I blamed them. But now I was stuck with housemates who felt the same way.

I leaned against the pole at the gates to the building and messaged Tyrell to let him know I was downstairs.

He appeared moments later, his full lips spread in a grin, his hands tucked into his bright-blue puffy jacket. "Hey. We could skip the movie tonight. I heard there's a party not to be missed on campus."

I gave him a warning look. "Not funny. Plus, I think Ainsley would combust if she saw me having fun at one of her parties."

"Now, that would be fun to see." Tyrell withdrew his

hands from his pocket, and for a moment, he paused. I thought he was going to go for a hug.

I stepped back as he gestured to the Platinum parking lot. *Not a hug.* I bit down on my lip and fell into step beside him, masking my disappointment.

"It would at least be more entertaining than robots turning into zombies?"

From the crease in Tyrell's brow, I knew this wasn't exactly the premise of the movie he'd suggested. His lips parted, and he hesitated for a moment, as if considering whether to take the bait. Then he sighed and scratched the small scar on his brow, as he always did before he went into one of his rants. "They aren't robots. They are artificial intelligence agents, and they don't turn into zombies. They—"

I covered my lips to stifle my laugh.

He raised a brow, opened his mouth, then closed it again, smiling. "I'm glad you find the apocalypse funny." He pressed his key card to the gates of the parking lot. The Bells was not important enough to have a gate. "We can watch something else if you want."

"And miss the opportunity for me to inaccurately recall everything for my own amusement?"

He held open the gate and rolled his eyes playfully.

I stepped through. "It's fine. Anything is better than being at The Bells."

The car chirped as Tyrell unlocked it. "That bad?"

"I spent half an hour looking for my cell phone, which Dani stole."

"Really? Even after the way you scared her off last week." He brushed a hand over his low fade.

I cocked my head.

He bit back a smile. "I know everyone else thinks you lost the fight, but as your—"

An unspoken word hung in the air. *Friend? Something more?* My chest tightened. I wished he had finished the sentence. I needed to know he understood that this wasn't going anywhere. It couldn't.

"I know you were just holding back." He finished quickly, ducking his head into the car before I could read his expression.

"And I have the bruises to prove it," I muttered, following his lead and entering the car.

It hadn't been much of a fight, and I'd fallen back into the desk, but according to everyone else, Dani had battered me to a pulp.

Tyrell pulled at his seat belt. "I'm glad to know Dani took your cell phone. For a while, I thought you were blowing me off."

An unsettling feeling clawed at my stomach. "No. Just Dani being Dani."

I spent two hours of the movie wishing the apocalypse would come and put me out of my misery, and fifteen minutes questioning my sanity as Tyrell raved about the movie on the way back to the parking lot. "With that ending, there will have to be a part two."

It almost sounded like a threat. "Sorry, I think I've made plans to spend the whole day with Dani."

"Well, if the movies aren't your thing," he teased.

"No, just that movie in particular. Or pretty much any of the movies you make me watch," I amended.

We weaved through a row of cars until Tyrell stopped by his. "You mean you're not hanging out with me for my love of movies?"

"No. You're lucky everything else about you is great."

He paused, running a finger through the slit in his brow.

I hadn't meant to say it aloud. I cleared my throat. "What happened to your eyebrow?"

He unlocked his car and smiled. "I was five and trying to get the last cookie. Unfortunately, so was my sister, and the dinner table was on her side."

I opened the door and entered. "You didn't get the cookie?"

"No." He put the key into the ignition. "But I got two stitches, so who's the real winner?"

"Katelyn," I said with surprising speed.

Tyrell had talked about his whole family, which also included his brother and parents, so much that it felt as though I knew them.

"You remind me of my sister sometimes."

I raised a brow. "Really? How?"

"She hates the movies I watch too. What about you? Tell me something about your family?"

I wanted to give him something, but the first memory that came to mind was the police knocking on the door. I tucked my arm against my body and sighed. "We're not as close as yours."

He opened his lips as though he wanted to ask more but thought better of it. It wasn't the first time he'd asked about my family, and answering was getting harder to avoid.

"How do you feel about the police commissioner campaign?" he asked, pulling his seat belt over himself.

I drew my head back, confused, but grateful for the change of subject. "The one Ainsley's dad is running for?"

He nodded.

I put on my seat belt. "Indifferent."

"For my next research project, I am going to follow the candidates and interview students to see how they are influenced. You up for it?"

"What would I have to do?"

"Keep up-to-date with all the latest news, and I'll interview you and other participants to see if or how your view changes as the election goes on. I'd send you different news—"

"How long would this take?"

"It would be from now until the results in a few months."

"Oh. It sounds like a great project," I said slowly, something sinking in my stomach. I'd let things get too far. Now he was making plans months from now.

"Just not one you would be interested in?"

I wet my lips. "I don't think, um… It wouldn't be a good idea. I… Maybe you could ask Jamie," I stammered. "He was by The Bells. He was arguing with someone, and they almost ran him over."

Tyrell blinked. "You can tell me if you don't want to do it."

"It's not that. It's just—"

"You don't know where we'll be a few months from now," Tyrell finished.

I kept quiet, swallowing the lump in my throat. I should

have stopped it because there could never be a future. And now he knew too. I braced myself as he parted his lips. He was going to do what I should have done a long time ago.

"I know we haven't had the discussion about us. But I just thought things were going well enough for us to plan things in the future."

He wasn't breaking things off. I expected to feel relieved, but my throat tightened. "When did you decide that?"

"It's not something I decided," he said carefully.

I bit down on my lip. When given enough time, everyone turned their back on me. When they got to know me enough, they didn't like what they saw. I wasn't going to be able to keep Tyrell at arm's length anymore.

He took a deep breath. "Things have been going well. I'm happy with us jus—"

"There is no us." I unbuckled my seat belt and scrambled for the door handle. "I'll find my own way back." I opened the door. "Good luck with your project, and thanks for everything. I appreciated the distraction."

His jaw went slack. "Distrac—" He scoffed. "Okay. So, this is the part where you push me away."

I slammed the door and heard shouts of my name. Something inside me was begging me to turn back. With every step, my heart felt like it was shrinking, which was perfect. I wasn't capable of love.

I passed through the parking lot, my feet sore from the walk in the cold. I expected to be met with a heavy stare, but there was nothing. The Bells had been deserted; only wreckage left behind. The wind picked up, amplifying the sound of clattering empty cans and bottles in the parking lot. I shifted on my feet and looked up at the drawn curtain. Sometimes, it felt like Dani could see through me. With one look, she would know something had happened with Tyrell. She wasn't there, but something was off. The curtain flapped with the wind. The window was broken, and only a few fragmented shards remained.

I quickened my pace, and a weight in my chest increased as I flew up the steps to The Bells entrance. I pulled away the fire extinguisher, and the door slammed with a heavy thud. The lobby was empty. Cold seeped into my bones, and I wrapped my arms around my middle. I walked to the hallway, and the corridor bulbs lit up over-head as I followed a trail of empty cans, bottles, and popcorn ground into the carpet. The air was a sickly mix of sweat and aftershave. The house felt different, hollow. I tightened the hold on my body in a futile attempt to stop the churning. The house was a mess because of the party.

Dani was leaving. Maybe the broken window was her parting gift, and the tightness in my chest was because of Tyrell. *I should have agreed to do his project.*

As I walked through the hall, my footsteps were the only sound. I brought out my key card, remembering how Dani had locked the door earlier, but it wasn't needed. The handle clicked, and the door swung back with ease. A small offering of light from the hall cast the room in shadows. Wind ripped through the room. Disappointment raced through me.

Dani was on the edge of her bed, not on her way out of state. The door slammed closed, and the curtain flapped, allowing through flashes of moonlight. Something was wrong. Dani didn't stir. A metallic taste filled the air.

"Dani?" My voice shook. My eyes darted around the darkness, looking for any subtle movement. I flicked the light switch, and my hand came back reddened and wet.

Light flooded the room. My body tensed. Dani lay slumped unnaturally. Her emerald eyes were vacant. Lips, normally upturned in a cunning smile, were parted and covered in blood.

I stepped back, shallow breaths coming hard and fast, but my body refused to take in any oxygen. Nausea raced through me. My whole body was numb.

Dani was dead.

TWO

"Hi, Sienna." A tall man dressed smartly in all black leaned forward onto the kitchen table and gestured to the chair opposite him.

I sat. My hands shook uncontrollably until I pushed them under my thighs.

"I am Detective Collins. I will be conducting your interview."

I nodded. The kitchen table was the only surface that looked remotely clean, but it was as though it had been wiped in a rush. Dry streaks lined the table, and a few crumbs were left in the corners surrounding a half-empty glass of water and a desk light lamp borrowed from the common room. I squinted through to see the rest of the room. Trash overflowed from the garbage can. Bloated chips and popcorn floated in the blocked sink. Shards of glass had been swept into a corner, and the bulb from the kitchen light was missing.

Collins cleared his throat. "I know it can't be easy after

what you have experienced tonight. I appreciate you talking to us."

He said it as though I had a choice. My roommates had been brought in here one after the other while I tried to understand what I had seen, wrestling with the rising panic because the police were coming for me. Well, to me. This wasn't the first time they'd wanted to speak to me in relation to a murder, but this time, Mom wasn't sitting beside me, a firm hand on my knee. The gesture had probably seemed like reassurance, like a loving mother comforting her daughter. Only I had noticed as she squeezed and pinched when my answers weren't good enough or I wasn't sticking to the story. She always said that the police were the reason for our broken family. I never disagreed because the alternative would be to blame me. Strangely, I wished she was here so I didn't have to go through this alone.

"This is my partner, Detective Shelley." Collins gestured to the narrow-nosed woman beside him. A couple of hours ago, she had collected my clothes and offered me something to change into, a small act of kindness as the bloody brown cotton clung to my body and burned my skin. We didn't speak, but her presence was the reminder I needed that all of this was real. Having her here now should have been calming, but her smile didn't quite reach her eyes.

"Hi," I breathed, my gaze focused on the table. They felt too close, their sharp eyes too invasive. I took a deep breath, my heart rattling in my chest as I pushed back. A screech filled the air as the legs of my chair scraped along the floor tiles.

Collins raised a brow, searching my face.

"Sorry," I muttered, gazing at the window. I was about to ask the detectives to open it when Collins spoke.

"I understand that you were the person who found Dani and called the ambulance." He clicked his pen, and his hand clasped around a notepad angled out of view.

I fought the urge to crane my neck and nodded.

"And when did you last see Dani?"

I swallowed. "Before I left, around ten, she was in bed. In my roo—our room," I amended quickly.

Collins made a note of something. "And how did she seem?"

I thought about that for a moment. It didn't seem like the time to mention that Dani was up to her usual tricks and had stolen my phone or that we'd had another of our many disagreements. "Normal."

"What constitutes as normal for Dani?"

I tried to wet my lips, my mouth dry. "She was lying in bed, avoiding the party."

"And where were you between ten and five?" He clicked the tip of his pen against his lips.

I swallowed hard. "I went to watch a movie, and then I went for a walk."

Another note. "And is there anyone else who can verify your story?"

I squeezed my fingers around my thighs. I had already decided I was going to leave Tyrell out of it. He didn't deserve to be interrogated or involved in any of this. I knew how the police could twist things. My chest tightened as I remembered his face when I walked away. "No," I croaked. "I went alone. I still have the ticket in my jacket if you need to see it."

"Okay," he said in a low voice and scribbled in his notepad. I looked to Detective Shelley. Her arms were folded over her stomach, and her eyes unwavering. Did she doubt what I was saying?

My throat felt uncomfortably dry. I grabbed the glass on the table with a shaky hand. I wasn't sure if it was for me or one of my housemates who'd been interviewed before me, but I gulped down the stale water.

Collins cleared his throat. "Did you speak to Dani before you left?"

"No. Not really. I was hardly in the room."

"Hmm." He breathed into his pen and lowered it to his lips.

I braced myself for the click, but he pulled away. "And when you were in the room, what did the two of you talk about?"

I pulled at the neckline of my dress. "Umm, she gave me some of my clothes that she had sto—borrowed. I left them in the utility room before I left." I remembered how much everything had changed only a few hours ago.

Dani had been as nosy and evasive as always. She knew everything about everyone while revealing nothing about herself. But there was something different about the way she'd acted. "I think she was leaving," I said. "She had two tickets for out of state under her pillow and a bag packed under her bed. When I tried to ask her about it, she didn't answer."

Collins hummed under his breath, and I tried to remember if the bag was there when I came back.

"Was that unusual behavior for Dani?"

"No. She only ever left The Bells to stay with her boyfriend."

"And who is that?"

"Michael. I don't know his last name. But he goes to Stedmond, as well."

"Did Michael ever come to The Bells?"

"Sometimes he would sneak in but never stayed the night."

"Sneak?" Collins asked.

Heat flushed the back of my neck. "Yes. He's an ex of Nia, one of our housemates."

Collins noted something down. I didn't mention the overlap between the two relationships, and while Michael may have sneaked, Dani wasn't half as considerate.

"How was Dani when you left?"

"She was fine. Ainsley came and said she wanted to talk to Dani in private, so I left."

Detective Collins tapped his pen on the notepad, scanned his notes, and looked up. "This is when you went alone to the movies and then for your walk?"

I nodded, ignoring the note of suspicion in the way he'd said it.

"And describe what it was like when you came back?"

I squeezed my hands between my thighs to stop the shaking. "She was dead."

I tried to shake the image of Dani lying there, her mouth open. I could have almost believed she was mid-sentence, about to make a witty remark, if not for her reddened skin and the bloody tears in her sweater. When I knelt beside her, my fingers searching for a pulse, I'd noticed it was actually my sweater. Seconds had passed, and my trembling body understood before I could.

My stomach churned, hot liquid rushed through my throat, and the skin around my neck tightened as I relived the moment. "I tried to feel for a pulse," I said. "But there was just so much blood. It looked like she had been stabbed, and she had slits in her skin." I raised my hand to my neck. "It was too late." I sniffed, and tears rolled down my cheeks.

Shelley drew her chair in closer and reached a hand across the table. "What did you do next?" she asked in a soft tone.

Heat rushed to my head. "I threw up. I couldn't breathe. There was all this blood on me." I remembered the sensation of wanting to claw at my skin and fought back tears that laced my lashes. "Then I called the ambulance."

Collins paused and allowed me to take a slip of water. "Did you notice anything different about the room?"

I looked up to find the detective eyeing me closely.

"The window was broken, and it was messier than usual, but I didn't check for anything."

"Does anyone else have access to The Bells?"

"To get into the building, you need a code. It's mainly for the cleaners, and it changes every week. We're not supposed to give it out, but Ainsley sent it out for the party. For our rooms, we all have key passes, but we don't always lock our doors. Dani was always losing her key pass, and we figured we were safe because we have the furthest room. We never thought anything like this would happe..." I trailed off and buried my head in my hands. Anyone could have walked in and killed her. "Wait, tonight she did," I said thoughtfully, sitting up straight. "The door was locked when Ainsley tried to come in."

Collins made a note. "And do you remember if it was locked when you returned?"

I remembered the blood and her cold body first, then I thought back and lowered my head. "No." I sighed. "It was unlocked."

"Was there anything that looked like it could have caused that harm to Dani?"

Tightness spread through my chest as I shook my head.

"Did you see anyone else when you entered the dorm?"

I shook my head.

"And did you have any problems with Dani?"

My head shot up.

Collins's face was passive, as though he hadn't just completely changed the line of questioning.

A hard lump formed in my throat. "We didn't always get along. We had disagreements in the past, but she didn't deserve to die. Not like this."

Collins hummed his agreement. "Did any of those disagreements ever become physical?"

I blinked. He already knew the answer to that. "Yes." He had probably already heard a version of the story from the other housemates he had interviewed. "Last week, she had taken some of my clothes. I tried to pull them off her, and I fell back into a table when I lost my grip. It wasn't really a fight."

"It must have been difficult sharing a space with someone who didn't respect your things."

I stayed silent. It wasn't a question.

"Can you think of anyone who had any problems with her?" He folded up his notebook and dropped his pen. "Anyone who would have a reason to want her dead?"

I took in a deep breath. "I don't know anyone who would have wanted her dead, but Dani wasn't always the easiest person to be around. She ruffled a lot of feathers, and I think maybe she just pushed someone too far."

"Anyone in particular you can think of?"

Five of my housemates sprang to mind. None of them had seemed fazed a few hours ago when Collins escorted me into the common room.

Red cups and empty bottles littered the long oak coffee table. Shelley was stationed in the corner by the pool table, wet with questionable liquids. The rest of my housemates were sitting on the nude sofas in the center of the room. They sat up straighter as we entered. The sandy-brown walls seemed to close in as their eyes leaped between my tear-streaked face and the police officers, waiting for an explanation.

"What's happened?" Raven asked finally. Her hair was split down the middle and gathered into two buns—one electric blue, the other black.

Either Collins hadn't heard or had chosen to ignore her, because he walked over to Shelley and leaned close to whisper something in her ear. Eyes trailed him, and I fell into the sofa beside Bianca. The damp chair pressed against my exposed skin, but I didn't care. Nothing could be worse than the blood.

"Where's Dani?" Bianca asked. She had changed out of her gym clothes. The ends of her green dress were scrunched in her hands. She curled and uncurled a fist, her eyes searching mine, then moved around the room. The other girls looked up, too, noticing for the first time that one of us was missing. Then they turned to me for answers; the unmistakable truth was already on my face and staining my skin.

Detective Collins stepped into the center of the room, capturing everyone's attention as he spoke. "Dani Bishop is dead."

Bianca gasped, covering her mouth with trembling fingers.

Collins towered over us, looking at each face in turn. Bianca cowered on the edge of the sofa, avoiding eye contact. Nia played with her hair, jaw tensed. Martina's fingers tightened against the book on her lap. Raven stifled a yawn, and Ainsley, the last person I knew had seen Dani alive, stared straight at me, something unreadable behind her dark eyes.

Collins's voice snapped me back to the present. "No one you can think of?"

I blinked. The kitchen came back into focus. The two detectives were waiting for an answer.

I pressed my lips together. My gaze fell to the floor. "No."

"Okay." Collins turned to Shelley with a questioning look. She gave a slight shake of the head, and Collins pushed his chair out. "Thank you for your time. I appreciate it. We will be in touch if we have any more questions."

I stood up, eager to leave and wash the blood off myself.

"Oh, Sienna," Collins called.

I spun around, my heart in my mouth.

He slid something across the table. "Here's my card. Give me a call if you remember anything that may help the case."

THREE

No one was prepared for the aftermath of death. Sleep was out of reach. Even if I didn't close my eyes, the scene replayed. Dani sprawled out, bloody and unblinking. Dead. The orange of daybreak flooded through the common room window. In my lap, I clutched a bag filled with the few essentials the police had allowed me to bring. I wasn't allowed back into the dorm, but I could still see it. I knew they had taken the body, but she would always be there.

Breaking news appeared in bold at the bottom of the TV screen. Police lights flashed. A lady clutched a microphone while her hair and clothes thrashed in the early-morning breeze. Positioned in front of The Bells, she addressed the camera.

"The body is confirmed to be twenty-year-old Dani Bishop. Although no arrests have been made, police are treating this as a murder investigation."

Bianca hands cupped her face. "I can't believe it."

"Her peers have described her as loving and happ—" The screen went black.

"I hope people lie about me like that when I'm gone." Ainsley blew out a breath. The remote was concealed under her oversized sleeves, and her other hand held a glass of water. "Martina's calling her family with the good news. I thought I should give her some space. They can't believe there's been another murder." She pulled a stool by the sofas, carefully inspecting it before she sat. "What did the police say to you both?"

Bianca's eyes darted to me before she lowered her head. I pursed my lips, not ready to recall the story of finding Dani again.

"I think it would be good if we all knew what happened tonight." Ainsley emptied an aspirin into her palm and swung the glass back.

"So, what happened between you and Dani after I left?" I asked.

Ainsley nostrils flared. "Nothing. I made sure she wasn't going to do anything to interrupt my party, and then I left. Which is exactly what I told the police. I also told them about your fight with Dani last week."

Bianca's eyes lingered on the floor.

I tensed. I already suspected they all would have mentioned what happened last week, but that didn't make me a murderer. I scrubbed at my knees, still feeling the blood. "I have already told the police everything. I don't need to speak to you about it."

Ainsley tilted her head, her eyes narrowing. "Did they tell you how she died?"

I controlled the widening of my eyes. I assumed they all knew she'd been stabbed, but it wasn't mentioned in the news report. I ignored her, turning to Bianca. "Can I stay with you tonight?"

"Um." She met my gaze, tears rolling down her cheeks.

Ainsley blew out a breath. "It's very optimistic of you to think you won't be spending today in a jail cell."

Bianca nodded slowly. "It's fine. I'm sure Mabel won't mind."

Mabel was the only roommate missing. Like Dani, she was in her second year at The Bells. Mabel was never around. She would turn up for a few days a month then disappear again.

Even if I wasn't going to sleep, I needed somewhere to wash off the blood. I looked up at the clock.

"Don't tell me you're still going to class?" Ainsley asked.

I shrugged. I'd thought death would be more significant, that the world would stop, but everything moved on despite my brain's attempt to keep me locked in that dorm room. Even if it was class, I welcomed the escape. I stood up, gripping my bag tightly, careful not to touch the sofa because there was still blood on my hands. I couldn't see it, but it clung to the end of my fingernails and embedded itself in my skin. It wasn't like Dani to let go. Quietly, I followed Bianca out of the common room and through the hallway. She opened the door to Number Three. It had the same simple layout as mine, with two sets of twin beds. A desk was placed against the cream walls, and a chest of drawers marked the middle. Blue tartan curtains blocked out the rising sun. Bianca turned on the light, chasing shadows from the room. A silver trophy gleamed from her shelf, and cut-up photos lined her desk.

Mabel's side was practically empty. Gray floorboards creaked as I mindlessly placed my bag on her bed.

"It's clean," Bianca said. "I change everything once in a while just in case she comes back." She swung a sports bag over her shoulder. "I'm going to go for a swim. It helps me calm down."

I nodded. My mind was already focused on the shower.

The water wasn't hot enough. I scrubbed until a purple hue appeared and my skin pruned. I changed into loose sweatpants, but the sensation of blood still clung to me as I walked through campus. Waves of panic and anxiety surged through my body. I kept my head down, focusing on the step ahead and not the whispers or the heated stares.

When I reached the auditorium, tiers of rows loomed over me. Large windows lined the sides, flooding the room with natural light. Students, deep in chatter, filled the seats.

When I walked in, silence descended. Then the room burst into a rushed whisper. My ears burned. I wished time would speed up as I slipped into the last seat in the third row, away from the concentrated pool of students in the center of the room. I didn't look up, even when someone behind me recounted my fight with Dani, ending with why she wouldn't be surprised if I'd snapped, or when another deep voice said it couldn't have been a coincidence I was the one to find her. Hearing tapping feet beside me, I looked up when a body blocked out the sun.

Ainsley and Raven stood in the aisle. "Either get up and let us pass, or move over," Raven moaned.

I took a deep breath. "There are plenty of o—"

"You are not the only one everyone is talking about," Ainsley snapped.

Something tightened in my chest. Our audience now included our teacher, Professor Locke. He watched through narrowed eyes, and I reluctantly shuffled three seats, placing my bag between myself and Ainsley, leaving Raven to sit at the end.

Ainsley leaned over, hands folded under her chest. "Have the police been in contact with you since they left?"

I shook my head. Professor Locke's watchful eye lingered. I was used to scowls and threats. Pity was something I would have to get used to.

"This Dani situation has made me realize that we all need to stick together," Ainsley said in a harsh whisper.

"A few hours ago, you accused me of killing her."

"And I'm not saying I've changed my mind." She riffled through her bag and brought out books. "But I would like to know what happened when you got back?"

Professor Locke tapped the microphone. "Hello, students."

Ainsley dropped her books, and they landed with a thud, drawing even more attention in our direction.

He cleared his throat, raising his arms, and the room descended into quiet. "I know it will be difficult for a few of you to be here today due to recent events." He pulled at his turtleneck sweater, letting his eyes slip over us. "Due to this, I will be stressing the importance of the various points of support offered by this institution. We have grief counselors, and I am also available to speak to any students. I was surprised to see the numbers this morning. If you feel overwhelmed, you are excused from today's lesson." He waited and scanned the room, which remained completely silent. His features seemed to blur. His dark eyes became lighter then transformed into a familiar shade of green. The room shifted, and I was back at The Bells. Dani lay there, relentlessly quiet. I scrubbed at my face and pinched my skin before my mind could completely trap me with her lifeless body. I needed class to start. It was easier to focus on my failing than it was to see Dani lying there.

"I hope you all remembered your homework from last week." He pointed up at the board. It read "reporting and interpreting financial positions."

Groans issued around the room.

"I would like you to discuss your answers with the person next to you. While you do that, Sienna, would you mind coming to the front?"

My heart pounded. Anyone who wasn't already staring at me was now. Ainsley muttered under her breath and stood up to let me pass. I moved down the steps, my head spinning.

Professor Locke met me at the bottom and held out an arm to steady me. "Are you okay?"

I blinked. It was the first time I had been asked that since Dani's death. It seemed insignificant. Dani was gone. She would never be okay again. "I'm fine."

He frowned. "Are you sure you want to be here today? I'm more than happy t—"

"Yes. I want to keep busy. It helps me not to think about —" I swallowed the lump in my throat.

Professor Locke nodded. "I understand. I'll try and make this lesson more interesting for you then." He smiled.

It didn't work. His words were white noise as he moved through the slides. My eyes strained, and I struggled to keep up. Lack of sleep was catching up with me.

"We are going to finish a little earlier today," Professor Locke called from the front. "There are a few people I would like to speak to."

I packed my books away, preparing for a quick getaway.

"I would also like to add that my thoughts are with all of you students. I know it must be difficult for you to deal with the loss of one of your peers."

Ainsley sighed deeply.

"He is not in this class, but one absentee I noticed today was Michael. I have tried to email and have not heard any response. I understand he was close to Dani, and I know he has a few friends in this class, so please, if anybody sees him, could you ask him to come to my office? I would like to speak with him and make sure he is okay."

Ainsley groaned. "If we have to go through the whole day of people pretending to care that she is dead."

I shook my head. "Not everyone is as heartless as you. He just wants to help."

"I'm sure," Ainsley said sarcastically.

"Before you guys go," Professor Locke said, raising his voice to counter the banging of the books and the small chatter overtaking the room, "we have the small matter of homework."

"Can't you see we are grieving?" Ainsley cried.

I shot her a look of disbelief.

"I understand what has happened is shocking, but we can't stop assignments. If you think you are struggling, apply for an extension. And, Ainsley, I would like to talk to you about another matter. Could you please stay behind after class?"

Raven and Ainsley shared a side-eyed glance.

"Make sure to check your online Atlas profile, and you will see this." Professor Locke pointed at the screen.

Low groans issued from the back.

"There are three questions, but I will only ask you to answer one. If I hear any more complaints, I will change my mind."

The room erupted, and a swarm of students headed for the door. Raven and Ainsley pushed through the crowd, and I followed the path they created until we were out of the hall.

Ainsley turned on me. "We need to talk?"

"Didn't Professor Locke want to speak to you?" I asked.

Ainsley rolled her eyes. "I heard."

"I don't want to speak about Dani." I tried to sidestep her, but Ainsley reached out, hands enclosing around my wrist. They were bandaged, the wrapping badly tied from her fingers to her wrist.

"What happened to your hand?" I asked.

She thrust her sleeves down. "Nothing."

It didn't look like nothing. Ainsley bit down on her lip. "I hurt myself while I was cooking."

I scoffed. "Do you expect me to believe that? You're determined to get some answers out of me but won't give me any." I pushed my way through the crowd.

"Wait," Ainsley called.

I didn't stop, keeping my head low as everyone watched. I didn't see their faces. I saw Dani lifeless. My chest tightened. My head throbbing, I crashed through the doors of the main building. My eyes pooled, and every blink stung. I allowed my legs to carry me toward the library. There was no distraction. Dani was all-consuming. But I knew nothing could hurt me at the library. And the last thing I could do was sleep.

FOUR

Like a dark smog, death hung over campus. People I didn't recognize muttered about Dani as I entered the library. Keeping my head down, I walked to the stairs then took the steps two at a time. A group of girls taking selfies by the tall windows paused when they saw me. My stomach clenched. I heard the sharp whisper of "That's the girl wh—"

Then I was gone. My head pounded with every step, and my vision came in and out of focus. I faltered on the second floor. I couldn't make it up any more stairs. There were five floors in the library. The first floor was known for its rowdy study sessions, and the fifth floor had been nick-named "solitary confinement," where the librarians were barely tolerant of the soft rustle of book pages. The higher the floor, the lower the level of acceptable noise. I caught my breath. Black circles swam before my eyes. I needed a friendly face—the only one I had left.

"Sienna." Khadijah, a bright-faced librarian, gasped then pressed a finger to her lips to silence a group who had just broken out in conversation, pointing in my direction.

She rounded the service desk. A pink hijab highlighted her rosy cheeks. "I'm glad you're okay," she said, placing a gentle hand on my shoulder. "I'm so sorry to hear about Dani." Her voice was kind in a way I didn't deserve.

Heat prickled behind my eyes. I couldn't meet her gaze. I wasn't sure what would happen if I did.

She clutched my arms. "Come and join me in the meeting room. Away from all of this."

I looked up. Eyes from every corner of the room were fixed on us—on me. The girl who'd had a fight with Dani the week before she turned up dead. I tensed, allowing Khadijah to lead me to a small room. The door was ajar, and discarded books and sheets of paper lined the desk. A mat was folded in the corner, scribbled notes filled the white-board-covered walls, and the air was heavy with the smell of dry-erase markers.

Khadijah pulled out a chair, and I fell into it. Fatigue wracked my body. My cell phone beeped. Khadijah looked down expectantly. I had ignored all my messages—some from strangers, different variations of calling me a killer or wanting more details on what happened. When Tyrell had called, I'd let tears roll down my cheeks as the call rang out. He still hadn't given up on me. I turned my cell phone over. My stomach sank. "It's Mom."

Khadijah offered a tight-lipped smile. "I'll give you a moment." She backed out of the room, closing the door quietly.

I clicked on the link Mom had sent me, already knowing what I would see.

"Twenty-year-old killed at Stedmond College. This is not the first time tragedy has stuck this institution. Members of the

community remember Viviane Marks, who fell to her death after being lured out to Brittles Cove by her classmates."

I knew the story of Viviane Marks. I'd found out too late to back out of sleeping in the same bed she had. Six Stedmond students had gone on a weekend trip to the cabin in Brittles Cove. One had been killed, three were jailed, one had escaped, and then there was Dani. She'd never spoken about what she'd seen, and somehow, she'd managed to evade being stuck as the girl who'd found Vivienne.

"Despite the incident not taking place on Stedmond grounds, all parties involved in the death of Marks were Stedmond students. Now, a year after her death, another life has been lost. Dani Bishop, 20, was found stabbed to death in her bedroom after a wild party that took place at The Bells accommodation."

Stabbed. My eyes snapped back to the word. This was the first time they had specified the cause of death, but the word didn't feel like enough. It didn't capture the cruelty of the scene. It was a frenzy, leaving multiple punctures and a deep slit across her neck. Whoever it was hadn't just wanted to kill her. They'd wanted her to suffer. This attack was personal.

"Despite many attempts, Stedmond representatives have refused to speak on the—"

That was all I could read before Mom came through with the inevitable call. I answered on the third ring, giving myself enough time for one deep breath.

"Someone has been murdered." Mom sighed. Never a good way to start a conversation. "Sienna, I should hear these things from you, not the news. You can't imagine what it's like after—" She huffed. "Are you okay?"

I glanced at the meeting room door. "Yes. I wasn't home when it happened."

"Was anyone else hurt?"

"No."

"I can't believe this. She was such a sweet girl. I remember the day you moved in. She offered to help you unpack and show you around the building." Mom tutted. "So young. It's such a shame."

Mom wasn't aware of my experiences with Dani, and I decided not to mention Dani had stolen some of the things she'd unpacked and never had shown me around, but I wasn't going to tarnish Mom's memory of a virtual stranger.

"Honey, this school seems to be getting out of control. They say she was stabbed." She paused, long enough for the image of Dani's body to seep in. I squeezed my eyes shut and inhaled deeply. "If another student so much as stubs their toe, you are coming back home, no argument. And I want you to call me with any updates immediately."

I pursed my lips. How could I tell her that I would rather stay in a place with all these murders than return home?

"Sienna?"

"Yes, okay, Mom," I promised.

"Good." I could almost hear her relief. "Your dad is still away on his business trip."

He had been on continuous business trips for over a year—one of the many consequences of our dysfunctional family. I wondered if Mom genuinely still believed the lies. No one else did.

"You will have to call and tell him yourself," she continued. "I've already told your brother."

A chill swept through my body. Khadijah's head popped through the door. I gripped the cell phone tighter.

"He is worried sick. Have you spoken to him?"

She knew the answer. This was just her way of making me feel bad about it.

I swallowed hard, not ready for her latest guilt trip. "Mom, I've really got to go now. I'll speak to you later."

Khadijah waved her arms, signaling that there was no need to hang up on her account, and I heard the start of Mom's protests before I hung up.

"She must be worried sick." Khadijah took the seat opposite me.

"Yeah," I breathed.

"I know it will be difficult, but you need to make sure you are getting some rest."

I blinked. My heavy lids threatened darkness. "I can't get it out of my head, and I feel like everyone thinks I had something to do with Dani's death."

Khadijah's mouth fell open. "Why would you think that?"

"Because of our disagreement last week."

Khadijah drew her head back. She knew all about Dani's antics throughout the year and had insisted they would stop if I killed her with kindness. *Well, she was half right.*

"I didn't. I could never."

She smiled softly. "Of course, I know you didn't."

Thickness built in my throat. I blinked back the tears and turned to the window.

"Did you speak to the police? As long as you tell them the truth, you should be fine."

Heat rushed to my ears. "I told them I went to the movies then for a walk."

"With Tyrell?" Khadijah's smile seemed to grow at this.

I nodded curtly. "But I told the police I was alone."

Her smile faltered, and her brows furrowed. "Sienna, lying to the police—"

"I know. I know." Shame burned through me. I could feel Mom's hands on my thighs and hear her low hiss as she reminded me, "It's not lying if it's to protect people you love." I slumped back in my chair, nails digging into my palm. "I kind of ended our *friendship* yesterday. I don't want him to be dragged into anything else to do with me."

"At times like this, you need to lean on your friends. You should speak to Tyrell and explain that, maybe." The pitch of her voice increased. "You got scared?"

I rubbed my ear. "Well, it's not every day you find your roommate dead."

Khadijah raised her eyebrows in a you-know-what-I-mean sort of way. "I understand how you feel, but this is a murder investigation. Lying to the police will do nothing to help you."

My stomach clenched. I turned back to the window. "Can we talk about something else, please? How is everything going with your boyfriend?"

"He is not my boyfriend. He is my fiancé," Khadijah corrected. "And it's going well. But let's talk about you. What you experienced yesterday is a lot, and you need to let the police do their jobs."

I turned to meet her gaze.

"And the best way for them to do their jobs is if they know the truth about what happened that night."

"I'm not sure how me and Tyrell falling out is going to help with their case."

"Sienna." Despite her best efforts, Khadijah's warning tone was just as soft as her usual voice.

I shrugged. "I will tell the police everything they need to know." It was true because what Khadijah believed and what I believed the police needed to know were completely different. "I should probably go now." I jumped off the chair.

"Okay, but please respond to my emails. I want to make sure you're okay."

"Why don't you just take my number?"

"Or we can use the college-provided email accounts." She beamed. "To protect your privacy, and this way, I know you're also seeing your emails for all your classwork."

"I don't care about privacy," I muttered.

"I wouldn't want to make you uncomfortable, and I know I'm not your teacher, but I think it's best we communicate on the college platforms," she said gently. "And remember, people react to shock in different ways. There is no correct way to handle this."

I nodded. "I know. Thanks for everything. I'm sorry to take you away from work."

"I was taking a break to pray anyway, and I want you to come to me anytime you need to talk."

"Thank you." I swallowed the lump in my throat. "Can you try to include something about the whole school not thinking I'm a psychotic, murdering bi—"

She interrupted politely. "I'll see what I can do."

FIVE

Laughter didn't belong at The Bells. The walls seemed to capture it, seizing joy before it could spread. The hairs on my neck stood on end when I heard the familiar deep rumble. I keyed in the new code, my jaw tense.

Tyrell sat on the waiting chair. Nia was beside him, pushing strands of blond curls behind her ear as she leaned into him and grinned. They stilled as the door thudded shut, laughter dying on their lips, smiles fading as they noticed me. Nia's big hoop earrings jangled as she shook her head.

"Sienna." Tyrell stood up, taking one hesitant step. "You weren't answering my calls. I heard about Dani. I wanted to make sure you were okay."

I took a deep breath, fighting the memory of all the blood. "I'm fine." I looked down at my feet. The room had changed. The floor had a new sheen to it, free from the spillage from the party and empty bottles. Even the fire extinguisher had been replaced.

"They were in your room too," Nia said, rising to her

44

feet. She straightened her cropped biker jacket and swung her bag over her shoulder. "Cleaning what was left of her." This was the first time I had seen Nia since last night. After the police questioned her, she'd stayed in her room, insisting that Dani wasn't going to be the reason she didn't finish her art project. "It was nice to meet you, Tyrell."

"Yeah." He wiped his palms along his thighs. "Thanks, Nia. You're a lifesaver. I'll call you so we can set a meeting up."

Nia beamed. I didn't know she could produce anything other than her usual scowl, but it could have something to do with Dani being dead. Nia had more reasons than most to hate her. Dani had stolen her boyfriend and flaunted it in her face for months.

She looked up at Tyrell through her eyelashes. Her blue eyes gleamed. "I'm happy to help."

I fought the urge to roll my eyes and stepped aside as she aimed for the exit. A strong, sweet floral scent trailed her. "Are you going to class?"

"No." Nia huffed. "Dani just died."

"To see Michael?"

Nia's face darkened, and she leaned in. "And why would I do that?"

I stepped back. A lump formed in my throat.

Nia didn't wait for an answer. She turned and slammed her palm into the exit button.

The door flew open, and I braced myself for the thud. The sound pounded in my head.

Tyrell parted his lips. I looked down, unable to meet his gaze. The word *distraction* was heavy in the air, and there was nothing I could do to take it back. Yet, he still came to see if I was okay. Shame burned through my chest. I stepped forward. "I shouldn't have—"

At the same time, Tyrell said, "I'm sorry you were the one to find D—"

We chuckled softly.

"You don't have to apologize to me." He shook his head.

I swallowed. "I didn't know you knew Nia," I said as lightly as possible.

Tyrell looked at the spot Nia had just vacated. "I don't. We just met. She let me in. I take it she isn't one of the ones you get along with."

There was only one person anyone really got on with. Mabel. "No. She isn't." I crossed the room and took a seat, and Tyrell settled in next to me.

"We started talking, and when I told her about my project, she offered to help."

"How nice of her."

Tyrell's arms twitched. I thought he was going to reach out. I wanted him to, but he gripped his hands, and disappointment gnawed in my stomach.

"Are you okay? It can't have been easy being the one to find Dani."

I swallowed hard, bile making its way up my throat. "It feels like everyone thinks I did it."

Tyrell turned, and our knees almost touched. He was so close, I could feel the warmth. "Anyone who knows you knows you could never have done anything like this."

That was the problem. No one knew me. Tyrell was the closest I'd let anyone in, and it would never be enough.

"Sienna." He ducked his head to meet my eyes. "You were with me, and from what I've heard, everyone was at the party. You couldn't have done it. The excitement of you finding Dani will wear off and—"

"Actually," I said, squeezing my hands into fists, "I didn't tell the police I was with you."

I wanted to take the words back. Heat rushed to my face. Guilt gripped my chest as he registered my words. His body stiffened. He couldn't understand. The police didn't care about the innocent as long as they got what they wanted. A shiver ran through my spine at the memories of the police station. Mom had not been there to direct me. The cold steel from the chair had pressed into my legs as I betrayed my family. Two pairs of disgusted eyes had bored into me as the truth spilled out and tore my family apart. They'd made me recount the story like they wanted to know it well enough to pass it off as their own, and each time I recounted it, their disgust had deepened. Then they had picked my story apart.

"You didn't tell them you were with me?" Tyrell rubbed the base of his neck.

"I'm sorry." The words came out in a whisper.

"Why?"

All the reasons felt insubstantial.

"I didn't do it, so it doesn't matter what I've told the police."

His brows furrowed. "If they do come to question me, do you expect me to lie?"

"No. But I've made sure they won't ask you any—"

"How do you know, Sienna? Because if they find out you've lied to them about this, they will wonder what else you could have lied about." He wasn't just talking about the police.

I wet my lips. "I know that. But it's too late to change my statement. I just—"

"Sorry. I didn't know you had guests." Bianca cowered behind the lobby doorframe, eyes darting between us and the exit.

"It's fine." Tyrell stood up. "I'm just leaving." He looked down. "I hope you know what you're doing."

My chest tightened. I had pushed him away, and he came back. I didn't want to lose the support again. He shook his head, taking long strides to the exit.

I shot up.

"Sienna," Bianca called. "The pol—"

"Ty, wait." I followed.

He didn't. Not even when the tall figure approached, taking long strides and fixing a penetrative glare on me.

I slowed. Tyrell wouldn't recognize him. I would make sure he never did.

Detective Collins raised a curious brow but said nothing. Shelley shadowed him, a tight smile on her lips—one I couldn't return. I stopped, allowing Tyrell to move farther away from me and all the misery I carried. My heart thrashed in my chest.

The detectives were here, and there could be no good reason for them to return to The Bells.

SIX

Arms folded across his chest, Collins studied The Bells, scanning every inch of the peeling bricks as though waiting for it to speak. I followed his gaze, noticing the slight differences in the exterior. The window in my room had been replaced. Graffiti had been cleaned. The inside was free from any reminders of Ainsley's party and the life taken that day.

Collins nodded to Shelley, and she walked to the entrance. I stepped forward, ready to supply the new four-digit code. Knots formed in my stomach as she keyed in the code and wedged the door open. In her hands, she held a master key card, a lighter, and a device I had never seen before.

I turned wide-eyed to Detective Collins. "Has something happened?

"I'm afraid you will have to wait outside for now, Sienna."

Someone had given them a key to The Bells. I swallowed the bitter taste in my mouth. My mind raced. They were looking for something.

Moments later, Bianca came out, head low and a throw wrapped over her shoulders. She pursed her lips as she passed Collins.

Then it was Martina, her fingers laced in a book, two mismatched fluffy slippers on her feet. "What's going on?"

Collins didn't answer. He craned his neck to see Raven and Ainsley behind her. "Is there anyone else in the house?" Collins turned to look at us.

Martina closed her book. "Just Nia."

"No." I shook my head. "Nia has gone out."

"Is there a reason you want to speak to us outside?" Ainsley sighed.

Raven looked over her shoulder. "She's going into our rooms." Her voice hitched. "Don't you need a search warrant for this?"

Collins produced a piece of paper from his jacket. Ainsley snatched it from him. Raven hugged her body and glared at the entrance.

Ainsley thrust the paper into his chest. "This is ridiculous. You didn't have to kick us out to do this."

"Actually—" he started, then Shelley stepped out.

I held my breath. Cold seeped into my bones.

She gave an almost imperceptible shake of her head, and Collins's jaw tensed.

"Can we go back in now?" Ainsley asked.

"Yes," Collins said after a moment. "But I would like to speak to all of you in the common room." He stepped back and gestured for us to pass.

Bianca didn't move, hand clutching her chest as she

worked through shaky breaths. No one else noticed. Their heads turned toward Nia.

"Why are you all outside?" She flinched, noticing Collins. "Oh." Wind swept her hair into her face. She didn't push it back, allowing strands to cover the redness and puffiness of her eyes.

"Please." Collins held open the door. We walked through. Muffled footsteps drowned out the rattling in my chest. Something had changed. I sensed it in the air. It was as though Dani were still alive, playing with us, and now she had us in the palms of her hands. The pounding in my head resembled her laughter, taunting me as I took my seat in the common room.

Collins stood, his right hand clutching his left. Martina sat beside me, her book gone. At least someone was taking it seriously. Raven had used the opportunity to go to her room.

Collins's jaw tensed when she reappeared.

"Sorry," she muttered, taking a seat beside Ainsley.

Collins cleared his throat. "We have received the results of the preliminary autopsy conducted on Dani Bishop. I wanted to inform you of the findings and how this will change the course of our investigation."

The room stilled.

"You may have seen the reports stating the cause of death. But the stab wounds to Dani Bishop were inflicted post-mortem."

I blinked slowly. The room was spinning, and I wondered if anyone else was experiencing ringing in their ears. It didn't make sense. I'd seen her body, the cuts, and the blood. I looked at the confused faces around the room.

Collins's head didn't turn, but I got the feeling he was taking us all in, reading our reactions, and storing them away. There was always the possibility that the killer was in this room.

"The actual cause of death was poison," he continued. "Carbon monoxide poisoning."

Bianca slumped forward, suppressing a gasp.

"Detective Shelley just tested the house and found the concentration levels were normal. However, there are signs in the utility room that someone had tampered with the vent for the gas water heater. The window in Dani's room was also sealed shut."

Something roared in my ears. The day Dani died, she didn't want to keep the window closed. She couldn't open it, and that explained the broken glass.

"The poisoning could have occurred over several days, weeks perhaps. Did any of you notice anything strange? Even the things you may think are insignificant may be very important to this case. Think about any changes in her patterns or behavior."

"She was sick for a few days before," Ainsley said.

Bianca nodded to herself. "She missed swim practice."

"You didn't mention this before?" Collins said.

"I assumed it was karma. Not poison." Ainsley smiled back at the dark-haired detective.

Collins mirrored her smile, probably storing it away for later. "Is there anything else any of you noticed? Anyone who could have had access to the room?"

"It doesn't have a key." My voice was small. "And everyone knew the code to get into the building." I didn't look at Ainsley, but I felt the weight of her scowl.

"They were coming to a party," she said. "I didn't invite anyone to murder Dani."

"You all have my card if you want to add anything else to your statements," Collins said. He left the common room, Shelley trailing behind him.

No one spoke. Bianca sobbed silently into her hands.

I needed to think. My brain was unable to attach to any thoughts other than that poison had no time frame. Everyone's alibis had just become useless.

Days. Dani could have been dying over several days. We all could. I looked up at the faces of my roommates, and a chill gripped my back. Someone hadn't poisoned Dani. They had poisoned the *house*. The others realized it too. Their jaws went slack, and their eyes widened.

Bianca jolted up, tears flowing down her cheeks.

"Where are you going?" Ainsley's voice stopped her before she could leave the room.

"We just found out that what happened to Dani was even worse than we could have imagined, and you don't even care." Bianca cried. "She didn't deserve this, and it could have been any of us." She choked back her sobs.

"Are you finished with this performance?" Ainsley asked. "Whatever happened to her doesn't change the fact that she is dead. It doesn't get any worse regardless of how it happened."

I disagreed. Something didn't make sense. Dani hadn't died from her stab wounds, but they were still there. The memory felt all too real. It was a targeted attack.

"We had over one hundred people here the day she died," Ainsley said.

"You had," I corrected.

She locked eyes with me. "And *we* managed to live with her for three months without resorting to murder. Anyone could have done it. It was Dani. Everyone had a reason."

Raven tipped her head up, stocky cheeks lifting as her eyes narrowed. "Why weren't you affected by the carbon monoxide? You slept in the same room."

Eyes snapped to me. "I—" My skin crawled, and a weight shifted in my stomach. "I don't know." I flushed. All the clues were there—the breathlessness and the fever—but we'd just assumed it was the flu. I'd had the same symptoms as Dani, but the night before she died, I didn't stay at The Bell's. I was with Tyrell, but I wasn't willing to share that with the girls.

I swallowed. "Shouldn't we all have been affected?"

"It would depend on the concentration levels and ventilation in the dorms. Your room was closest to the leak. It makes sense why we weren't as affected." Martina gestured to the rest of the girls, drawing her hand in a circle, omitting me. "But you were sleeping in the same room as her so…"

Nia watched me closely, her head tilted to the side. "You weren't here the day before she died."

My breath hitched.

Raven looked between us. "What makes you think that?"

Nia shuffled uncomfortably. "Michael slept here."

The rest of the girls glared at me, waiting for answers.

"Poison happens to be leaking into the house, and you weren't here," Ainsley said. "Where were you?"

"Does it matter?" I shot back.

Ainsley leaned forward. "Seeing as this house was

poisoned, and you were the only one who was gone, I think it does. Do the police know you weren't here the night before the murder?"

No. But I had a feeling they were going to.

"Can we go now?" I asked.

They looked at each other. I wasn't helping my case, but I refused to be interrogated for something I hadn't done. Without waiting for an answer, I pushed myself up before I remembered I couldn't get back into the room without Bianca. She hesitated for a second then wiped her cheeks before hurrying out of the room.

Nothing had been moved. The small bag with my belongings sat by the foot of the bed. The bed I hadn't slept in was still neatly laid.

"Poison," Bianca said as she switched on the bedside lamp. "Who could do something like that?" She drew back her curtain and opened the window. "They could have killed us all." She stiffened.

Except me. She didn't say it, but I saw it in the quiver of her lips.

She sat by the desk. The detectives must have interrupted her, because she was enclosed in a ring of photographs, tape, glue, and a thick picture book.

Bianca looked up. "Coach has paused practice for this week." She picked up the glue, smothered some on the back of a picture, and gave a weak smile. "Scrapbooking is the only other thing that helps me to relax."

I glimpsed some of the pictures. Her swimming team by the pool held medals to the camera.

She straightened the stack of photos and banged them against the table. "Usually, I go back to happy times, but today, I could only focus on Dani. I didn't realize how good she was at avoiding cameras till now. We spent most days together training, but I could only find two pictures with her." She pulled out her drawer and placed the book and materials inside.

She frowned. "Today can't have been easy for you. I got slashing noises every time I passed."

I parted my lips, not quite sure how to respond.

"I think it will get worse if you don't tell them where you were."

I played back the night of the murder. All that time, Dani had been dying slowly. It was a coincidence. There was no way the killer had known I wasn't going to be at the house. Only Dani, Tyrell, and I guess Michael would have known I wouldn't be back. Bianca hunched over her desk, busying herself tidying strips of paper.

"What about you?" I asked. "Did you find Ainsley after I left?"

Color drained from Bianca's cheeks in the dim light. "No. I didn't think it was the best idea to try and convince Ainsley to turn down the music, so I just returned to my room."

"You didn't see Dani?"

"No, I didn't leave the room again until Raven knocked on everyone's doors, saying the police were here." Bianca turned her back to me, pulled a hairband from her wrist, and tied a messy bun in her bedside mirror.

"So, you were here when it happened?"

Bianca's reflection contorted under the lamplight. She gave a simple nod.

"Why do you think this happened to Dani?"

"I don't want to speculate." She shifted away from the mirror, keeping her head down. I couldn't see her face as she rushed into the bathroom and slammed the door shut.

SEVEN

I couldn't fight it. A cry lodged in my throat as I glared at Dani. Her skin reddened as she clutched and clawed at her throat. The air thickened, holding me in place, forcing me to hear the gargling noise that escaped her pale lips. I strained, waiting for her to form something coherent. I tried to move, to ask her who'd done this. Then the scene transformed. A man held out a hand, and a weight pressed on my chest. I recognized him. His features were burned into my memory. His eyes, framed by creases in the corners, were filled with tears. My gaze followed them as they rolled down his cheeks and pooled by his mouth.

I held back a scream, begging my body to move, my legs only shaking from the effort. My eyes were locked on his mouth. It had been a while since I'd had this dream, but I knew what he would say. His thin lips parted, and time slowed as he croaked, "Help me."

I jolted awake, blinded by a bright light. I squinted and lowered my eyes. Bianca's feet stood by the foot of my bed.

"Sorry," she said meekly. "I didn't mean to wake you."

She dropped the flashlight from her cell phone. "You were moaning and tossing in your sleep. I just wanted to check you were okay."

Sweat lined my forehead. My heart thundered. "Yeah."

Bianca shuffled back in the darkness. The bed creaked as she got in. I didn't remember falling asleep. I grabbed my phone, now facedown but still playing an episode of my latest reality TV fix—the same episode. I had felt trapped in my head for hours, but it had only been forty-five minutes. I sat up and wiped the back of my hand across my forehead.

"Goodnight," Bianca said.

A flush crept across my cheeks, and I slid back into bed, wondering what she had heard or seen. Dani was the only one who'd known about my nightmares, and now she was a part of one. My eyes burned with exhaustion. My vision blurred at the edges. I pulled back the covers, relied on the cold to keep me awake, and put on my headphones. I got lost in a world where Jenna's biggest worry was choosing between two men to marry. The threat of nightmares still lingered as I finished the series, and the curtains struggled to keep out the rays of light.

Bianca's soft snores continued as I got ready. The dark circles around my eyes were easy to obscure with makeup, but it took a while for the bloodshot red to leave the whites of my eyes.

I wasn't going to class today. I didn't have it in me to deal with all the suspicious looks or whispers. It would only get worse when everyone found out about the poison. I left Bianca's room and turned right in the hallway. Heavy steps carried me to the door of my room. I squeezed my eyes shut. In the back of my mind, I could still hear my screams.

Taking a deep breath, I opened the door to the utility room, a small room tucked away at the back of The Bells. I expected something to cry out at me. Someone had come in here and put us all at risk. It was the reason Dani was dead. But everything was normal. Bianca's swimsuits and Nia's uniform from her part-time work filled a basket, and a bag of Mabel's clothes was stuffed between the cleaning supplies that packed the shelves. Brooms and mops were leaned against the back wall, a basket of clothes sat next to a bottle of detergent on top of the washing machine, and on the wall behind the dryer was the gas water heater.

I didn't know what I was looking for. My eyes roamed over the small control panel at the front then to the ventilation pipe. Nothing had changed. I turned, but something caught my eye—my bag, filled with the clothes Dani had given back to me the day she died. I swallowed. I had enough clothes to get me through the week, and right now, I didn't need any more reminders of Dani. I closed the door behind me.

The sizzle of oil drew me to the kitchen. Martina stood by the stove, headphones on over her damp and tousled hair. She turned, and her skin flushed as she noticed me. "I didn't think anyone else would be up. Excuse the look." She pushed the headphones around her neck. "I went for a run." She cracked an egg and dropped it into the pan. "What are you doing up?"

I chewed on my lip. "I-I couldn't sleep."

Martina nodded. "I couldn't stop thinking about it either. It could have easily been any one of us." She walked over to the trashcan and dropped the eggshell in. "How are you feeling after last night?"

"You mean everyone implying that I murdered Dani?"

Martina shrugged. "I meant Jenna choosing Jake over Paul, but I guess that too."

I laughed for the first time since Dani had died, and it felt wrong. Martina felt it, too, and lowered her head. I walked to the table, which had an empty water bottle, a steaming mug of coffee, and a book on top. I took a seat, avoiding the interrogation chair. Everything had changed since that interview with Collins.

"None of it makes any sense," I said.

"I googled the effects of carbon monoxide poison." Martina flipped over her omelet. "It could even have been an accident." She wiped her hands over her joggers, pulled out her cell, and tapped on the screen before placing it on the table. "Look, there are twenty accidental deaths from monoxide poisoning in this country every year."

I looked down at the article. Carbon monoxide was colorless, odorless, and deadly.

"It wasn't an accident." I handed her back her cell phone. "Whoever it was blocked the vents and then repaired them after Dani died. The police saw signs someone had messed with it. It had to be intentional. And I saw her." I cleared my throat. Bile threatened to rise to the surface. "The poison might have killed her, but for someone, that wasn't enough."

"Good point." Martina placed her cooked egg onto toast and took the seat opposite me. "But how did the police miss it in the first place? They say that the poison turns the skin red."

It didn't feel like she was asking how the detectives missed it, but how I did.

"She was pretty much covered in red. Blood was everywhere. I didn't focus on her skin."

She scrubbed her face with her hand. "Of course. I'm sorry. I can't imagine how scary it must have been to find her."

"Yeah," I breathed.

Martina studied me, chewing her toast. "You know, my sister always said Dani was the type who would never get a good ending."

Maria was the only one who had evaded the police after the death of Vivienne Marks.

"I know we aren't supposed to say it, but I think most people felt the same way." Martina bit into her toast with a soft crunch, then wiped at the crumbs on her mouth. "I wanted to believe it was an accident. It makes sleeping easier at night, but plenty of people wanted to get rid of Dani."

I swallowed the lump in my throat. I couldn't disagree. I was one of them, but I would never have been able to do what the killer had done. I looked up at Martina, wondering if she believed that or if this was just her way of getting me to open up—like she had with Maria. Everyone knew Martina had turned her sister in to the police, but Maria still managed to get away.

I wet my lips. "You never talk about your sister." Anything we knew about her was from the news reports and the many false sightings that kept Martina on edge and kept the bad reputation of The Bells alive, well, until Dani's death.

"Would you?"

Something hardened in my chest. I had my own reasons for not wanting to speak about my sibling—a secret only Dani knew. "Have you heard from her?"

Martina tensed. "No, but if I had, she wouldn't have anything good to say. She will never forgive me. I still think about where she is all the time. She didn't push Vivi. I thought it was for the best that she just turned herself in." Martina sighed and pushed her plate away. "We didn't want to betray her, but my parents and I would rather she faced the consequences of her involvement than live out on the streets." Her brow furrowed. "She doesn't see it that way. I don't want to think about what she would do if she saw any of us again."

"Did she threaten you?"

Martina's smirked. "No. Dani did. She said she knew where Maria was."

"And you believed her?"

Martina laughed. The tension in her shoulders seemed to ease. "I made a habit of never believing anything Dani said, but I didn't need her to tell me my sister wanted nothing more to do with our family."

"When was the last time you saw Dani?"

"Why?" She paused as she brought a mug to her lips. "Do you think I could have done it?"

"No." Heat rushed to my ears. "I jus—"

"It's fine." She smiled. "If anything, I'm flattered someone thinks I was capable of standing up to Dani. But I didn't kill her." Martina held my gaze. "And I'm not going to pretend to mourn her. I almost got kicked out because of her. And after what happened with my sister." She chewed the inside of her mouth. "My family can't afford any more drama."

My eyes fell to the table. Dani had stolen Martina's work, and when they'd both submitted it to the Atlas portal, it was flagged as plagiarized. Martina was threatened with expulsion, and they'd fought about it. Then, suddenly, a few days later, Martina was voluntarily doing the work for Dani.

A question rattled inside my head—one everyone wanted to ask but never did. I wet my lips and checked the door. "Why did you carry on doing Dani's work?"

She tapped against the side of her mug. "It was easier that way. I'm the sister of the criminal, and Dani was the poor girl who witnessed a murder and had to redo the year. The teachers would always be on her side. The assignments weren't hard and didn't take up much time." It wasn't bragging. Everyone knew Martina was among the smartest students, her head constantly buried in a book. "It kept her off my back. That way, I always had something Dani needed."

It was true. The best way to deal with someone like Dani was to have something over them, but wouldn't things have been easier if Dani weren't here at all?

EIGHT

"What time does the meeting start?" Nia's hair fell in her face as she looked down at the gold watch.

"Ten minutes ago," Bianca muttered, wringing her fingers. She bounced on her feet, eyes constantly darting to the common room door. She had sent a message into our group chat asking everyone to meet at seven o'clock, and we were still waiting on Martina, Raven, and Ainsley.

"I've got to leave in twenty minutes." Nia shrugged and increased the volume on the TV.

Even through the TV screen, the resemblance was undeniable. Aaron Crawley shared the same rich-brown skin, plump lips, and almond-shaped eyes as his daughter. He waved to the crowd, stepped up to a podium, and waited for the applause to die down. A reporter narrated.

"Aaron Crawley has stated he is committed to tackling the rising levels of gang crime, but not everyone is able to put their trust in the police."

The screen cut to a woman with graying hair, hunched over as she recalled the death of her son due to gang crime.

My stomach tightened, and I zoned out, my eyes drifting to the movement of the sign language interpreter in the corner, until Ainsley's dad was back, talking about how he wanted to improve youth employment rates within the force.

Nia scoffed, shaking her head.

A knot twisted in my stomach. I thought of Tyrell. We hadn't spoken since he left The Bells. If I had agreed to do his project that night, maybe I wouldn't have been the one to find Dani, the nightmares wouldn't be back, and Nia wouldn't be pretending to be some political expert.

"I am a proud father of two," Aaron said. "And just this morning, my children gave me amazing advice. Strive to unite the peop—"

The screen went blank. "I haven't spoken to that man in weeks." Ainsley threw the remote onto the sofa. When we first moved into The Bells, he sent a gift every week: a new bag, shoes, and jewelry, then suddenly, it stopped.

"I was watching that," Nia said through clenched teeth.

Ainsley fell into her seat and crossed one leg over the other. "And now you're not."

Nia said something under her breath I was glad Ainsley didn't hear.

Bianca sprang up, clasping her hands. She blew out a breath as Martina and Raven entered the room.

"What's this about?" Martina asked.

Ainsley groaned. "What isn't about Dani these days?"

Bianca straightened. She had called the group meeting, but she looked surprised that everyone had turned up. "Thank you all for coming." She bumped into a side table as she walked to the center of the room and cleared her throat before she started. "I know we all had complicated relationships with Dani." She grimaced but continued, not discouraged by the blank stares. "And, um, we all know how important swimming was to her. It was where she was her happiest. So, the rest of the team and I have decided to race in her memory this Friday. The cost of entry will be a donation to support her family with the funeral costs. We want it to be available for everyone, so there is no minimum fee because every little bit helps."

"So it can be free?" Raven asked.

Bianca scratched the base of her neck. "N-No. Everyone has to pay something."

"Did you have to bring us here to tell us this?" Ainsley said. "There is the reason we have the group chat."

Bianca opened her mouth, closed it, then said, "I thought you would have pretended not to see the message."

Ainsley shrugged, a soft smile on her lips. It was exactly what she would have done.

Bianca flexed her hands. "I also think it would be good if someone was willing to say a few *nice* words about Dani, maybe tell a story about our time living with her."

"Good luck with that," Raven said. "Why don't you tell the one about how she beat you at the championships and then taunted you by leaving the trophy around the house for you to see?"

Bianca frowned, her face draining of color. "Mabel would be good," she said, ignoring Raven. "Has anyone heard from her? My calls haven't been going through. She might not even know that Dani is dead."

Mabel had known Dani the longest and was the kind of person to see the good in everyone—even Dani.

"She always comes back eventually." Martina sighed. "We will just have to wait until then."

"Great." Ainsley clapped her hands together and stood. "Anything else?"

Bianca thought for a moment before shaking her head. Ainsley, Raven, and Martina marched out of the room.

"Do you think they'll come?" Bianca asked in a low voice.

"Yeah," I admitted. "Not for Dani, but they wouldn't want to miss out, and since the killer is still out there, it would only look suspicious if they didn't."

Nia flicked her wrist. A glint of gold shimmered as she checked the time then switched the TV back on. Aaron's opposition, Nolan Davis, addressed a crowd.

"I didn't know you were so into the elections," Bianca said.

Nia leaned back into her seat. "I'm not. I'm doing it to help a friend."

I clenched my jaw. She had only known Tyrell for a few days.

"Not to annoy Ainsley?" Bianca asked.

Nia bit back a laugh. "That's just a bonus."

A deep voice came from behind. "Thanks for the code. I—"

We turned.

Tyrell stood by the entrance. "Hey." The word caught in his throat as his eyes landed on mine.

Bianca's jaw dropped. "After everything that's happened, I think it's best if we stop giving out the code."

Tyrell rubbed at the scar on his brow. "Sorry. I didn't know when I was coming, and I didn't want to leave Nia waiting in the lobby."

"It's fine." Nia waved a hand.

Bianca pursed her lips, keeping her thoughts to herself, but her shake of the head betrayed her. Tyrell stepped aside as she strode out of the room.

I didn't move. My heart thumped, and Tyrell came closer.

"You'll be glad to know I've been watching the news," Nia said, oblivious to the tension. "A lot of it was about Dani, and there was that video of the cat playing the drums. Have you seen it?"

Tyrell laughed. "I hope you made time for the election updates between your cat videos."

"Of course. I even made notes."

"Notes?" Tyrell questioned.

"I am taking this seriously."

Something burned in my chest, and I thought maybe they had forgotten I was still there until Nia looked between the two of us. "Do you need something?"

My jaw tensed. "No."

Nia drew her head back. "How exactly do you two know each other?"

I opened my mouth. I didn't know what would come out. Then I decided to let Tyrell define whatever we were.

He licked his lips. "I helped her out at the library a few times."

Nia nodded. "She needs all the help she can get."

My body tensed then relaxed when Tyrell bit back a laugh.

Nia walked to the door. "I just need to get my notes, then I'll be ready."

She left, and Tyrell shook his head, a stupid grin on his face.

"What's so funny?"

"I think I'm starting to see why you don't get on with your housemates."

"And that was Nia being nice." I backed into the sofa and sat down. "Did she tell you Dani was poisoned?"

Tyrell's eyes widened. "Wha—"

I filled him in on what the police had said about the carbon monoxide. "And I think…" I tried to control the quiver in my lip. "I think the only reason Dani died and I didn't is because I was with you."

His expression softened. He ran a hand over his forehead. "But no one knows you were with me." It was a statement, not a question. "And you're not going to tell them."

My gaze dropped to the floor.

He shook his head. "I don't get it. I really thought we were getting somewhere."

I couldn't bear the thought of him looking at me differently because of who I was or what I'd done. But we could never be more than what we had. "We were."

"But?" Tyrell prompted. "You can be honest with me."

I shifted in my seat, pushing my hands under my thighs, and welcomed the tingling sensation as they numbed. I already knew what he was going to ask.

"Why did you lie to the police?"

I felt faint. I swallowed the lump in my throat. "I had been questioned by the police before Dani's death." Heat rushed through my face. "It was one of the hardest things

I've had to do, and I didn't want to tell them any more than I had to because they twist things, and I didn't want them to do that to—"

Us.

I cleared my throat. The unspoken word hung in the air. He seemed to digest this for a while, not that it mattered. It only sped up what was going to happen anyway once he realized I couldn't give him what he deserved.

"Why were you questioned by the police before?"

I blinked, trying to stay present, battling fatigue and an overwhelming sense of dread. "Does it matter?" I asked, spots blurring my vision. "I didn't kill Dani, and everyone here thinks I did. The only person who knows I didn't is you."

He blew out a breath.

Anger brewed in my stomach at his disbelief, and I stood up. "Why would I want to kill Dani?"

He cocked his head.

"Okay, *how* could I? I'm not capable of murder."

"I wouldn't know what you're capable of."

My jaw dropped. The words were like a slap.

"I don't know anything about you. You don't tell me anything about your family, friends, your past. The only thing you would talk to me about is how much you hated Dani. We spent every day together while carbon monoxide leaked into this room, and the day Dani died, you broke things off."

I opened my mouth to protest, but it came out as a choked sob. He was right. He didn't know me, but I'd thought he knew enough to know I wasn't capable of this.

Pain shot through my chest. I swallowed, afraid any attempt to talk would end in tears.

"But it's not that I don't believe you."

I met his eyes. He scrubbed his hands across his face, wrestling with himself. "I just don't know why I should."

I felt the tingling of tears behind my eyes. "I didn't do it."

"So why won't you tell the police the truth?"

I opened my mouth then closed it. I knew the answers he wanted, and I couldn't give them to him. "I can't."

Tyrell closed his eyes. "I don't know where I went wrong or why you can't trust me, but I really liked you, Sienna."

Liked.

He pushed his hands into his pocket. "If you're ever ready to tell the truth to the police. Or me," he added quietly. "Let me know."

"We can still—"

"All done?" Nia was back, a binder under one arm and an eyebrow raised.

Tyrell didn't meet my gaze.

I spoke through a scratchy throat. "Yeah, all done."

The heat of Nia's stare pinned me as I scurried out of the room. I turned right, taking deep breaths to fight the tears. I couldn't face being in a room with Bianca or in the same building as Tyrell.

I rushed through the lobby and threw open the door to The Bells. Cold air blasted over me. I gulped in breaths and leaned against the brick walls. A sharp buzz started in my pocket. I picked up the call without checking the screen.

"This is a prepaid call from…" The sound was muffled,

and my hands trembled at the deep, familiar voice. "August, an inmate at the—"

I hung up, my ears pounding. My legs were moving. I didn't know where to go, but I needed to be away. I shivered as I walked through the iron gates of Stedmond Park. It lay in darkness, but I could still see trodden earth on the low-kept grass and empty bottles and wrappers in the bushes. I walked to a bench by a flickering streetlight, and my shoulders hunched as I felt the back of the steel bench. I pressed my lips pressed together tightly and lowered my head so no one heard while I sobbed.

The Bells was quiet when I returned. I knocked softly on Bianca's door. The creak of a bed sounded before the door swung back, revealing a smiling Bianca.

"What are you smiling about?"

The small bedside lamp lit the room. She walked backward to her bed, sat cross-legged, then perched her laptop on her lap. "We sent out a link for people to buy tickets for Dani's memorial, and we've already sold fifty tickets. I couldn't buy an ice cream with the amount Raven and Ainsley donated," she muttered. "But I guess it's still good they will be there."

I kept my head down as I crossed to Mabel's side.

"Unfortunately, her family don't want to come. Not while the killer is out there."

Bianca had fought to have Dani kicked off the team, but it never worked—perks of being the best. Dani had lost most of her gold medals and trophies after she'd started placing them in the kitchen and common room to taunt Bianca, because Bianca had started throwing them away. Yet now she was planning a fundraiser for the very person who'd made her life difficult.

"Why are you doing all of this?" I asked.

Bianca blinked rapidly. "I'm just glad I can do something for her."

"It's great that you want to help, but why?"

Bianca flinched and looked down at her hands. Seconds passed. I didn't think she would answer, then she looked up, tears in her eyes. "I feel so guilty." She clasped her hands together to stop shaking. "Sorry. That's not the best thing to say after someone has been killed." She laughed with no trace of humor. "Dani knew things. I don't know how she would find out, but she always knew how to use it against you." She sniffed. "So, sometimes, I can't help feeling relieved that she's dead, you know?"

I did. Dani knew my secrets too.

"And then I feel sick because who thinks that way?" Tears rolled down her cheeks. "I'm sorry." She sniffed, wiping her face with the back of her hand.

The right thing to do would be to comfort her, to tell her it was okay because we all had those thoughts. But someone had acted on them, and there weren't many people who hated Dani more than Bianca did. I decided to give her a moment alone, closing the door behind me with a soft click before going to the kitchen.

The dishwasher hummed. An empty glass was on the counter, and a drawer was half open. I closed the drawer and picked up the glass.

"Where did you go?"

I stilled then turned and found Raven behind the kitchen door.

She dropped an unpeeled orange onto the counter and raised her palms. "It's just me."

I swallowed.

"It looks like you've had a rough day." She touched her eye with her index finger and dragged it down her cheek. "Everyone here thinks you did it."

I turned my back to her, placing the glass in the sink. "Thanks."

I heard shuffling, and moments later, Raven was beside me, holding my gaze. "Did you?" Her voice had a note of expectancy.

"No."

She smiled. "Everyone in this house had a motive." She held up two hands and six fingers. "She stole Nia's boyfriend." She tucked her thumb in. "She's been beating Bianca at swimming from before I can remember." She folded her index finger. "I can admit Ainsley and I have had our differences with her over the last few weeks." Another two fingers. "Martina was sick of doing all her work." She dropped her left hand and tapped her index finger on her chin. "And then there's you," she said, narrowing her eyes.

I forced myself not to lower my head, determined not to show any signs of guilt.

"Where were you the night before Dani died?"

I stepped back. "Did you come here to accuse me of killing Dani?"

"Nope." She pushed up from the kitchen counter and threw the orange peel in the trash. "Just wanted an orange."

She picked up the discarded orange and headed for the door. "But you should know secrets always have a way of coming out."

"Wait," I called.

She turned to face me. Amusement lingered.

"You said you and Ainsley had been arguing with Dani. Why?"

She smiled faintly, swinging her wide-framed body around the door. "Good night."

NINE

The picture didn't do Dani justice. Her smile was wide, and her green eyes twinkled. She looked happy. She held up the medal around her neck to the camera. It failed to capture how dishonest, manipulative, and cold she was, all the reasons why someone would want her dead. The image had been printed onto the coral-blue T-shirts for her memorial.

The depiction was a stark difference to the lifeless way my mind forced me to remember her whenever I slept. But now my eyes played tricks on me. I thought I saw Dani wink, her mouth curving into one of her knowing smiles, but when I blinked, it was gone. The girl wearing the T-shirt shook a bucket in her hand. Metallic chimes and rustles rang out. I took a deep breath to ease the pounding in my head and pulled the change from my pocket. It clashed with the hum of chatter as I dropped in the change.

Dani wasn't popular. She was infamous. Dani was the best swimmer at Stedmond, the girl who'd stolen her roommate's boyfriend, the one who saw Vivienne Marks die, and now, the girl who was dead.

I joined the line to enter the rec center. Three long tables, manned by people checking off names, blocked the entrance, a familiar figure behind them. My neck stiffened as I locked eyes with Detective Collins. He was cloaked in black, standing out in the sea of blue. He tipped his head forward then continued to scan the crowd. I shuffled forward.

A fair-haired girl smiled as I approached the table farthest from Collins. "Have you donated already?"

I nodded and gave her my name.

She checked on her laptop. "Great." She passed me a wristband. "Please feel free to donate more. All proceeds go to helping her family." She gestured to a collection bucket with a different photo of Dani taped to the front. In the picture, Dani looked up at the camera, irritation etched on her face. She was wearing my yellow flowery dress, which I hadn't noticed was missing until now.

"The program is about to start. Please make your way into the rec center," a silver-haired lady repeated robotically into a megaphone.

The crowd flowed through the automatic doors. The murmur of conversation echoed in the reception area. The front desk was empty. The bulletin board sign-up sheets and schedules were covered with a photo of Dani. The smooth floor turned rough as we reached the pool. I tasted chlorine in the warm air. Refreshments were crammed onto a table at the back of the room, and chairs lined the blue-and-green patterned tiles framing the pool.

I walked toward the pool. Its clear and inviting water

shimmered above Stedmond's crest. I wasn't a strong swimmer, but for a moment, I imagined diving in and watching all my problems sink to the bottom, and I understood why Dani had loved the water.

"It's hard to look at the pool and not think about her," a hoarse voice said beside me.

I turned to find Michael. I hadn't noticed when he arrived.

He ran his hand across the stubble on his face, his sunken eyes never straying from the pool. "Thanks for coming, Sienna."

I swallowed, unsure what to say. I wasn't here for Dani. Her death had affected me for selfish reasons, and here I was, faced with someone experiencing genuine grief. His shirt hung off him. His black trousers were low at the waist, and his face was more hollow than I remembered. My stomach tightened. I liked Michael, mainly because having him around had meant Dani behaved better than usual. He made her tolerable, but she'd never hidden her scheming nature, and I couldn't understand what Michael had seen in her.

"She would have been happy to have you here."

It wasn't true, but I smiled politely.

"I wanted to talk to you earlier, but..." He exhaled. "I don't know if I really want the answer to my question."

My heart sped up. The crowd continued to bustle through the room, edging closer to the podium, apart from one person at the back of the room. I shifted, feeling Detective Collins's cold stare.

Michael stilled. "Do you think she suffered?"

There Dani was—bruised, cut, and pierced. Every inch

of her was covered in blood. I tried not to react. I wasn't sure if he could see it in my face. Michael's eyes were no longer on the pool. They were on me.

"She died from the poison. She probably didn't even know what was happening. Maybe it was like falling asleep." That was a truth I could offer him to save him from the nightmare.

He parted his lips, but someone tapped on a microphone before he could speak. The sound traveled through the room, and his eyes moved to the podium.

"Hello." The swim coach leaned over the microphone. "Thank you all for coming. For those who don't know me, I coach the swim team, and I had the pleasure of coaching Dani for two years. Anyone lucky enough to have spent time with Dani knows she was not afraid to tell you what she thought."

The crowd hummed in agreement.

"Some people who knew that better than most were the swim team." Coach gestured to the girls standing to the side of the podium.

Michael's jaw tensed.

"They were heartbroken when they heard the news, and they decided to do something for her. So, today, we are going to race in her memory."

The room applauded.

"It's rare I ever come across the natural talent Dani had. I could stand here all day and talk about how much of an amazing swimmer she was and how she was always true to herself. You never knew what to expect with Dani. Like all of us, she was flawed. I know I had been on the receiving end of her sharp tongue more than I would like to admit." She blew out a breath. "But we can hear about Dani from someone who knew her better than anyone. Michael."

"I'll speak to you later," Michael said in a low tone. He kept his hands in his pockets as he approached the podium.

Soft applause filled the space. People tapped and squeezed him on the shoulder as he passed. He kept his head low and withdrew his hands as he reached the bottom of the steps. The swim team stopped clapping, attempting to give Michael a touch on his back. He stilled, turning to face them. I couldn't see his lips, but something had made Bianca go three shades redder. They pulled on smiles as the room watched.

Michael climbed to the podium then addressed the room. "Dani would be surprised to see you all here." He placed both palms on the edge of the podium and craned his neck over the microphone, his voice low and thick. "Because she knew how much most of you hated her."

Hesitant laughter rang throughout the room.

Michael waited for silence, no trace of humor on his face. "What I loved about Dani was her ability to make a way. She never took no for an answer and always wanted to be the best. Most of the time, she came up short. Academically, I'm sure some of you have submitted assignments suspiciously identical to Dani's. Or others have stayed up all night because they had two of the same assignments due."

Teachers shook their heads and frowned as affirmative grunts could be heard in the room.

Michael looked up. "Sorry, Dani."

"Wrong direction, buddy," someone murmured, and

quiet laughter broke out from the back of the room. A teacher headed in the direction of the voice.

Michael scoffed and snatched at the microphone. "She never cared what any of you thought. She saw through all of you. She didn't pretend to be perfect. In fact, there was one place where she never had to pretend."

Michael looked at the pool and took a deep breath. Some of the swim team flinched as Michael jabbed a finger in their direction. "She was the best swimmer on that team, and they all knew it."

The tight masks slipped from a few of the girls' faces. Rachel, the only one who had opted for a blue sweater instead of sporting Dani's face, rolled her eyes.

"She wanted to graduate, be an Olympic swimmer, travel the world. Like all of you, she had plans." Michael paused. His cold eyes settled on the audience. "But she was robbed of the chance."

"Whoever did this to her is still out there." He threw a finger out in front of him. "Or in here."

Uneasy looks passed through the room.

Coach was up, her silver hair bobbing as she crouched past the front row to reach the podium.

Michael closed his eyes. A tear rolled down his cheek. "I won't stop until Dani gets the justice she deserves." He dropped the microphone.

I covered my ears as sharp microphone feedback rang through the room, drowning out the scattered applause. The swim team stepped back as Michael flew past, wiping his cheek.

"Thank you, Michael." Coach gave her own brief applause. "Our captain, Diane, would also like to say a few words about Dani. And please, everyone, remember to donate as much as you can. All the proceeds will help Dani's family pay for the funeral."

A petite blond girl approached the podium. She ironed out a piece of paper. "Hi, everyone. Before I start, I have a poem I would like to read." She took a deep breath, and the room fell silent—completely silent—until the door at the back of the room opened. I turned quickly enough to see Michael's back.

A few people in the crowd tutted. Then all eyes were trained on the captain. I crept to the back of the room as she started the poem. My neck prickled at the stares. Wearing a sweater more green than blue, Tyrell leaned against a wall and raised a questioning brow. I ignored it and focused on catching up with Michael. The captain continued her poem about a bird flying home. I didn't look back when the door creaked open and thudded shut behind me.

The air got lighter as I walked through the corridor of the rec center. Diane's voice quietened as I walked to the entrance. The lobby was deserted. I slowed, careful not to trigger the automatic doors.

"I know what you did." It was Michael, his voice low.

Someone laughed, high and cruel. "Your girlfriend is dead, and you still care about this?"

I inched forward.

Ainsley was leaning against the ramp railing. Amusement traced her lips. "I'm not sorry for your loss. I'm sorry you couldn't see Dani for what she was." She stepped forward, lips curled inches away from Michaels's face. "She used you. She would have left you behind to clean up her mess." She enunciated each word. "I didn't kill her, but I did see her that night. She gloated that she had one ticket out of Stedmond and was never coming back."

That was a lie. I'd seen two tickets.

The words had the desired effect, though. Michael's body slumped, and Ainsley's lips twisted into a smile.

Michael's fist pulsed by his side. "You're lying, and I will tell everyone about what you've done."

Ainsley shrugged. "You'll have to prove it first." She groaned, pushing up from the railing. The double doors pulled apart, and she craned her neck to see me. "Do you always have to involve yourself in things?"

Heat burned my cheeks. I shuffled forward.

Ainsley leaned into Michael. "It's over now."

I ignored her glare and stepped aside as she passed.

Michael drew in a long breath, head in his hands. "She shouldn't be here. She hated Dani."

If that was the criteria for being here, the rec center would be empty.

He pressed the heels of his palms into his eyes.

I shuffled closer and leaned on the rail beside him, an uncomfortable lump in my throat. "I saw Dani's tickets on the day she died."

Michael looked up, his eyes glistening.

"There were two." Knowing Dani, it was impossible to be sure who the second was for, but this seemed to calm Michael.

He lowered his head and exhaled into a fist. "I couldn't face coming to this memorial. It makes it seem real, and no one really cares. People avoided me because I was with Dani. Now they avoid me because she's dead. They don't know what to say, or they pretend like they loved Dani all along."

"Stedmond is offering grief counselors, and Professor Locke wants you to come to his office whenever you are ready to talk." I hadn't used the services offered, but that didn't mean it couldn't help someone else. "I think it could be good to talk to someone who isn't a student and didn't have a relationship with Dani."

Michael rolled his eyes. "I don't need to talk about it. He doesn't care about Dani or me. She always hated that guy."

"That doesn't mean much. She hated everyone."

"Yeah." He laughed, and the sound turned into a sigh.

I swallowed. "Did you speak to her before…"

He winced, running a hand through his unkempt hair. "We argued. It's so pathetic when I think about it now."

When he didn't continue, I asked, "Why?"

"Nia." He closed his eyes and sighed. "What Dani and I did was wrong. Dani liked to play games, but I didn't want to hurt Nia more than I already had. We were supposed to be leaving on the day Dani died, and when everything came out, I was too proud to give Nia a proper apology, so I figured I owed her at least that if I was never going to see her again." He swallowed. "Dani didn't want me to tell anyone we were leaving. She was adamant. Maybe if I would have listened…" His voice broke, and he cleared his throat. "But I didn't."

"How did Nia take it?"

"I thought she hated me. But she didn't want me to leave. She said she still loved me and thought we'd work it out."

"Do you think Nia m—"

"No." Michael let out a wet laugh. "Nia's not a killer. I told her I wanted to be with Dani, and even though she thought I was making a mistake, she accepted it." He swiped a hand through his hair. "It was Dani who made things hard. She couldn't help but rub it in Nia's face."

"Have you spoken to Nia since?"

"She came over after Dani died, but we didn't speak." His gaze lowered to the ramp. "I wasn't ready. I made my choice. I only wanted Dani."

To me, everything about Dani screamed *run*, but here was Michael, who loved her for what she was. I pushed aside thoughts of Tyrell, an uncomfortable sensation settling in my stomach.

Michael looked up at me, his eyes narrow, as though he were choosing his words carefully. "Did Dani have something on you?"

My hands gripped the rail, and I kept my face still as my throat closed in on itself. "What do you mean?"

Michael smiled. "Dani liked secrets. She knew things about people you couldn't imagine. Most of which she shared with me."

My heart thumped.

"Did she know something about you?"

I swallowed and considered my options. *Is he asking because he already knows?* I couldn't meet his gaze. Something tightened in my chest as I looked at the abandoned campus. It felt like Dani was back. I took a slow breath. "Yes."

He huffed out a laugh. "Then she liked you more than you think."

I blinked. Confusion clouded my face.

"She loved annoying you, but I think, deep down, she liked you."

My lips parted. My thoughts jumbled. "She didn't tell you anything?"

He shook his head, and a small feeling of gratitude grew for Dani. She knew my darkest secret, something she would never let me forget, but she hadn't done anything with it. She hadn't even told Michael, who knew everything else.

A thought flashed through my mind. "What did she tell you about the rest of the girls?" It would be easier to get information from Michael than it ever was to get anything out of Dani. "One of the secrets could have been the reason she was killed."

"That's more of a reason I should keep them to myself." He ran his palms over his face and sighed before pushing himself up and dusting his hands. "You should be careful around the other girls."

Ainsley immediately came to mind.

"All of them," he added, as if reading my mind. "Thanks for this." He seemed calmer than before, but I couldn't help but feel disappointed I had no new information.

"You're welcome, and I'm sorry for your loss." I didn't realize how much I meant it until it was out. It weighed heavily in the air.

"Thanks," he muttered. "I should go back inside and try not to accuse everyone in the room of murder." The rec center doors slid open, and he walked through.

I followed at a distance, my mind whirring. Dani had been a complicated person while alive but even harder to understand in death. It wasn't enough that Dani was leaving. Someone needed her silenced permanently. I took a deep breath. Something rang in my ears. *To think someone could do that then show up and pretend to mourn for her.*

We were by the pool entrance. Michael looked through the glass panels in the door before he pushed open the door. Heads swung in our direction. I tried to hold their gazes. No one could be that heartless. Something would show in their eyes, but the crowd only offered a fleeting look before turning their focus back to Coach, who was at the podium.

"As a coach, you want to work with the very best. And that's what Dani was."

The dryness in my mouth made it difficult to swallow the lump in my throat. I walked to the back of the room, where tables were lined with drinks and cookies. I snatched a small cup of lemonade and finished it in three gulps before going for another.

"Everything all right?" Tyrell asked in a low tone and leaned against the drinks table. "I saw you talking with Michael."

"Yeah. Everything is fine." I sipped my lemonade.

"Be careful around him. Ever since Dani, he's been lashing out. He was hanging around Platinum and fought with Jamie the other day." Tyrell nodded to a window of the gym overlooking the pool.

Jamie stood with his head pressed against the glass, eyes rimmed red. Professor Locke had an arm over his shoulder as they listened to the story of how Dani had won the team a championship. I pursed my lips. Michael didn't seem dangerous. He was grieving.

I turned to see Nia breeze past and lean into Tyrell.

"If I have to sit through one more speech," she said.

Now I saw her in a different light. She'd known Dani was leaving. She also had access to The Bells and a motive.

"I don't think I can pretend to be interested in any more stories about Dani." Nia looked up at Tyrell and pouted. "Can we get out of here?"

"We can't leave now. We'll look bad."

"It's not like Dani's going to notice," Nia moaned.

I pointed in the general direction of the pool. "I'm just going to…" I couldn't think of an excuse, and neither of them noticed as I walked away. It didn't surprise me that Nia had latched on to him. Maybe the police would be less suspicious of her if it looked like she had moved on from Michael.

"We need one last push," Coach said into the microphone.

The crowd gathered poolside as the team began to line the pool. Bianca appeared first, head low as she walked to the end of the pool, clenching and unclenching her fists, her eyes fixed on the water. With Dani gone, she was the favorite to win, and even though this was to raise money for Dani, Bianca would be taking it seriously.

"Please donate as much as you can and give a round of applause for the Stedmond College swim team."

Cheers and claps echoed. Low chatter filled the room. Coach called out a second name, and a short, fair-skinned girl stood beside Bianca.

"Hey." Martina weaved through bodies to stand beside me. "Have you ever seen her this nervous?" She nodded to Bianca.

"Maybe she's just focused." I looked back at Bianca.

She rubbed her hand along her black swimsuit then across her neck.

"No." Martina shook her head. "She doesn't have the shield of Dani being the best, and I don't think she copes well under pressure. I watched them a few times in practice."

I raised a brow. I didn't think Martina would have ever willingly gone to see Dani practice.

"Sometimes it was the best way to catch Dani." She shrugged then clapped along, and the crowd roared for the captain, the fifth and final girl.

Coach left the podium and positioned herself at the end of the pool, timer in hand.

Martina leaned in close. "Bianca beat Dani when I was there."

I narrowed my eyes. "I thought Bianca never beat her."

Coach blew out a long whistle.

"Dani let her win. Bianca knew it. And so did everyone else."

I tried to imagine the frustration—no, the hate—I would have for someone who constantly reminded me that my best was never good enough, who made sure I was never able to celebrate my wins.

"Take your marks." Coach raised her arm, and silence fell.

Bianca's face was a picture of focused determination. The girls took their starting positions behind the blocks. A loud buzzer sounded from the speakers, and the racers exploded into the air, arms stretched out above their heads as they lunged into the water.

Bianca was out in front, gliding smoothly, then strong

strokes hit the water, slicing through. Ripples expanded behind them. Bianca was level in first place with Diane. Their strides quickened, and the motion of their legs strengthened, but for Bianca, it wasn't enough. Diane propelled into first place. Her fingers gripped the edge moments before Bianca finished. She turned to see the captain. Her shoulders rose and fell with her deep breaths. Her nostrils flared as she clamped down on her lips.

The room applauded as all the girls finished the race, rushing to congratulate their captain, clapping and smiling. Everyone but Bianca. Her eyes widened in disbelief, then she blinked and left the pool, ignoring the extended towel offered and strutting toward the changing room, snakes of water running down her back. Coming in second would have been a win with Dani here, but Dani was gone, and Bianca still couldn't escape her shadow.

Michael stepped into her path. He leaned close and whispered something in her ear.

She staggered back then ran around him and into the changing rooms.

Martina blew out a breath. "Have they said anything about when you can move back into your room? Because Bianca is the last person you want to share with right now."

TEN

A dainty-looking woman peered at me through her spectacles. The bottom half of her body was hidden behind the desk, and printed on her Stedmond lanyard were the words *I'm Claire! How can I assist you?*

"Student ID?" she asked.

I slid the card through the opening at the bottom of the glass barrier. Martina was right. I didn't want to spend another night sharing a room with Bianca. I had been too afraid to let myself fall asleep, not only because of the nightmares but also because of the secrets they might give away.

Claire pressed the rim of her spectacles, her gaze flicking from me to the photo I submitted before college. My hair was its natural shade of black, tied back in a high bun, highlighting the oval face, curved brows, and high cheekbones I shared with my brother. Now, I wore my brown highlights down, strands of my coils covering my brows. My heart thundered as recognition flashed in Claire's eyes.

"Sienna Bassey?"

"Yes." I nodded, swallowing hard.

She hummed under her breath, and her long nails clicked the keys on her computer.

"But I didn't put the sock over the fire alarm." A student on my right huffed.

Claire tapped a claw-like nail under the glass shield. "Your key pass."

I slid the pass to her, and she swiped it through a slot. "I am going to reissue access to Room Four at The Bells," she said, barely moving her lips. She dropped the card on the table. "I have to advise you we have fixed some of the issues, but not everything will be the same as you left it."

I hoped she was right, considering the last time I was there, there was a dead body on the floor.

"The college is not responsible for any missing or damaged property." Before I even touched the pass, she called out, "Next."

The first thing I noticed was the chill. It swept through the dark room, whistling in the air until the door clicked shut behind me. I squeezed my eyes closed, embracing the darkness as my hand glided along the wall in search of the light switch. I forced away the memory of the wet blood that had been there the last time I touched it and blew out a breath as light penetrated the room.

No blood.

My mattress lay with the edges curved over the head-board, stripped of its bedding. Dani's bed frame was bare. Papers, books, and cosmetic products were scattered on the floor beneath the slats. Some drawers were ajar. Others had been removed and were upturned on the floor. Books lucky enough to remain on the shelves were stacked at odd angles. The bag Dani had packed the night she died was gone. Her family didn't want her things back. They didn't want anything that could remind them of her time here. All that was left of her was swimming accolades coated in dust. Strange rustling and crunching sounded under my feet as I moved through the room, instinctively avoiding where I'd found Dani. A limp arm, reddened skin, and vacant eyes flashed through my mind. I blinked, shaking the image away, pulled back the curtain, and opened the window as wide as possible.

I knew the poison had gone. The Bells also had carbon monoxide alarms, but I couldn't relax. The air seemed to stiffen as I packed what was left of Dani's life into trash bags. I had been so sure I hated her, but now I just felt pity. There wasn't much to show for the life she'd lived.

I walked on the balls of my feet, afraid blood would start to seep from the floor as I threw the last of her things into the trash. Dani's side was empty, but I couldn't help looking over my shoulder. The unnerving silence and absence of her glare would be hard to get used to. The cold tried to fill the gap she'd left behind, sinking in my skin. My breathing slowed.

The poison was back. I rushed into the utility room, beads of sweat running down my back. Nothing was out of place. The carbon monoxide alarm levels were normal. My bag of clothes Dani had returned was still behind the door. I opened it and pulled out my hooded sweatshirt, drew it over my head, and rubbed at my arms, hoping the shivering would stop.

"There's no poison," I muttered to myself. I tried to relax, but my body threatened the promise of sleep. I hung

94

the bag over my shoulder, checking the carbon monoxide alarm one last time.

I knocked lightly on the door to Number Three. Maybe I wasn't ready to return to the room, but the whispers of staying another night with Bianca quickly vanished as the door swung back. Small eyes and a red face poked through the gap.

Bianca stepped back. "It's you."

"Yeah, just coming to get my things." I walked into the room.

Bianca's gym bag lay in the middle of the room. Her swimsuit and joggers were strewn along the floor, crumpled pages of her scrapbook next to it.

"Oh." She sniffed and slumped onto her bed. "You're going back?"

I nodded, stacking my books on the table, careful not to take any of Mabel's things. "Do you think Mabel will be back soon?"

Bianca glared. She drew her brows tight together, and a crease formed on her forehead. "I've heard sometimes she sleeps somewhere else on campus. Maybe she heard about Dani and wanted to stay away. I wouldn't blame her."

That didn't sound like Mabel. If she knew that Dani had been murdered, she would be here, forcing us to stick together and think of happy memories of Dani. We never had perfect harmony in The Bells, but the closest we ever got to it was when Mabel was here.

I zipped my bag. "She's in one of my classes, and I haven't seen her in weeks."

Bianca peered at me. She opened her mouth to speak

then bit down on her lip and lowered her head. She sniffed quietly, and something tightened in my chest.

"The fundraiser was a good idea," I offered.

Her face fell. "Thanks."

I remembered the moment Michael approached her after the race, and a question fixed on the tip of my tongue. I swallowed it, extending the grace Michael had offered me. Bianca wasn't a murderer. If Michael thought she was, things would have gone differently. It didn't seem like him to taunt someone after a loss. That was exactly what Dani would have done.

Bianca pressed down on her lip.

"Thanks for having me." I heaved my bags over my shoulder.

"It was nice having someone here." Her voice shook.

I opened the door. I saw a tear roll down Bianca's cheek before it clicked shut.

I walked through the hallway. The lights were suddenly more ominous as they lit the way back to Number Four. I pressed my key card to the door and pushed it open. Nothing had changed. My eyes still darted around, looking for anything out of place. The window wasn't open as wide as it had been before, but the room was colder.

Or is that my mind playing tricks on me? I hugged my middle. A crunch sounded from the pocket of my hoodie. My heartbeat slowed as I slid a hand into the pouch. Inside was a sticky note. I unfolded it. Then my blood froze at the thick red letters written on it.

IF YOU SAY ANYTHING, I WILL KILL YOU.

ELEVEN

The weathered note wasn't meant for me. Creases and folds covered it. Cotton from the inside of my hoodie stuck to what was left of the adhesive strip. The paper had been in the pocket for longer than the four days since it was returned. This was for Dani. A threat that had come true.

I stared up at the ceiling, taking deep breaths and studying the small cracks and flakes of peeling paint. I should have called the police. I'd found a direct threat to Dani's life and something that could lead back to the killer. I reached for my cell phone then stilled. There was no way for me to prove this note was for Dani or that I didn't write it.

Mom's grip was back on my thigh. Stale coffee felt heavy on my tongue as detectives pinned me with their disbelieving glares.

I couldn't go back there. I wouldn't give the detectives more reasons to consider me a suspect. My hand still hovered over my cell phone, and something tightened in my chest. There was a time when I had friends to call.

Now, they'd blocked my number, and they crossed the street when they saw me, which was better than the neighbors who'd left posters demanding us to leave. There was a reason we'd stopped getting invited to things. People had celebrated when I moved away for college.

Mom thought it would get better. I knew it wouldn't.

I swallowed through the thickness in my throat and got ready for my first night back in my room, placing the block letters of the note downward. Maybe I could show the note to someone else? I thought of Michael. Dani might have confided in him about who wrote it, but would he tell me?

I sat on the edge of the bed. I was used to being alone, but I had never felt it more than the night Tyrell left The Bells. How would he react if I told him the truth about me? I blew out a breath and laughed. My only friend was a librarian.

I jumped. The sound of my cell phone sliced through the air, and the screen lit up to reveal an unknown number. My fingers clasped around the phone, and I picked it up—my first mistake.

"Sienna?" a deep voice said in a hushed whisper. "I heard ab—"

I hung up. My muscles tightened. Slow breaths became a quick series of exhales. I closed my eyes, trying to gain control. That was my next mistake.

Dani lay there, a vise-like grip on her reddening throat. She couldn't breathe, and there was nothing I could do to help her. She outstretched her arm, freeing her neck, and tried to speak. The garbled words merged with the ringing in my ears.

I couldn't open my eyes. My heavy eyelids were fused shut, and sleep threatened to pull me under.

I pried my eyes open, biting back a scream. My brother's familiar deep voice played in my head. The walls closed in around me, and this time, I didn't have the option to run. I was confined to the house where Dani was found, and everyone in it had a reason to kill her.

I leaped to my feet and snatched the note. The room spun as I walked to Dani's side of the room. A cruel breeze ripped through, and the mental image of her lifeless body became more vivid in the moonlight. She was suffocating, unaware she was breathing in poison. Her wheezing drummed in my head as I picked up a black dry-erase marker and stuck the note to the whiteboard on the wall.

I wrote Dani's name in the middle and drew lines around it, each leading to the name of someone with a motive to kill Dani. It was a long list, ending with me, because I needed to prove my innocence as well as the killer's guilt.

Everything I knew went on the board—a timeline of swim meets, parties, fights, and her relationships. I created six different social media accounts and searched for everyone I knew who was at Ainsley's party. After Dani died, Bianca looked through the posts—videos and selfies of a night they would never forget.

Except now they were gone.

My heart thudded as I scrolled through the list of Ainsley's followers. There was no trace of the party. It couldn't be a coincidence. Ainsley had even deleted her outfit of the day.

I private messaged anyone who'd been at the party. On

some accounts, I claimed to be a reporter, and on others, I claimed to be a student. By Monday morning, I had thirty-three replies, and every single one refused to talk.

I scrubbed a hand over my tangled coils. Yesterday was supposed to be wash day, but I was too caught up in finding Dani's killer. I had only left my room twice—to stock up on refreshments and to print at the library. The dorm room walls were now covered with every newspaper article I could find about Dani, as well as the previous codes to enter The Bells and everyone I knew they had been shared with. I barely slept. My head lolled, and my eyes burned with determination as I glared at the walls in silence.

Silence? I couldn't hear Dani anymore. The wheezing had stopped. I didn't know when it had. Maybe now that her life was spread across the surface of the walls, her misery wasn't just confined to my head.

The walls were overflowing with information, but there were gaps in the story.

Why was Dani so desperate to leave?

Names stared back at me. Jamie. Michael. Everyone at The Bells. The swim team. students who were at the party. I needed to cross people off the list, but there was nothing new to learn in my room.

I ran the shower as hot as possible and got ready to go back to class.

"I didn't ask you to turn it down. I asked you to turn it off." Raven's voice carried through The Bells. I heard the commotion before I opened the door. Muffled sounds amplified as I walked through the hallway to the common room.

Nia sat on the sofa, the TV remote on her lap and one leg crossed over the other, a smug grin on her face as Raven blocked her view of the screen. "I heard."

I saw press videos of Ainsley's dad playing on the screen through the gap Raven had left.

"I am watching it." Nia tucked the remote under her arm, but Raven still gripped it. "You know what?" Nia let go, leaving Raven to fly back. "Take it."

Raven fell back onto the coffee table.

"Move, Sienna," Ainsley drawled, bumping my shoulder as she entered the room.

Raven pushed herself up, rushed toward Nia, and stopped once she saw Ainsley. She looked between the two girls.

"What's going on here?" Understanding flashed in Ainsley's eyes. "Oh." She stepped back, her lips pressed tight. "You don't need to stop watching on my account."

Raven gave a clenched half-smile.

"Come on," Ainsley said. "We'll be late to class."

I looked at the clock. We still had fifteen minutes, and Ainsley was never early, but she turned and left. Raven followed her.

Nia settled back into the sofa. "You look terrible."

"Thanks." I tugged at the hem of my shirt. "How is everything going with Tyrell's project?"

"I've never been into politics, but he makes up for it." The screen showed an opposing candidate, and Nia flicked through her notebook. "Ainsley's dad's obviously going to win. Every time I turn on the TV, this guy has a different scandal." She pointed to the round-faced, balding man on the screen. "He crashed into a car and tried to run as if everyone in this city doesn't know who he is." She scoffed. "But he's relatable. Ainsley's dad tries to be too perfect. There's something off about the whole family."

Something in Nia's words stuck. "Did you go to Ainsley's party?" Nia's name had been the first to go onto my board. She had access to the utility room and our dorm room, and she had a good reason to stop Dani from leaving.

Nia laughed. "I had better ways to spend my time."

"Where were you?"

"In your room, stabbing Dani."

I rolled my eyes and parted my lips to speak.

Then her lips quirked upward. "That's what you wanted to hear, isn't it?" Nia curled her fingers through her hair.

"Only if it's the truth."

She wore a bored expression as she stroked the length of her hair. "I met up with a friend."

"Michael?"

She tensed. Her hand twitched, and loose strands fell flat before she tucked them behind her ears. "It's none of your business."

"You wanted to get back together." I could see the whites of her eyes and the fist clenched on her lap. "It must have hurt when he chose Dani over you. I would be mad too. She stole your boyfriend, and after just three months, he was willing to run away with her."

"And I've moved on." Her tone was clipped.

My stomach hardened, jealously bubbling inside. I didn't know if she was talking about Tyrell. As far as I knew, she was just helping with his project.

"You hadn't when Dani died," I challenged. "And now

you think you can use Tyrell to mask the fact that you're not over Michael, and maybe you were willing to kill for it."

She sneered. "Over Michael? Dani was leaving. I had no reason to kill her."

"You would if you wanted Michael to stay."

"Dani's dead. Michael's still here, and I haven't so much as looked at him." She lifted her chin and crossed her arms. "Tyrell approached me, and I do pretty well in class, so I had no idea who he was before Dani died. It's great that you think I'm this mastermind, but I had nothing to do with Dani's death."

I bit down on my lip. "Tyrell doesn't deserve to get caught up in this."

She cocked her head, her lips curled at the edges. "Looks like you were hoping your study sessions with Tyrell would turn into something more."

My face flushed.

"You're jealous?" She turned off the TV, and loud clicks of her heels filled the silence as she stepped forward. "Good to know."

TWELVE

The glares were unapologetic. I kept my head low, red-rimmed eyes threatening to seal shut. Makeup only concealed so much. The dark circles were gone, but the effects of Dani's murder lingered. I blinked. the screen at the front of the lecture hall blurred as my heavy eyelids closed around Professor Locke's tight-lipped smile. He must have given an instruction, because the hall burst into chatter.

Then he was calling my name. "Sienna, please, can I have a word before you start?"

I stiffened. Heads snapped in my direction. Murmurs died, and my legs carried me past the students in the narrow row, down the stairs, and to the podium at the front of the room.

Silence.

Professor Locke cleared his throat. "Thank you. You can all get back to work now." He turned off the wireless mic attached to the collar of his white designer shirt, and students reluctantly obeyed.

"Hi, Sienna. I just wanted to check in and make sure you're all right. You haven't replied to any of my emails."

I swallowed. "I just needed time after everything that happened."

He nodded, rubbing at his smooth chin. "I know. I didn't expect you to be back in class so soon. You also have to take care of yourself. You haven't spoken to the grief counselor."

"I know. Maybe I will this week." I tried to smile. My head pounded from the effort.

"If you don't feel comfortable speaking with someone else, you know my door is always open." Professor Locke was only a few years older than us and cared about his students in a way other teachers didn't.

I nodded. "Thanks for looking out for me." I turned and made my way back up the steps.

"One minute left," Professor Locke's voice boomed around the hall.

"I could show you what I've got so far," Sweaty called, the loudest person in any room. There wasn't a party on campus he missed.

I shuffled along my row, the hairs at the back of my neck on end. Students no longer glared at me. They looked over their shoulders at Sweaty as he cupped his hands over his mouth. "But you'd be missing out. You will be blown away if you give me an extra five minutes."

Professor Locke straightened out his shirt, a trace of a smile on his lips. "Are you trying to manipulate me into giving you extra time?"

Sweaty raised a brow. "Is it working?"

"No." Professor Locke raised his palm. "And I'd like you to give feedback first."

The hallway was pandemonium. Students streamed in all directions, clutching backpacks and piles of notes and books. A cell phone skidded across the floor, narrowly avoiding being crushed under boots, and its owner pushed through the crowd to retrieve it. I leaned back against a wall under the staircase – the only place for safety. Students rushed up the steps, laughing and shouting as they hurried to their next class. The light above filtered through the footfall and highlighted Sweaty's face. "This is cozy," he said. "To what do I owe the pleasure?"

"Were you at Ainsley's party?"

His brows furrowed, then an amused look spread across his face. "Look."

I suppressed a shudder as he placed a hand on my shoulder.

"I can't just sit around waiting for you. I know it must be hard for—"

"Ew. No." I shrugged him off. "I need any pictures or videos you took that night."

He arched a brow. "If that's what you're into."

"Of the party." I sighed through gritted teeth.

Sweaty brought out his cell phone. "Why?"

I swallowed. No one was paying any attention, but I lowered my voice as I decided to part with some of the truth. "I want to see if Dani was in any of them."

His hand slacked, then he pressed the cell phone against his chest. "Ainsley's asked us to delete them, and I don't want to ruin the chance of having another party at The Bells."

I practically fought the urge to rip the cell phone from his grasp. If Ainsley didn't want anyone to see them, it was because there was something there. I took a step forward. "Please, it's important."

He tipped his head back. "Considering we have history."

The closest we had been was the hand he had placed on my shoulder earlier, but I wasn't going to challenge that now.

"I'll show you, just you," he added. "I don't need these getting to the police."

"I won't show them to the police," I promised, reaching for the cell phone.

"But."

My hand twitched.

"I get to call in a favor."

"A favor?"

"I can call it in any time, no questions asked."

"I'm sure I'll have plenty of questions."

He grinned. "Don't you trust me?"

"No."

He shrugged. "But right now, I have something you need, and Ainsley's already convinced most people to delete their pictures. They already have their own reasons why they don't want the police questioning what happens at these parties. So I won't ask why you're doing this, and you can see all the pictures you want."

I hesitated. No favor Sweaty could call in would be

good news for me, but I needed the chance to see the party firsthand. I took the cell phone.

"Swipe right at your own risk."

I scoffed and carefully swiped left. The first few were selfies of Sweaty and his friends taken outside The Bells. I passed through variations of the same picture from a different angle. Sweaty watched over my shoulder, amused.

The pictures moved inside. There was a picture with a girl, another girl, then another girl. I cringed and felt Sweaty's grin grow. I swiped faster. Then I paused, my pulse racing. My eyes widening, I swiped back. I pinched my fingers together and zoomed in on the image.

"Nia was there?" I dragged the face hidden behind blond curls into the frame's center.

"Yeah, doesn't she live there?"

My chest tightened. Maybe after meeting Michael, she was angry enough to stab Dani. "She does."

"Was she not allowed to be there?" Sweaty asked.

I looked up. I had been frozen on the same picture for too long. I pointed to the screen. "Do you mind if I send these to myself?"

The corners of his mouth ticked up. "You know there are easier ways to get my number."

"Do you have to hit on everything that moves?"

He pulled at his ear. "Just the special ones."

I rolled my eyes. "I'm going to send a few of these to myself."

"I'll think about that favor while you do."

Sweaty was annoying but, for the most part, harmless. I should have known better than to make deals with anyone, but right now, I needed answers. "Fine." I grunted and returned to his camera roll, selecting all the pictures until they became photos of lectures slides.

"Two hundred and thirty-two pictures?"

"Yeah. It was a fun night."

I sent the pictures then returned the cell phone as an onslaught of buzzing ensued from my pocket. "Thanks."

"No." He smiled. "Thank you."

I walked away, fighting the urge to snatch his cell phone and delete my number.

THIRTEEN

The date for Dani's funeral was set. That was the first thing I heard as I stepped into the lobby of The Bells. I closed the door quietly behind me, making sure the back of Raven's half-blue hair didn't turn from the hallway. She leaned forward, addressing someone in room one.

I strained to hear the hushed voices. Ainsley's voice was barely audible. "Her family have invited everyone, including the police. You're so lucky they didn't search our rooms properly the last time they were here."

I stared unseeing at the floor and moved closer. My heart thudded in my ears.

"Where is it now?" Ainsley hissed.

"In my room," Raven said.

"Are you crazy? Get rid of it."

I stilled. My mind raced as I waited for them to continue. They didn't, and it only took seconds to understand why. I looked up to see Raven glaring.

Then Ainsley pushed past her into the lobby. "Argh. They still haven't arrested you yet?" She moaned. "Personally, I don't think you should be locked up for Dani's murder. It should be for bringing that freak into Nia's life. Do you know how painful it is to hear her talk about how happy she is?"

I clenched my teeth.

"It makes me wish Dani was here to take this one too," Raven said. "He's already practically moved in. Now I can never get Nia out of the room."

"Is Tyrell here now?" I asked.

"No." Raven rolled her eyes. "They are meeting up later. I don't plan to be here when they do."

Ainsley neatly tucked a smart gray shirt into her pencil skirt and straightened a big designer bag over the crook of her elbow.

"Where are you going?" I gestured to her outfit.

"I have an interview for a part-time job over the next break."

"You're not going home?" I asked.

She cleared her throat. "Not everyone wants to spend the holidays with their family."

It was something I understood. I opened my mouth then closed it. "I need you to send me all the pictures from your party and a list of people you sent the invites to."

Her head fell to the side, then she hunched forward and laughed. "What makes you think I would do that?" She caught her breath. "I already sent that over to the police."

"Really?" I asked. "*All* the photos?"

She craned her neck to look over my shoulder. "My cab's here." She brushed me as she walked past. "You should leave the police to do their jobs."

The door slammed shut, and Raven's throat worked. "Why do you want pictures from the party?"

I shouldn't have asked. They wouldn't tell me anything. I clenched my jaw. "No reason."

The pictures had already revealed one thing. Nia was perfectly positioned when Dani was killed, so if she had nothing to do with her murder, why lie?

Light filtered through the narrow slit in the curtain, and the dry-erase marker squeaked as I posed the question to the space beneath Nia's name on the board. Then I glared at the rest of the names on my board. The pillow shifted beneath me as I sat back on the balls of my feet. So many people had reasons to want Dani dead. It should have high-lighted the dangers, but I needed to solve this. I needed life to go back to what it was.

The board was full with notes, questions, and motives. I stood up, taking the pillow with me, and dropped it on the floor by the adjacent wall. My head spun, and I leaned against the wall. Sticky notes crackled beneath my trembling hand. Then I lowered myself to the ground.

Dani couldn't have my dreams, so now she haunted my senses. Food lacked taste or stung with the coppery taste of blood. Sometimes I thought I could hear her voice or see her smirk in the faces of others. Then I would blink, sleep threatening to pull me under, and when I opened my eyes, she would be gone. Now, I held my breath as shadows stretched and morphed across the notes and pictures on the wall. I squeezed my eyes shut and blew out a sharp breath before I opened them again.

It was real.

My cell phone buzzed in my hand. I glared at the two

hundred thirty-three notifications from an unsaved number. All of them were photos except one. The newest notification was for a message from Sweaty: *Can't wait to call in that favor.*

I felt a pang of regret and hoped the pictures would be worth it. I dragged my pile of pens and sticky notes closer, sent the photos to my laptop, and opened the screen. Sweaty's gray eyes were a blur behind my laptop screen. I clicked through selfies and deleted all the useless ones. Most of them were selfies, which I flicked through absent-mindedly, then I had to remind myself that I was looking for something. But that was the problem—I wasn't looking for anything in particular. Just anything that seemed odd. Sweaty was in the midst of all the action. No two pictures were of the same people or location.

The space somehow looked bigger with the party in full swing. There were more people there than I had seen at The Bells. In a video, Sweaty's clothes were plastered against his skin. He wiped an arm across his forehead then draped it around a red-haired boy. They cheered to the camera before it panned to a bleary-eyed boy. His glasses askew, he threw up, and I made a mental note never to sit on the right side of the sofa again. The camera spun back to the pair of boys laughing. I paused, ready to swipe, but there was something eerie about the still. I zoomed into the background, recognizing some of the figures from Dani's swim team. Raven was a blur, but I could make her out from her white dress. The boy Sweaty had his arm wrapped around reminded me of Mabel, her bright blue eyes, and the shock of curly red hair.

Red.

That's what's wrong with the picture. I leaned forward. I blinked, half expecting the picture to change. Red coated the side of Raven's dress. Lack of sleep had been playing tricks on me, but if Ainsley wanted everyone to delete the pictures and videos, maybe this was why. It couldn't be a coincidence that Raven looked like she was covered in blood the night Dani died. I felt like I was finally closer to the truth. I held down the screen until the metadata for the picture came up. The original was time-stamped just before midnight, more than two hours after I left. I added the photo to my evidence folder, eyes wide in concentration. Only the clicks from the keyboard broke ghostly silence.

I needed to create a timeline of the night, and now, I had a main target. I scanned the pictures for the white lace, ignoring the gritty sensation behind my eyes. I saved any picture featuring someone who lived at The Bells and noted the original time the photo was taken. Nia disappeared from all pictures around eleven, and Bianca made an appearance among her swim team. I noted the times and updated the folder but kept my focus on finding Raven after midnight. I scanned over Sweaty's bathroom selfies until I found Raven's distinctive blue-and-black hair. A rush of adrenaline shot through me. A fitted black halter dress had replaced the white dress, and she hunched into Ainsley's shoulder, a wry smile on her face. She was hiding something. At this very moment, there was something in her room that she and Ainsley didn't want the police to see, and that was where I needed to look.

There were three more pictures from Martina. She had deleted most of them and only recovered the three she'd sent to a friend. A group photo, one mirror picture, and a hazy sea of cameras pointed toward the lens. Washed-out faces smiled past the camera, blurs of movement. It was hard to identify any of the bodies except for one. My heart lurched. I scrambled to view the timestamp, then I zoomed in. At 1:30 a.m., familiar brown hair fell into Dani's pale face.

FOURTEEN

I held freshly folded printouts of the pictures from the night Dani had died. My eyes darted around the library. Light flooded in from the bay windows, and rows of bookshelves shielded me from the chattering students. I tapped my feet against the floor, my head pulsing to the beat.

Tyrell liked to study on the second floor, and it was also where I'd met him. I peered at the entrance, willing him to walk through. My heart quickened as a flash of blond entered. I leaned forward in my seat, my vision blurring.

I blinked. It wasn't Nia.

I moved back, waiting for the doors to open. I didn't know when my head started to droop. By the time I had registered what had happened, my eyes were closed. Cool glass pressed against my temple, and the room quietened. I tried to remember why I was there.

I needed to search Raven's room, but first, I had to be sure Nia and Tyrell were out, and if they were out, they would be here.

My body drooped. Lips parted, releasing slow, labored

breaths. Seconds passed slowly. Everything went black. My heart thudded. I tried to open my eyes, but my body froze, and there was nothing I could do to stop it.

She was coming.

"Sienna?" A soft hand pressed on my shoulder.

I drew back my head from my slumped position. Khadijah's kind features, framed by a pink-and-white-striped hijab, softened. "Are you okay?"

"I'm fine," I managed through my dry throat.

"Why don't you wait for me in Meeting Room Five?"

I frowned. "I can't. I'm waiting fo—" There was no way to end the sentence without worrying Khadijah more. "I'm just tired. It's been hard to sleep lately."

She nodded. "I can take a break, and you can talk about it."

I chewed my lips.

"I just need five minutes." Khadijah peeked out from behind the shelf and beckoned Mary over.

I lowered my head, earning a scowl from Mary as she approached.

"I'll meet you in the meeting room," Khadijah said. She leaned in and whispered in Mary's ear.

I rose slowly from my chair, only catching the beginning of Mary's complaints as I walked to the meeting room.

Sunlight streaked through the windows. Notes lined the whiteboard on the walls, and the sharp smell of dry-erase markers filled the small space. I pulled down the blinds, blocking the view overlooking the platinum building.

Khadijah entered, holding two bottles of water. "What's happened?"

I rubbed my dry eyes. "How long have you got?"

"Only fifteen minutes. Mary has a dentist's appointment at four." She sighed. "Sienna, you're supposed to be taking care of yourself."

"It's hard when people think I did it. Every time there's new evidence, somehow, it incriminates me. I can't sleep or eat. It feels like I've lost everything, and my only friend is the librarian."

"Frie—Sienna." She dropped the bottles on the table and held my gaze. "I know you are not capable of murder."

My throat caught. "How?" When everyone else doubted me, I wanted to understand what went on in the mind of someone who didn't. How could anyone trust me when I couldn't give them the whole truth?

"You are one of the most amazing students I have ever met. Even when Dani was taunting you, you were always calm. You gave grace when you didn't have to. When things got hard, you came to me or Tyrell. You chose to vent to people who care rather than lash out." Khadijah smiled. "You need to keep doing that and know that things will always get better."

I bit down on my lip and nodded.

"Have you spoken to Tyrell?"

"I think you're the only person I can vent to right now."

Khadijah's brow wrinkled. "What's happened?"

I sighed. "He wants to *know* me." I looked up at Khadijah to find a grin on her face.

She chuckled softly. "That doesn't sound too bad."

It was. I shifted in my chair. Khadijah's gaze wasn't intrusive, and the silence that followed was a polite offering I couldn't take. There were some things I wasn't ready to talk about. "I just think he would see me differently."

"And you won't tell him why?"

"No."

"You don't have to tell him anything you are uncomfortable with, but you can let him in a little. He cares about you."

I pushed my hand under my thigh. "Or you can distract me by taking me to get something to eat tonight?" I looked up through my lashes.

Khadijah blushed. "I have plans with my fiancé."

"I thought we just established that love is dead."

She laughed. "Maybe you should think about going home for a few days. I'm sure your family would love to see you."

I shook my head. The room seemed to move with it. Dark spots clouded my vision.

Khadijah arched a brow. "Have you been keeping your family updated?"

My sunken expression gave her the answer. "It's been in the news." I shrugged. Then I saw it—bright-blond curls and a tall figure. I blinked. They were here.

Now, I needed to get back to The Bells and find a way into Nia and Raven's room.

I stood up. "I don't have any updates. And I'm not going to tell her that everyone thinks it was me." Something clawed in my chest. "You don't understand what that would do to her."

"Your family must be worried sick."

"Yeah." I breathed.

Khadijah had seen flashes of Mom's good nature during our visit to Stedmond. Mom made an impression, and Khadijah was clinging to it. It was hard for her to see Mom as anything other than loving and caring, and I didn't want to burst the bubble.

Mary entered without knocking, her handbag clattering against the door. "I'm going now. Khadijah has to get back to work now." She turned to me as though I hadn't just heard.

"Thanks for listening," I said quickly, tucking the folded photograph under my arm. "I will see you later," I called over my shoulder and left.

I knew The Bells was empty, but I scanned the hallway for the third time, pacing by the doorframe of Number Two. I had no plan on how to get into the room. If I could steal Nia's ID, I could go to Stedmond's accommodation center or call security and pretend I'd lost my key card, but that would mean going back to the library to get Nia's ID and hoping that if I asked nicely enough, they would overlook the fact I wasn't white with blue eyes.

I smoothed shaking hands down my thigh and reached for the door handle. My pulse was racing as I pressed down, waiting for the welcoming click. The door swung back slowly.

I couldn't believe it. I bit down at my smile. Tension eased from my shoulders. Then I froze.

"What do you think you're doing?" Nia asked.

My heart beat dully. My hands dropped to my sides. Tyrell and Nia sat on her bed, hunched over a local newspaper article on her lap. I looked between Nia's glare and

Tyrell's confusion, waiting for the ground to swallow me up.

"Sorry," I croaked. "I didn't know you were in here."

"In my own room? Were you planning on coming in here while I was gone?"

Yes. "No, I just got confused." I backed away, trying not to look at Tyrell. I could imagine his expression, and my chest tightened. *Pity? Anger?* I didn't want to know, and yet, I couldn't help but meet his eyes.

His furrowed brows highlighted his scar and the story he had shared with me. Even now, when I hadn't given him anything back, his intent gaze tried to penetrate beyond the surface. No judgment. Just someone who wanted to understand.

I swallowed the lump in my throat and closed the door behind me. My head was pounding as I ran to my room.

FIFTEEN

There were two of her. Piercing green eyes floated from Dani's picture. Two sets of lips overlapped, and I could almost hear the laughter ringing in my head. I wondered if the killer had been affected too. Did they see her face every time they closed their eyes? Or was that a special punishment just for me? I glared at the names and notes across the walls. The room zoomed in and out of focus. I squeezed my eyes shut, tears rolling down my cheek, as I tried to stay balanced. Then three soft knocks issued from the door.

I knew who it was. I crossed the room and practiced a smile, and my lips cracked from the effort.

I wiped my cheeks then unlocked and pulled the door back. "Hey."

Tyrell ran a hand across his face, the index finger tracing his brow. "Are you okay?"

I wasn't. But I wasn't going to lie. "I'm sorry for interrupting you and Nia."

"Don't worry about it." He glanced behind him to the empty hallway. "Can I come in?"

I stepped back. If it was possible for him to think lower of me than he probably already did, it was about to happen. He stepped into the room. His eyes slowly roamed the walls as the door clicked shut behind him. I didn't have to think about how my room looked through somebody else's eyes, with the board with all the suspects, motives, alibis, scattered books, and sticky notes on the walls at all angles with the timeline of the night Dani died. My tangled bedsheets were unfit for sleeping but perfect for late-night brainstorming. Pillows were stacked on the floor by the whiteboard, the indent of my knee firmly sculpted.

I waited silently, my nails digging into my palms, as Tyrell took it all in.

He closed his eyes and took in a deep breath. "Are you going to tell me what this is about?"

I swallowed. "What do you mean?"

"Why were you trying to get into Nia's room?"

"Oh." I released a shaky laugh and nodded slowly. "That."

"Don't worry." He waved around the room. "I'm working my way up to this."

My breaths quickened. My mind raced for an explanation, anything that could minimize the truth. But he could see it. It was written on the walls.

"I think Raven might have had something to do with Dani's death." Saying it out loud brought down the weight of the words. It was a big accusation to make. I searched Tyrell's face for signs of doubt.

"Raven?" He narrowed his eyes. "Why?"

I hesitated. There was so much about myself I wasn't ready to share. But I could give him this. I walked to Dani's side of the room, where the notes started. "This is a timeline of the night Dani died." I pointed to the first sticky note. "Around nine p.m., I left to meet you, leaving Dani alone with Ainsley in this room. They had been arguing about something for weeks."

Tyrell stepped through the room, reading through the timeline.

"But whenever I was around, they would stop, but I heard them today. There is something in Raven's room they don't want the police to find, and Ainsley wants her to get rid of it."

"Look." I pointed to the picture of the red-stained dress. I'd printed it at the library.

Tyrell leaned in. "But, Sienna." He pointed at the clock barely visible at the back of the photo. "Dani was killed arou—"

"Two a.m.," I breathed. "I know. I think this is when Dani fought with someone. Because here she is." I pointed to the last picture of Dani at one thirty in the morning. "I know this is just before she died, because she is wearing my sweater."

"Why would she change into your clothes?"

"To spite me," I offered, and knowing Dani, it could have been true. "After her fight with Ainsley and Raven. Ainsley hurt her hand, and Raven had all that blood. So they got changed, but they were angry. They couldn't have a fair fight, so they had to get a knife."

Tyrell pressed his lips together. "Sienna, why don't we give this to the police? You shouldn't keep obsessing ove—"

"I'm not obsessed."

"You literally have a murder board."

I chewed my lip. "It's not a murder board. It's just a board about a murder." I took a step back. "These pictures alone don't prove anything. But maybe if I had some physical evidence." I tried to control the increasing pitch of my voice. "By peeking." At Tyrell's questioning look, I reiterated, "Just *peeking* into one of their rooms."

Tyrell cupped his cheeks. "Sienn—"

"Think about it." I cut him off. "We are trying to build a puzzle without all the pieces."

"Because that's for the police do."

"If I leave it to the police, I could be the one who ends up in jail."

He met my gaze, his eyes softening. "Raven and Ainsley would never let you anywhere near their rooms."

"I know. But I just need a key."

"And you think they would give you one?"

"No. Because it doesn't need to be their key." I looked at him with bright eyes. "It could be someone who shares a room with them."

Tyrell's face dawned with understanding. "Like Nia." He shook his head slowly. "You can't just break into people's rooms."

"The killer broke in and killed Dani. How do I know they won't do the same to me?"

He ran his hands over his head. "What would you even be looking for?"

I bit down on my lip. "Anything. I don't think I'll know until I see it. I'm still finalizing a plan," I said, walking over to the threat left for Dani in my sweater. "But I think I should use this."

Tyrell's eyes widened, and he took the note. "What is this?"

"Someone left it for Dani."

Tyrell's mouth fell open. "Someone was threatening to kill her?"

"Plan A is to go into the room and see if I can find anything." I sat on the edge of my bed. "And plan B is to confront Raven with that. Because we can assume the killer wrote this."

"Can we?"

"Yes," I said quickly. "And we are assuming Raven or maybe Ainsley is the murderer."

"We are?"

"Yes. Everyone knows that Raven would kill for Ainsley, and she would never get her hands dirty."

"Sienna," Tyrell said, his voice controlled.

My stomach twisted. I couldn't read the expression on his face.

"I'm sorry." I stood then staggered, blood rushing from my head. I turned my back to Tyrell and steadied myself. "I'm not asking you to get involved."

"You can't do this alone."

I didn't want to do it alone, but it wasn't fair to ask.

"I'll help."

I turned. Lightness flooded my chest.

"On one condition." He held up a finger. "I need you to get some sleep."

I closed my eyes for a moment. It was quick. But enough time for Dani to seize my mind. She lay there cold and limp. I opened my eyes. "I can't." My gaze dragged to the spot where I found her. "I'm sorry."

Tyrell opened his mouth.

"I'm not tired," I added, and my dry, traitorous eyes twitched. "Plus, we need to make a plan. Raven could hav—"

He gripped his hands and placed them behind his neck. "Raven will be in class at three because that's where you should be. Nia and I have plans at four, and she said she would be out until then."

"So we have an hour? What ab—"

"Uh." Tyrell raised a finger.

"Dani was m—"

"Nuh."

I furrowed my brows. "What are yo—"

"I don't want to hear anything else about this until you've slept."

I frowned. "Are you hoping I'm going to change my mind?"

"No. I know how stubborn you are. I just think you could use some sleep." He grabbed my woven cotton pajama set and threw it to me.

I wanted to be mad at him but focused more on why I hadn't picked out a cuter set.

"Get ready."

I obeyed, went to the bathroom, and washed off the unconvincing makeup. It couldn't hide the damage from the sleepless nights. Dark circles hung from my dry eyes.

When I returned to the room, my ruffled sheets had been straightened, and pillows had been freshly changed and fluffed. The soothing sounds of lapping waves filled the room.

Tyrell turned his laptop to show me a three-hour video of the sounds of the ocean.

I smiled. "Really?"

"I'll stay until you fall asleep."

I slid into bed and closed my eyes. "Thanks."

"It's been weird not seeing you around," Tyrell said. "I've missed you."

I was grinning like an idiot, and with my eyes closed, I had no idea if he could see it. I opened my eyes. He was smiling back.

I tried to capture that smile, to focus on it, but I could hear her coming. I sat up. "You don't have to stay here."

"Why not?"

I chewed on my lip. "Every time I close my eyes, all I have are nightmares."

He frowned, turning down the volume of the waves. "Okay. Lie back and close your eyes."

I did.

"Imagine the first day we met?"

I concentrated, trying to picture the second floor of the library. It had been quiet, only the first week of college. Excitement buzzed in the air. The dream of what it was like to be a college student hadn't been crushed yet. But Mary was making a start. She shuffled through the room, letting everyone know only quiet speaking was tolerated on this floor.

"You were stuck at the printer," Tyrell prompted. "A handsome guy behind you."

I bit down on a smile as the buttons on the machine became vivid. I couldn't figure out how to work it. I had been back to my laptop twice, but nothing had come out.

"Um." A deep rumble sounded from behind me. That was the first time I had ever heard Tyrell's voice. "You know you've been sending them all to the wrong floor."

I checked the printer. Only one print was scheduled. It was for a Tyrell Kenzie. He was right.

I sighed, looking back at my laptop. "Okay, just wait. I will print it again to the..." I looked around.

"Second floor."

I nodded. "Right."

"You do know you're being charged credits every time you print. You could just go upstairs and collect your print-outs already there."

That was a reasonable suggestion, but at the time, I raised a brow and drew my head back.

He held his palms in the air, a trace of a smile on his lips. "I will keep any further suggestions to myself."

"Thank you," I muttered, selecting the second floor in the printing options.

"Do you have any other hobbies besides destroying the environment?"

"Ignoring strangers."

He grinned. "Does that mean I can't get a name?"

"Sienna."

"Would I be pushing it if I asked for a number?"

"Maybe if you see me again."

My muscles relaxed. I wished I hadn't been so reserved. I wanted to enjoy this memory longer, but I took my paper and walked away. I was glad he'd seen me again. No matter how many times I pushed him away, he came back. He saw past the hard exterior in search of the truth.

"I've never lied to you." My lips were moving, but I

couldn't be sure I was speaking aloud. "Will you forgive me?"

"There's nothing to forgive," a voice said.

Tyrell's?

The scene was changing. I was going down the library stairs, but the paper ripped from my hand. I grasped at air, then my body froze.

I knew what was coming. "I don't want to see her."

Tyrell's voice sounded far away. "Who?"

She was already here. This time, Dani wasn't lifeless. She sat upright on her bed, a newspaper on her lap.

"Vivienne Marked for death by jealous friends."

"It must be weird reading about something you were there to witness," someone said in a voice that sounded like mine. "You never talk about what happened."

She grinned, a sly grin I didn't know it was possible to miss until now. "We all have our secrets, Monroe."

My body reacted. Pulse thumping in my throat, my chest heavy, I couldn't hide the shock on my face.

Dani folded the newspaper on her lap. "They would have killed me."

I swallowed the lump in my throat. "Who?"

She looked past me. "It's too late." She didn't seem to be talking to me. "I should have stopped it."

Were the words for me? I tried to step forward. The room transformed, and drops of dazzling white swirled behind the blackness behind my eyelids. I couldn't open my eyes. I was floating. The sounds of the lapping water rebounded in my head.

"I'm sorry," I said. "I couldn't stop it. I want to help solve it. I don't want anyone else to die because of me."

I thought I heard Tyrell's voice before darkness took me.

SIXTEEN

I opened my eyes and sat up. The glow of sunlight crept through the curtain, penetrating the black. The room was still, the usual pounding in my head quiet. I blinked, trying to remember what had happened.

"Ty?" I leaped up, scanning the room before I opened the bathroom door. Empty.

I was alone, but something was different. The hairs on my neck stood up. A new sticky note clung to the bedroom door. I stepped toward it. It wasn't my scrawny scrawl. My heart raced, then my shoulder relaxed as I recognized Tyrell's neat handwriting lining the pink paper.

You looked peaceful, and I started to feel like a creep. Just call me if you need me. x

I smiled, grabbing my cell phone to message back, but when I tapped the screen, there was already a message from Tyrell: *Is it too much to hope that you've changed your mind?*

I haven't. But it's okay if you have, I replied.

Dots appeared on the screen then disappeared. My chest tightened.

I got the key last night. I'll see you at three.

I blew out a breath, excitement bubbling in my stomach as I got ready. It was easier now. Dark circles didn't weigh down my eyes, and even my hair seemed more willing to cooperate. My tight curls framed my face. The only problem was my stomach. I couldn't remember the last time I had a proper breakfast, and the growling made me think it was long overdue.

I walked into the kitchen. The buzz of the blender filled the air, heavy with the smell of fresh oranges.

Martina looked over her shoulder and turned off the blender. "Smoothie?"

I nodded, then took two slices of bread and pressed them down in the toaster.

"Is everything all right?" Martina asked, pouring two glasses of the smoothie and handing me one. "Nia was looking for you last night. She kept banging on your door. You must have been out. Something about her room."

My mouth went dry. "What about her room?"

"You barged in, and she said you looked…" Martina's eyes widened before she waved a hand. "It doesn't matter." She threw her head back and gulped down the smoothie. Then she pointed to the table with croissants, pancakes, tiny cakes, and muffins. "Nia's out until the afternoon, so maybe you should stock up and hide in your room."

"What's this?"

She bit into a muffin. "Bianca is having some of the girls from her swim team round," she said through a mouthful and looked down at her watch. "I've got to go. See you." She dropped her dishes in the sink and left in a half jog.

My toast popped up, and I jumped as a knock sounded at the door.

"Good morning." A bulky, long-haired man stepped into the room. "Nia?" He had a thick accent I couldn't place.

I shook my head.

Before I could open my mouth to speak, he continued. "I got call that she was locked out."

My eyes widened, and my heart raced. I had hoped she wouldn't realize we had taken the key so quickly. "Um. She is not here." I stepped forward, hand outstretched. "Do you have the key? I could give it to her."

He sighed. "The key is inside the room. I am only here to open door."

He walked away, and tension eased from my shoulders. If Nia thought the key was inside the room, the plan was still in place.

"Gloves." Tyrell glanced over his shoulder at me. He held Nia's key pass inches away from the door. "Shouldn't we have gloves or something?" He stepped back, eyes wide.

I scanned the hallway, heart thudding. I had been so focused on getting into the room, I hadn't thought about any of the logistics. There were holes in my plan, things I could see with a clearer mind. But we were so close to finding out what Raven was hiding, and it was too late to back out.

"We just need to be careful with what we touch," I said, pulling at my sleeves. "And we can cover our hands so we don't leave prints." I held up my arms, and the ends of my sweatshirt flapped over my fingers.

Tyrell gestured to his short sleeves. "I left my jacket in your room." He turned to go back, then he stilled. Something sounded at the end of the hallway.

We had seconds. I held my breath, waiting for Tyrell to decide. It was my fault he was in this situation. He gave a subtle shake of his head and bit down on his lip before he pressed the key pass on the door. It unlocked. Tyrell entered, and I rushed in behind him, carefully closing and pressing my ear to the door.

We waited. It couldn't have been Nia or Raven, but that didn't mean it was safe. I thought about the man who'd come to retrieve Nia's key. I'd forgotten to mention that small detail to Tyrell, and there was no way I was going to do that now. He paced the length of the room, head in his hands.

There was no sound. No one was coming.

"It's okay," I whispered. "It's just us."

The room was an inverted version of mine. Every room in The Bells had the same basic layout—two of everything: a bed, desk, closet, bedside table, and attached bathroom. But the feel was different. Nia's side was bright, with pastel-colored notebooks with doodles, brushes, half-filled canvases, and paint crammed onto her desk. I recognized one painting from the first day we moved into The Bells, a painting of Nia and Michael. It had been changed. Nia's arm was embellished with flowers and butterflies. They spread across the canvas, covering Michael's features. Nia gazed at the flowers. Her blue eyes gleamed. She hadn't altered her bright smile or the blush in her cheeks. She didn't completely erase him. Thin stems exposed parts of his skin. I edged toward her desk. She'd never wanted to let Michael go, and she had every reason to want Dani dead. "Maybe we should snoop through Nia's things, as well."

Tyrell shook his head. "I couldn't."

I shrugged. "I could."

He sighed. "I have barely come round to going through Raven's things."

"Fine," I mumbled.

I hovered over her desk, my eyes fixed on a vase on her bedside table and a mirroring half-finished painting. The desk and glass-paneled window were outlined in light pencil. Clusters of small, dainty blue petals exploded across the canvas. Cornflowers. My favorite. They were polished with a perfect shine. Each stem was too symmetrical to be real. My heart swelled. I used to fill my dorm room with them, grateful for the color in the sea of black. Dad used to buy them for me, and they reminded me of the life I longed to go back to but couldn't. A heavy weight filled my chest, tightening its hold as I read the note.

To Nia,

Thanks for your help. You are a lifesaver.

From Tyrell.

Tyrell caught me staring, and I swallowed. "I sat through four hours of a robot zombie apocalypse. I think I'm the one that deserved flowers." I hoped he didn't notice the thickness in my throat.

"You barely paid attention to the *two-hour* movie. Plus, I had those flowers before I met Nia. They were..." He trailed off, his face falling.

I grimaced, and realization flooded through me. They had been for me.

"She's just painting it for an art project." He gestured to the room. "So, where should we start?"

"Oh." I turned. Pain flickered in the back of my throat. "From my experience, people always hide things in places that are accessible but hidden. It's more about it being out of sight, out of mind than never being able to find it, and Nia isn't like Dani. She would never go through Raven's things.

"Is snooping something you do a lot?"

I paused and thought of my brother.

Tyrell raised a brow, his mouth falling open. "I'm going to take that as a yes." He pursed his lips. "Did you ever look through my room?"

I pointed to the closet. "You know, over here might be a good place to start. The best thing we could find would be the white dress."

"Really?" The volume of his voice increased. He slapped a hand over his mouth.

"No," I whispered. I didn't add that his interest in me seemed too good to be true, and I was tempted to see if he had any other girls in his life, but I had no right. Not when I was keeping secrets. "What were you worried I found?"

Tyrell lifted the pillows on Raven's bed. "Nothing."

I walked toward the closet. "Nothing could be worse than your taste in movies."

He smirked. "Help me?" Tyrell lifted one side of the mattress and nodded to the opposite side.

I heaved up the mattress and lowered my head between

my raised arms, and my chest tightened. Nothing. Not so much as a speck of dust.

We dropped the mattress with a dull thud, and I stepped back to take in the room.

Raven's eyes bore into me from a picture on her desk. It captured her narrow eyes, more invasive than the rest of her family. They smiled, bright eyes and broad smiles. The picture next to it was a collage. One photo showed Raven holding a fat ginger cat. Another was a selfie in a red frame. Raven grinned in the center, and a surprised-looking Ainsley stood behind her, eyes wide and mouth half open. If someone didn't know her, they could have mistaken this for a smile. There was another picture of Ainsley alone, leaning back on a sports car. Something about it seemed familiar. Her thick hair was tied into a bun, sunglasses lined her crown, and the sun kissed her brown skin. She looked gorgeous, but my eyes couldn't help but fall back to the car. I had seen it before. My stomach rolled. I picked up the frame, a sour taste in my mouth.

I turned to Tyrell, who crouched down by Raven's nightstand. "This is the car I saw on the day Dani died. The person inside had been arguing with Jamie." I pulled out my cell phone, took a picture, then turned the frame. "It looks like they have a connection to Ainsley."

Silence.

"Ty?"

His head snapped up. "Where did you say Dani was going on the day she died? I think these might be her tickets."

I walked over to Tyrell and peered over his shoulder. He held up two small rectangular papers.

I reached for them, head spinning. I remembered when she put them in her pocket before I left. So Raven must have gone into the room to get these, but she also would have had to take the tickets directly off Dani. I held the tickets in my hand, Dani's means of escape. "Maybe this explains the picture. Dani came back out because she needed the tickets. They stopped her from leaving, and when Dani didn't give up, they stabbed her." I pushed the tickets into my pocket.

"Sienna, you can't take anything." Tyrell reached out for the tickets. "We need to leave everything as we found it."

I flattened my hand over my pocket.

"We can't let them know that you were here."

"Fine." I handed them back to him. "What else is in there?" I nodded to the cabinet.

"Nothing interesting." He moved back, giving me a chance to look through it myself. I pulled out scraps of paper, scanning old notes, concert tickets, and museum tickets.

Then my heart lurched. I had to steady my hands at the realization of what I was holding. My brother's face glared at me from last year's newspaper clipping. The headline was bold and clear: "August Monroe is arrested for murder."

The article below was incomplete. Someone had been careless when ripping it out, and words were crossed out and underlined.

"Have you found something?" Tyrell called from the other side of the bed.

No one else knew. I steadied a shaking hand. Raven must have gotten this from Dani. I stuffed the newspaper clippings into my back pocket. "No." I swallowed. "Have you?"

"No. Let's go now."

"We need more time," I said.

Then I heard it.

"You need key?" The familiar voice from this morning rang through the door.

We exchanged looks of horror.

I looked around. The door was the only escape.

"Hello, you are Nia?" a familiar voice called from the hallway.

We were both frozen in place, hoping for a false alarm. My heartbeat slowed as no sound came. "I came this morning, and now you call again," the man continued.

I couldn't hear Nia's voice, but she must have said something because the man continued.

"I need to see ID."

"Closet," Tyrell said in a hushed whisper. He took me by the arm and led me to the tall oak closet in the corner of the room. "I'll message Nia to meet at Platinum to give us a chance to leave." He pulled open the door and pushed aside clothes hanging from the rail. Then he climbed in and held out a hand.

I hesitated. This could be my chance to confront Nia.

"Sienna." Tyrell's voice was low but firm.

I wouldn't be the only one affected by my actions. I bit my lip and took his hand, and the world fell into darkness as the closet door shut.

Tyrell wrapped an arm around my waist. I could feel his warm breath on my neck, then it stopped. We both stilled as movement sounded around the room.

Tyrell let go and slowly pulled out his cell phone. A chill snaked through my stomach as he typed. I waited for a ping on the other side, but nothing came. I bit down on my lip.

If we couldn't get out because Nia's cell was on silent.

Soft thuds came from inside the room. I leaned forward, pressing my eye to the beam of light between the two doors. Only a thin strip of Raven's bed was visible. I squinted as an arm reached out. Then Tyrell pulled me back. I could feel his heart racing, and despite my disappointment, it felt good to be back in his arms. His cell phone lit up. He released me slowly, and I remembered the secret that burned in my back pocket. A shudder swept through my body. I couldn't let myself fall back into this. If I couldn't tell him everything about me, we could never work. There wasn't much space in the confined closet, but I shuffled forward, my feet brushing against something different from the soft cotton of clothes. Plastic rustled quietly. I started to crouch, but froze mid-movement, catching the slow shake of Tyrell's head.

He held up his cell. A message flashed on the screen. Nia had agreed to meet him at Platinum. We couldn't relax yet. Hurried footsteps rang through the room. Drawers opened and closed until finally, the door to the room opened and shut with a click.

We waited. Our breathing was the only sound.

"Let's go," Tyrell said.

I pushed open the door. My eyes fell to the floor as they adjusted to the light.

"Sienna," Tyrell called, already moving to the exit.

I couldn't follow. I turned, and my body drew closer to

the closet, where a dress wouldn't look out of place. I opened the door. The clothes on the rail had been separated pushed to either side. Some had fallen, and a loose hanger lay at the bottom. I reached down, sweeping across the floor. Something rustled. I closed my hand around the cold plastic.

Tyrell huffed and circled back. "Sienna, we have to—"

I pulled out the wrapping and let it drop to the floor.

Tyrell and I stared down. Quiet protests died on his lips, and we gaped open-mouthed at the blood-stained dress.

SEVENTEEN

It had been over an hour since Tyrell and I had searched Raven's room. I bit down on my thumb, pacing my dorm room. Each time, a sticky note caught my eye—a different suspect, clue, or motive. But nothing was more condemning than the bloodstained dress. Raven was at the party. She had easy access to Dani's room and had to have been there at some point to take the tickets from Dani. Then she could easily have slipped back into her room and changed without being seen.

But what was her motive? I circled the room, skimming the walls for an answer. Ainsley and Raven wanted her gone. *But if Dani was about to leave, why take away her means of escape?*

Unless it was a secret that only stayed hidden with Dani dead. But even in death, she had found a way. I hadn't expected to find the newspaper clipping of August in Raven's drawer, now hidden between books on my shelf. Its presence was still felt. Judgement, following me around the room.

I slumped down on the bed. My heart thumped. Tyrell insisted we had to leave Raven's room the way we'd found it, which included the bloody dress tucked away in her closet. We wouldn't be the ones to find it. The police would.

We had agreed to call with an anonymous tip after he finished meeting Nia. But there was no guarantee Raven wouldn't have gotten rid of the evidence before then.

I tapped the screen of my cell phone. No new messages.

I pinched my lips. I couldn't wait until Tyrell came back. The longer I took, the longer Raven had. My stomach sinking, my throat tightening, I pressed the number-nine digit.

Then I heard the screams.

Dread rushed through me as I raced to the door. My bare feet slapped against the floorboards, the sound drowned out by Ainsley's cries.

"What's happ—" The question died on my lips.

Figures lined the hallway. Bianca and Martina watched from the kitchen doorframe. Bianca's hands were pressed to her cheeks, and Martina's were folded over her chest. The door to Raven and Nia's room was wide open. An officer held Ainsley back.

"What do you think you are doing?" She threw an arm back, her elbow connecting with the officer's shoulder.

"Careful." Detective Collins stepped out of Nia's room.

Only a few paces away from my room, I took a step back and swallowed.

Collins turned. He looked at me—through me—before his gaze flicked to Ainsley. I expected him to reprimand her for the assault on his officer. Instead, his lips ticked up. "You have to be careful with one of our key witnesses."

Ainsley's face dropped. "Witness?" she said breathlessly.

Collins held her gaze then looked in turn at me, Martina, and Bianca. "Raven came to the station this afternoon, and she has confessed to the murder of Daniella Bishop."

My jaw dropped, and the hall rang with Ainsley's deafening screech. The sound reverberated in my head even after she'd stopped screaming.

My legs buckled beneath me. I was right. I couldn't believe it. My body shook as I placed my hands on my knees.

"She had nothing to do with this," Ainsley shouted.

Two officers came out of Raven's room, a bloody dress tucked under one of their arms. Ainsley couldn't mask her horror. "No." She gasped.

The officer let her go, and she almost fell to her knees before she clung to Collins. "She's lying."

Collins looked down, unmoved by the nails gripping his arm. He sighed. "Miss Crawley…" He didn't have to finish. Ainsley had dropped her grip, her hands flying to her mouth instead. Even Collins frowned.

I moved toward the room then craned my neck to see inside. The closet door was ajar, and items of clothing had been dumped on the floor with less care than Tyrell and I had taken. The mattress was propped up against the desk, and an officer stood where I had been only an hour before. She pulled out a plastic bag to package something from the bed. I couldn't breathe. I shook my head, speechless, as the officer bagged a knife.

"Is that—" Martina was over my shoulder now.

Bianca had crumpled to the ground, whispering into her palms.

"She couldn't have," Ainsley muttered. "Raven didn't do it."

For the first time, I believed it. The knife hadn't been there when I checked, and if Raven had been busy confessing to the police, someone else had planted the knife.

"Why would she confess to something she didn't do?" Bianca asked in a small voice, and I wondered the same thing.

In The Bells, we all had different ways of getting everyone's attention. Dani would steal and wait for us to notice. Ainsley barged into rooms and demanded to talk. Bianca asked for meetings using our group chat. But Nia, she screamed.

I uncovered my ears to open my door and immediately regretted it. Nia stood by the threshold of her room. Tyrell was a few steps behind her, index fingers pressed to his ears to shield himself from her wail. His eyes bulged in question when he saw me, and he jerked his head to Nia's room.

I shook my head. "Nia," I hissed. The last thing I needed was her scream to summon Ainsley. She was in a bad enough mood already. When the police left, she had searched the room herself, as though expecting to find a handwritten explanation from Raven. Then, Ainsley blamed Bianca for letting the police into the building. Bianca must have been remembering the same moment, because she scanned the hall before deciding it was only safe enough to poke her head out of her dorm room.

"The police searched your room," Bianca said meekly, the sound somehow enough to break through the scream.

Nia's face tightened. "For what?"

Bianca's eyes fell to the floor. "Raven confessed to killing Dani."

Nia's face drained of color as she blinked back at Bianca.

"The police found a knife in her room," Bianca continued.

"A knife?" She clapped her hands over her mouth.

Tyrell's eyes snapped to mine, and I tried to convey all my thoughts and questions with the widening of my eyes.

"Yes," Bianca said. "I'm sorry. We tried to clean up as best as we could."

"Raven?" Nia's voice dropped. She drew her head back, confusion etched on her face. "Oh, I didn't think—" She shook her head. "Tyrell, can we finish this later? I have to sort out this room."

"Sure." Tyrell blew out a breath. "Can I help?"

"I'd rather be alone."

Tyrell nodded, and Bianca slunk back into her room.

Nia's door slammed shut, leaving Tyrell and me alone in the hallway.

He held out his palms in question.

I motioned to my room, and he followed as I walked back to Number Four.

"It couldn't have been Raven," I said as soon as Tyrell entered the room. "The knife wasn't there when we looked."

The door clicked shut, and Tyrell leaned back against it. "Maybe she moved it." He shrugged.

"No," I said. "She was turning herself in when we checked her room. Someone else had to have planted it. When I heard her and Ainsley talking, they were trying to get rid of something. Raven is not stupid enough to move the murder weapon then go to the police."

"It makes sense if she murdered Dani."

We fell into a beat of silence.

Tyrell sighed. Thick brows framed wide eyes, imploring me to stop. Part of me felt like I should. Not many things beat a confession, but the whole thing felt wrong.

"I don't think she did it. If I tell the police that the knife wasn't there, they will at least need to consider the people who have access to Raven's room."

"You mean the *person* who has access to her room."

I shrugged. "It's the most logical place to start."

"What are you planning to say? 'Excuse me, officers, while I was breaking into the room of the self-confessed killer, I noticed the murder weapon wasn't there.'"

"That's it." I smiled. "But with a little less sarcasm."

"Okay." Tyrell pinched the bridge of his nose. "Let's forget about the confession. How do you explain the bloody dress, the tickets?"

I opened my mouth then closed it.

"And even if she didn't do it. You wanted to investigate because you thought the police would come after you. If they think they've got the killer, let them." He stepped closer. "I don't know what we are to each other."

Something clawed at my stomach.

"But I care about you." His eyes wandered around the walls to all the notes and pictures.

The murder room.

"No one is going to think it's you. You can relax. Sleep, eat, and eventually even go to class." His mouth pressed into a line. "I heard you say you don't want anyone else to die because of you."

The thing in my stomach was thumping now. Like a caged animal, it had its own heartbeat and was desperate to escape.

"You don't have to explain anything to me. But I want you to know you are not to blame for Dani's death, and you don't have to be responsible to prove who is."

I let the words comfort me. We stood paces away from where Dani had died. Could I sit back while a killer was out there? *Again.*

I swallowed, my throat dry. "And if Raven is innocent?"

"She confessed."

She had. *But even if she did do it, why now?*

"I was beginning to think you were avoiding me." Mom's voice drawled on the other end of the call. "You haven't answered any of mine or your brother's calls. We started to worry."

Two seconds into the call, she had already mentioned August. "I'm fine. They arrested someone for Dani's murder," I said, steering the conversation into somewhat safer ground.

Murder seemed to be a common talking point in my life.

I hadn't spoken to my brother since he was arrested. And Mom never let me forget it.

"Really?" She sighed dramatically. "I'm so relieved. You still need to make sure you're keeping safe. I don't know what I would do if I lost another child."

Another one of her pity tactics. I held a finger over the button to end the call and decided it wasn't worth the headache later. "How are things at home?"

"Sally-Anne across the road is having her fiftieth birthday this weekend, and she's invited the whole town."

That doesn't include you.

"Even Maisy is back. Her mom is trying to make them wear matching outfits." Mom's voice was laced with amusement.

"How do you know all this?"

Her voice darkened. "I overheard while I was getting groceries."

"Mom." I sighed.

"You should come back. You and Maisy are best friends. You should be here."

I opened my mouth, but she continued.

"Plus, I was thinking about making my famous mac and cheese. I'm sure she would appreciate it."

"I don't think she would."

Mom's voice choked on the other side.

"Please don't speak to the other neighbors about this. They had—"

"If we don't try, how do you expect them to move on?"

"It's been over a year. Have any of your attempts so far worked?"

"Am I supposed to just give up? This is my home."

150

Home was the place where everyone called for her to be arrested and branded her a murderer. They didn't even have the decency to whisper it because everyone else thought the same thing.

"If I don't reach out my hand, of course, there will be no one to take it. This place hasn't been the kindest to me, but if we want everyone to move past everything that has happened, we should give them the same grace we deserve."

We weren't talking about Kinwick. We were talking about August.

Mom's voice cracked. "I miss the family I had."

"I wasn't the one who tore it apart."

"No, but you're stopping us from putting the pieces back together, can't you see? We are supposed to love each other unconditionally. You can't turn your back on your brother because the whole town did."

"That's not—"

"He might still be home, and we would have been a family if you hadn't done what you did. You can feel guilty, but don't take it out on him. He is ready to forgive you."

Sick. I felt sick. Bubbles of bile clambered up my throat, the same way they did when I lied to the police then to my friends.

"You are supposed to be willing to do anything for the ones you love."

Every word felt like an attack. She had addressed the one thing I knew I would never be capable of. Love.

"Could you imagine if it was you who made a mistake? Don't you think we would do anything to keep you safe?"

They would. But would it really be love if I let them risk everything?

There was a pause. The question wasn't rhetorical.

"I know you would."

"And could you imagine how you would feel if we all turned our backs on you?"

A small piece in my resolve cracked. I swallowed. "I wouldn't put you in this position."

"You don't know what you would do."

I opened and closed my mouth.

Her voice softened. "Speak to him, please. For me."

"I don't think I'm ready yet."

"I knew you would need time to get through this. But I didn't think you would be this selfish."

Selfish. I squeezed my eyes shut. The word settled on my skin. "Bye, Mom."

I hung up and threw down my cell phone. As it fell, the screen lit up with a call from Tyrell. We were getting too comfortable, blurring lines. I tried to stop it before it went too far. I couldn't risk caring so much that I lost myself. Maybe he would figure out who I was first and hate me anyway. I let the call ring out. Then I deleted his voicemail without listening to it. I didn't need anyone else in my life.

EIGHTEEN

The next morning, a louder-than-usual hum filled the auditorium, halting for only a moment each time a student entered. The volume of chatter increased with each person who didn't have a wide frame and distinctive blue-and-black hair. I had gotten to class early. The nightmares were back, and The Bells felt suffocating.

I hid behind my laptop, ignoring the shouts of my name and the gestures trying to get my attention. A paper airplane sailed past my head and into the row in front. Professor Locke issued a warning into his microphone, and the calls stopped.

I kept my head down, rereading the last message from Mom.

Will you speak to him today?

Shortly after we spoke yesterday, there was an all-too-familiar call from an unknown number. I didn't answer it. In the same way, I hadn't answered any of the messages or calls from Tyrell. I put my cell phone facedown on the table.

Even Professor Locke's attention had started to turn to the door each time someone entered.

Raven wasn't going to walk through that door, and everyone else was starting to realize it too.

"Let's get started," Professor Locke said to the room. He tapped against a wireless microphone attached between his shirt's buttons, and hands flew to heads to shield from the feedback. "I need everyone to be focused." He flicked to his first slide.

Students leaned forward and brought out laptops and notebooks.

"We are starting a new topic today, and I also have an announcement to make that will affect all of you, so make sure you are taking adequate notes. It won't just be for your sake."

I spaced out and thought of last night. Professor Locke must have given an instruction, because the lecture room broke out into groups. A girl with a short bob turned to me. I blinked in confusion, and she sighed, turning to work with someone else. I fought sleep. The battle was harder each time I thought about Raven. It didn't make sense.

Murmurs about the classwork exploded into gasps. I looked up as Ainsley strode into the room. Her braids hung over one shoulder, baby hairs sleek and styled, her catlike eyes adorned in silver. The only crack in her exterior was her glossy lips pressed together as she walked into the room. Everyone had forgotten about the task.

Professor Locke raised a hand. "If you are not talking about the principles of financial accounting, I don't want to hear it."

Eyes trailed Ainsley's walk up the steps. She strode past

my row, her eyes finding mine and narrowing before she fell into a chair at the back.

Professor Locke cleared his throat, and stares peeled away from Ainsley. "I know a lot is going on, and everyone is on edge, but the most important thing you should be worried about is your grade. So, I have organized a group project to bring your attention back to this class and ensure accountability." Professor Locke smiled despite the groans in the room. "You have all been placed in pairs. The list of all your partners is already available on your online Atlas profiles at the end of the lesson—"

It was too late. A rush of clicks and swipes on keyboards raced through the room.

Professor Locke placed a hand on the podium and shook his head. "That's my fault. I should have held onto that for later. But now you have started, I will give you five minutes to see your pairs and introduce yourselves, if necessary."

I woke up my laptop, which was never a good sign in class. I logged into my Atlas profile. There were seventy students in my class, not a single one I would want to be shackled to for a project. I scrolled through the list, barely recognizing some of the names.

Feet scuffled, and people scanned the room in search of their partner. I looked for my name, surprised to see even Mabel had been given a partner. She would have been the perfect partner for me, but she was paired with Jorge Diaz. The name wasn't remotely familiar.

"My partner is in prison," Ainsley's voice drawled.

"Yes, I am aware of that. Please stay behind after so I can sort that out for you, Ainsley."

Sienna Bassey. My eyes instantly snapped to the name beside mine. *Beverly Haines. Another unfamiliar name.* I looked up, waiting for a look of recognition or a nod. When nothing came, a swell of hope that I could do this alone grew. Then I heard a painfully familiar voice.

"Isn't this perfect?"

I didn't turn my head. It wasn't that I didn't want to confirm who my partner was. I couldn't. My body was physically frozen, refusing to make this nightmare a reality.

"Beverly?" I let the name roll off my tongue with distaste.

A tall figure sank into the empty seat. "Sweaty," he corrected. "Should be fun, us working together. You can always take me up on operation make Tyrell jealous, and I've finally figured out what I want that favor to be."

I lost all hope he had forgotten about the pictures. I didn't want to know what the favor was. I could only handle one tragedy at a time.

Professor Locke clapped from the front of the hall. "Okay, time is up. You should all be able to recognize your partner, at least. Any further discussion can be had outside of class."

"Can't wait to discuss this with you later." Sweaty grinned and tapped on the table before he shuffled out of my row.

Professor Locke changed the slide to show a question in bold. "Ben and Molly have a struggling business, and they want you to advise them on what they can do to improve. If you check your Atlas profile, you will see their whole case study. Quotes from employees. The business values. Financial statements. I expect you to detail ways they can improve. Here are some books that can help. I suggest you get all three, but one will do." He moved on to a slide showing the book titles and authors. Everyone rushed to make a note. I brought out my cell phone and snapped a picture, determined not to make it one of the many in my gallery to never be seen again.

"You may also be able to find some copies in the library if you are lucky."

I emailed Khadijah the picture of the books, ignoring the sixty unread emails in my inbox.

Professor Locke went back to the lesson objectives for the last class of the semester. I tried to follow the class, but I couldn't make out any of the words, and when we broke into groups, no one turned to work with me.

When Professor Locke finally dismissed the class, bodies flooded to the exit. A smaller stream of students made its way to the podium where Professor Locke stood. Some people had been left without partners. Others wanted to swap. Sweaty strode through my row and dropped his bag onto the desk.

"I make good grades, and that's not going to change because of you." He gestured between us. "We will need to work through whatever we have going on here."

I raised an incredulous brow. "Which is nothing."

"Have you got any of the books?"

"I'm going to get them from the library now."

"Good. And then we can meet at my place and get started on a plan."

"At your place?"

A smile ripped across his face. "Sienna." His voice

dripped with sarcasm. "Are you only capable of thinking of one thing?"

"Library," I demanded. "I need to go there now to pick up my books. It has all the resources we could need, and most importantly, it's public."

"You don't trust yourself around me. I understand, but we are only coming up with a plan, and Platinum has study rooms."

It also had Tyrell.

"The library will be busy," Sweaty said, picking up his bag. "We'll have to look for seats. People will stare at you and ask you questions about Dani's death and Raven. And they won't know we are doing a project. Do you really want to be seen with me? *Publicly*. At Platinum, you can be in and out."

"Fine." I nodded, stood up, and packed up the last of my things.

Sweaty rose, too, bowing dramatically for me to pass first. "No. You go."

He smiled, walking down the row slowly. The hall was mostly empty now. Professor Locke was wrapping up with the last student around his desk.

Ainsley was still in the front row. Professor Locke fell into the seat beside her. Sweaty chose this moment to speed up. I pleaded internally for him to slow down. I couldn't hear any of their words as I turned out of the lecture hall, but Ainsley wore a look I had never seen before. Sadness.

NINETEEN

Mary waited by the entrance to the library's second floor. She pushed a trolley with a stack of books, pausing every few paces to bring a finger to her lip. I waited for her to pass before I headed to Khadijah. A baby-blue scarf was tucked into her white dress. She was sitting by a table, hunched over a laptop and surrounded by books. Four were stacked to the side with my name on a note on top.

"You got them." I knotted my hands. "Thank you."

"They are in such high demand all of a sudden. I heard about your project when I asked one of your peers what it was for, and I thought it would be good for you to have this book, as well." She held up a thick book: *Market Principles and Practice*. "I know Professor Locke, and he always appreciates wider reading."

"Thanks," I said, taking the seat beside her. "What this?" I nodded to a pile of invitation cards beside the books.

Her grin wide and bright, she partially closed her laptop screen. The screen darkened, and spreadsheets disappeared.

"These"—she picked a card from the top—"are my wedding invites, and this one is for you." She pushed a card toward me. It was teal, framed with silver. The cursive writing read Khadijah Weds Adam.

My heart swelled with happiness.

"There's no pressure. It is in a few weeks. I checked with the higher-ups to make sure it's okay, and you are welcome to bring a plus one so you are comfortable because I don't expect you to sit around talking to Mary the whole time."

I stifled a laugh at the thought. "I'm going to file a complaint about her one day." I eyed Mary as she hassled a student hoarding stacks of books at her table.

"She is just doing her job," Khadijah said. "It would be nice to see your mom again."

I shot her a look.

"But I imagine you'd have much more fun with Tyrell instead."

I frowned. "I won't need a plus one."

"Has something happened?"

"No," I said, and nothing had. I didn't answer Tyrell's calls and messages, and life continued—a sign that he was better off without me. After the call with Mom, something inside me had shifted. I knew who I was. I didn't want anyone else to make me question myself. Even now, as Khadijah chewed her lip, knowing something was wrong, she wouldn't pressure me because there were boundaries. She wasn't in a position to use our relationship against me the way Mom did, and Tyrell would if I let him.

"I heard about Raven." Khadijah stacked the cards neatly and placed them in her handbag. "I am glad that you're all safe now."

"I don't think it wa—" I swallowed. "Yeah."

"Is that a friend of yours?" Khadijah asked.

"I doubt it." I looked up to see Bianca wave from behind a bookshelf. I raised my hand in acknowledgment, but she didn't stop.

"I think she is calling you." Khadijah smiled. "Don't let me keep you."

"Oh," I said, tucking the books and invitation under my arm. "Thanks again," I said.

Gazes rose from books to me and followed as I crossed the library floor to Bianca.

"Hey." She pinched the skin at her throat. "Sorry to interrupt. I just wondered if you had seen Ainsley today?"

"I saw her in class. Why? What happened?"

"I think she has something to tell us. She wants all of us to meet in the common room tonight. I tried to ask her what it was about, but—" Bianca froze. Her gaze lifted to something over my shoulder.

I turned.

Michael's sunken eyes darted between us. "Is it true?" He clenched and unclenched his fist. "About Raven confessing to killing Dani?"

"Yes," I confirmed.

He closed his eyes and looked at the ceiling. I hadn't seen him since the memorial, but his hurt had become a spectacle. Even now, glares bore into him. Everyone wanted to see if they could push him to explode, and from what I heard, it didn't take much.

"I-I…" Bianca stuttered. "I'm sorry."

"No. You're not." His voice was thick.

Bianca's cheeks reddened. She stepped back then hesitated as Michael stormed toward the exit. She chuckled and rubbed her neck. "I think he hates me. Surprisingly, he was a lot nicer than Ainsley."

The books in my arms seemed to grow heavier. I propped them against my hip.

"Are you going to go to this meeting?" Bianca asked in a small voice.

Nothing good could come from a meeting organized by an angry Ainsley, but it could give me the opportunity to answer some of my questions. "Yes, I'm coming."

"Tyrell's not here."

I met Sweaty's amused smile. My eyes had been fixed on the study room door behind him, waiting for Tyrell to pass.

"Why are you telling me?" I pulled the book *Leadership in a Changing World* closer and placed a finger at the beginning of the sentence I had been trying to read for the past five minutes. There were only four rooms on this side of the Platinum halls. Tyrell was in 801, a heavyset guy I couldn't remember the name of in 802, Jamie in 803, and Sweaty in 804. I had been to Platinum countless times, and I'd never seen Jamie. That explained why the study room was so small. Sweaty and I took opposite sides of the square table split vertically with a blurry divider. A small shelf hanging from the wall held classic books, the spines unbinding and fading, and a cushioned sofa chair was placed by the window.

Sweaty slid his copy of *Principles of Financial Statements* over the table. "I think we should focus on their finances. Everyone else will avoid it, so our work will stand out."

I pushed the book back. "Everyone is avoiding it for good reason."

"Aw." He adopted a baby voice. "You don't think you can analyze a statement of accounts."

"I'm not five. I just don't think we need to make things harder for ourselves."

Sweaty leaned back in his chair, the front two legs off the ground. "So, what do you suggest?"

"We write an article about how their poor leadership has affected the productivity of their employees."

"Boring."

"We could be sure about the quality of our work. Most of it is subjective, so we don't have to worry about numbers or messing up on the day."

"You're scared."

I glanced at the door. "Or I don't need to draw any more attention to myself."

Sweaty took a deep breath. "People don't care nearly as much as you think they do."

"You don't know what it's like being one of the girls from The Bells and the person who found Dani. At least twenty people have asked me about Raven today. You were in class."

"I don't really pay any attention to all that." He shrugged. "Dani was crazy, and Raven's not my type. I'd like to ask you about Ainsley and Martina, though. Maybe not Martina. I think I might have made out with her sister once."

I cringed but disregarded his last point. "You knew Dani?"

He pointed across the hall. "Her ex-boyfriend lives right there. She used to be over all the time."

"I forgot. I hardly see him." My breath hitched. "How has he been since…"

Sweaty dropped his chair, and its legs smacked against the vinyl floor. "I don't know. I never ask. Not sure how to ask how he feels about his ex's murder during our daily nod hello. If you ask me, it's Michael you should check in with. He's all over the place. He's lucky Raven confessed, because if the police had any sense, they'd be looking at him."

"You think Michael had something to do with Dani?"

"I'm just happy Raven confessed. Now the parties can be fun again, without everyone thinking there was a killer on the loose."

There is a killer on the loose. As the day went on, I became more certain that Raven was innocent.

"How about a prerecorded presentation? So you don't have to deal with your stage fright. We record a presentation here, then we play it to the class then take some questions afterward."

"Yeah, that's not a terrible idea."

Sweaty turned. The light from the hall had dimmed. Jamie's tousled, straw-like hair fell into his face. The cut on his lip had healed. Only a faint line remained.

He nodded briefly to Sweaty, who reciprocated the gesture, then, combing his fingers through his hair, he turned to me.

"Sienna, can I speak to you after? There's something I want to show you."

TWENTY

Dani was everywhere. Her old, battered sneakers were on the shoe rack by the door. Her perfume and creams were neatly arranged on the desk, and the sturdy metal base of a trophy, one of her many accolades, gleamed on the mantel. The layout was an inverted version of Tyrell's room. The small living area was equipped with a double sofa, a small dining table, a TV, and a row of shelves that divided the small kitchenette from the bedroom area. I kept my head still, glancing at the rest of the room from the corners of my eyes. It was frozen in time, before Dani had died. Photos of Jamie and Dani were scattered around. A photo captured them baby-faced by his bedside table. Another photo in the kitchen showed her blowing out a number-eighteen candle on a cake. The first thing I had wanted to do when I got my room back was clear out Dani's things, but I hadn't been in a relationship with her for almost five years.

Jamie didn't acknowledge all the traces of Dani as he gestured for me to take a seat in his living area. I didn't. I leaned against the arm of his sofa, my eyes drifting to thick, fading words sprawled in Dani's loopy handwriting.

I didn't want to wake you, going to sleep at The Bells. See you tomorrow. Dani xx

I furrowed my brows. How long had that message been there? If I hadn't known better, I would think Dani was coming back.

I tried to relax as Jamie turned.

"Tyrell told me about Raven. I still can't believe Dani's gone. It's hard to know she lived under the same roof as her killer, someone she considered a friend." He ran a hand over his forehead. "I know I have to accept that Raven confessed, but—" Jamie swallowed. "I don't think it was her."

The hairs on my neck stood on end. He had given voice to the thought I couldn't seem to settle. "Why?"

"That's what I wanted to show you." He crouched, grunting with the effort, and steadied himself against the shelving unit separating the kitchen and the bedroom. He buried his head in small boxes and folders, rustling through notebooks and more photos. "Sorry." Jamie looked up. "I don't remember where I put all of them."

I still didn't know what he was searching for, but I smiled politely, leaning back into his sofa as he stuck his head into another tray.

Jamie exhaled loudly, laying a palm behind him and slowly lowering himself to the floor.

An image flashed in my mind—Ainsley leaning against a silver sports car, the same one that was at The Bells the day Dani died. "How's the leg?" I asked.

He didn't look up as he tapped on his thigh. "Good as new."

"Did you work everything out with your friend?"

He paused. His brows arched as his eyes met mine. "Why the sudden interest?"

"Just wondering."

Jamie pulled out a drawer. "You saw what happened. We haven't kept in contact."

I crossed my arms over my chest. "Who was it?"

Jamie's jaw tensed. "Here it is," he said through gritted teeth and brought out a gray notebook. Circular patterns were printed on the cover. He flicked through the pages until something flittered to the floor.

I choked on a gasp.

Jamie bent down to retrieve a small square-shaped note identical to the one I'd found in my sweatshirt.

Jamie rose to his full height, towering over me as he held out the note.

I WON'T WARN YOU AGAIN.

I didn't take it. My stomach clenched as I blinked down at the words.

"Did she tell you about them?"

"No." I slipped a fist into my pocket. "How did you get this?"

He turned, rifling through the shelves, pulling out more notes. Each one held a different promise. A different threat.

"She started getting them after swim practice." He stepped back, leaning into the shelves. "They would always tell her not to say anything. That they would make her life miserable. That they would kill her. Everyone on that team was jealous of Dani, and she knew a lot of things. It was hard to know which secret they were talking about. But I knew it had something to do with me." His teeth clamped down on his lip, and beads of blood broke the surface.

"Why?"

"I sold drugs to some of the girls on the team. It's the reason I lost her." His eyes rose to the message on the board, promising a tomorrow that could never come. He hunched over and scrubbed at his face.

Swimming was the only thing Dani cared about. I could only imagine the fury of her boyfriend enhancing her competition. "Dani found out?"

"She was livid. I told the girls I couldn't sell to them anymore, but Dani told me not to stop, and then the notes started."

My brows furrowed. "She asked you not to stop? Did she say why?"

"That was just Dani." He smiled. "I thought it meant everything was okay between us. She stayed here every night after that. I'd meet her after practice. We were good. And then it ended."

"Because of Michael?"

Jamie's jaw ticked. "Because she couldn't trust me anymore. She would never have looked at Michael if she hadn't felt betrayed."

I shuffled my feet. "Okay, and did you figure out who sent the notes?"

"No, but Dani did."

"Did she tell you who it was?"

"She didn't say much to me after Michael got his claws into her. Didn't even say goodbye. One day, I was blocked, and she was with Michael."

"Do you know the names of the girls you deal to?"

Jamie considered this for a moment, letting the question hang in the air so long, I thought he wouldn't answer. He lowered his head as he said, "Rachel, Sam, and Bianca."

My eyes widened, and a buzz swept through my head as I stepped forward. "Are you sure?"

"I loved her." His voice broke, and he coughed to clear it. "If I had done things differently, we would still be together. I would have protected her. I have nothing left of her."

I fought the urge to look at literally any corner of the room.

"I was barely allowed at the memorial. They won't let me come to the funeral."

Michael's interaction with Bianca in the library resurfaced.

Maybe the reason he didn't like Bianca was because he knew she was writing the notes. She had been doping and still was unable to match Dani. That itself might not have been a motive for murder, but Dani threatening to expose her would. It would be just like Dani to want another thing to have over Bianca's head. It would explain Bianca's behavior since Dani's death and why she was so nervous about the meeting.

The meeting.

I tried to move back, but the arm of the sofa pressed into my spine. "Sorry." I stepped over the notes of threats made to Dani. "I have to go."

TWENTY-ONE

The only sound was my breathing, hoarse and ragged. My arm stung. There was an unnatural calm to The Bells. All the doors were closed. The automatic hallway lights lit up ahead. I held my breath. My muffled steps were jarring in the stillness. I was hyperaware of each corner of the hall, concealing what lay in the quiet. The silence shifted halfway through the hallway, into something tangible, blocking out the rest of the world. I moved through the heavy air before a voice sliced through.

"Good. You're back."

I stilled. An erratic rhythm beat in my ears.

Ainsley didn't seem to notice or care. She looked down at the books under my arm, then her cold eyes met mine. "Common room, now."

She turned, and despite myself, I followed, my heart rattling.

I was the last one in the common room. Bianca sat nervously at the sofa's edge, chewing her nails. Martina was cross-legged with a book in hand, and Nia's eyes followed me from the single armchair. Ainsley stood in the center of them all. I took the seat opposite her, avoiding the stain from the party and ignoring the sixth figure. An invisible, dark, and heavy thing that snaked through the room.

Everything had changed since the last time we had all been together.

"Raven didn't kill Dani," Ainsley declared. "And I know one of you did."

I should have felt relieved. There was finally something Ainsley and I could agree on, but unfortunately, she counted me among the suspects.

Nia tutted. "Your only friend has gone to prison, and now you think one of us is responsible."

Bianca bounced her foot, and without looking up, she muttered, "Raven confessed."

"I don't know who pushed her into it," Ainsley said. "But I know it's a lie."

Martina removed a finger and slipped a wrinkled receipt into her book. "Why would she lie?"

Ainsley's eye twitched. She opened her mouth then closed it.

It was the question everyone was thinking. Who would confess to something they didn't do?

"I am the one who found Dani," I said. "And I wasn't at The Bells when she was killed."

"She was poisoned," Ainsley hissed. "If anything, I don't think it was a coincidence that you just happened to be out."

"It wasn't a coincidence. You were throwing a party I didn't want to attend."

"You weren't invited."

Nia scoffed. "Is this what you brought us here for? To confess?"

"I haven't heard you deny it," Ainsley shot back, her finger tapping an unrhythmic, disjointed beat. Her neck was poised, ready to snap in anyone's direction.

"I did not kill Dani," Martina said slowly.

"But you wanted to." Gone was Ainsley's usual cold tone. Her voice was sweet and enticing. The quick change added a note of uncertainty.

Martina shuffled back in her seat.

"No," Bianca whimpered quietly.

"We all did," Ainsley continued.

Eyes fell to the ground.

"She knew our secrets. Things we would have killed to keep quiet."

It was the one thing we all knew to be true. But I knew too well, even with Dani dead, it didn't mean our secrets died with her.

Bianca balled her hands into fists. I didn't think it was possible for her to drain off more color, but then Ainsley thrust her head in Bianca's direction.

"We all know you would have killed her just to win a race, but even with her dead, you couldn't achieve that, so it must have been something else."

Bianca's throat worked. The sound of her breathing increased.

I imagined Dani finding the threats amusing and planning all the different ways she would have taunted Bianca.

"What was it?" Ainsley leaned forward.

Bianca tightened her arms around her waist. A vein in her forehead twitched. "I didn't hurt Dani."

The other girls watched intently. Nia hid a reluctant look of pleasure behind her hands, as though unsure if Ainsley would turn to her next.

"Then who did?" Ainsley asked.

The room fell into a heavy silence. No one dared to look up.

"Nia? Maybe you killed her before she had the chance to take another one of your boyfriends," Ainsley said. "Martina?"

The eyes in the room flew to Martina. Her brown hair was tied back in a high ponytail.

"You fought with her a few weeks ago."

"She stole my project. I almost failed class." She added, "*Almost*."

"What about you?" I tilted my head at Ainsley. "Are you going to tell us how you hurt your hand?" I nodded to the dark marks around her knuckles.

Ainsley's eyes narrowed. Her nostrils flared. "If I was willing to kill, do you really think it would have been Dani?"

"What happened to your hand?" I asked again.

Silence. All eyes that were on Martina had shifted to Ainsley. Bianca even sat up a little straighter.

"Dani changed that night into some of my clothes," I continued.

"She never did have taste," Ainsley quipped.

"I always thought she got into a fight with Raven that night, but now..." I glanced down to Ainsley's hand. "I think you got into a fight with her that night, and she changed because there was blood on her shirt."

"For all we know, it could be yours."

"Remember, I wasn't here. I left Dani alone in the room. With you."

"Yes, and when you came back, Dani was dead," Ainsley said mockingly. "We've heard your version of events, but you have no way to prove that."

I had intrusive thoughts of locking Ainsley up in a room with the real killer and hoping for the best.

Martina stepped in. "Even if you think Raven is innocent, it doesn't make one of us guilty. People don't confess for no reason."

Ainsley's face darkened. She leaned back, changing tact. "I know you all think I am the enemy. But I am just trying to help Raven. We should be doing everything we can to make sure Raven doesn't go to prison for something she didn't do."

"Why are you so sure she didn't do it?" Nia spoke up. "She was acting really weird that night, not to mention the knife found under her bed."

My lips twitched. I looked at Nia, but she gave nothing away.

Ainsley rolled her eyes. "Anyone could have put that knife under her bed."

"And made her confess?" Martina added.

Ainsley's face tightened. "I just know she doesn't have it in her."

"Then it must be true," Nia muttered.

"I don't want to believe it was her either," Bianca said. "But if she admitted to it herself, there isn't anything we can do."

"Do you think Raven would leak poison into the place she sleeps in every night?"

"And we would?" I asked.

Ainsley pinched her lips together. "Then maybe we need to look at people outside the house. Dani had enemies everywhere."

Nia sighed. "Why don't you just talk to Daddy and ask him to make this all go away for Raven?"

Ainsley flinched; her eyes widened.

I leaned forward. "Ainsley, I think you need to give the police all the pictures from that night and the names of all the people you invited to the party."

"And I think they got the wrong roommate, so maybe it's best if we keep our thoughts to ourselves," Ainsley snapped. Her eyes darted around the room. "Does anyone have any useful suggestions that don't involve the police?"

Then loud shots rang through the air. Everyone went still. I brought my hands to my ears. My muscles went weak, and my pulse raced.

All heads turned toward the window as we heard a familiar spluttering engine. The parking lot was out of sight, but we all knew what it was.

"Did you know she was back?" Martina turned to Bianca.

Bianca dropped the hand that clutched her chest and gave an almost-inconceivable shake of the head.

Moments later, the door clicked, and footsteps came through the hall. Then, we saw a shock of red.

"Hi, guys," Mabel cried, grinning around the room.

Nobody seemed able to muster up any enthusiasm in response.

Mabel didn't seem to notice. "Aw, it's so cute to see you

all hanging out together." She walked past Ainsley, brushing her fingers lightly over her braids. "So pretty."

She doesn't know.

Mabel's forehead creased. "What did I miss?" She dropped into the chair next to Nia, flashing Bianca a smile she didn't return.

I wondered where Mabel went when she disappeared. Between the news coverage and the college gossip, everyone knew about Dani.

We exchanged unsure glances before Nia turned to face her. "Dani's dead."

TWENTY-TWO

Unlike the rest of us, Mabel was in her second year at The Bells. She had known Dani a year longer. That should have meant an extra year to hate her, but Mabel always saw the best in people, especially Dani.

In disbelief, she searched our faces, which held no remorse, just contempt for the dead. Her lips lifted, and she brought a shaky hand to her chest. "You're joking," she said breathlessly.

Bianca opened her mouth, but nothing came out.

"No." I leaned forward. "She's dead."

"No," Mabel croaked. Her head fell into her hands, and red curls covered her face. The room had shifted.

The invisible figure grew heavier, bearing down on my shoulders.

Ainsley leaned back, pursing her lips, and crossed her arms.

Can she feel it too?

It was easy to forget Dani was a person, flawed like

everyone else. Just as there were people relieved about her death, there were people who cared. Lives had been ruined. She'd left a void that could never be filled. I had seen it with Michael and Jamie, and sometimes, I felt it myself.

The Bells mourned Dani, even if we didn't.

"How?" Mabel managed through the tightness in her throat.

"She was poisoned," Martina said.

Mabel lifted her head, brushing back her curls to reveal a look of confusion.

"And then stabbed a bunch of times," Ainsley added.

"Oh." Mabel moaned through trembling lips as though that were a more fitting way for Dani to have died. "Is it safe to be here?" she asked through sobs.

"Yeah," Nia said. "Raven has confessed, but Ainsley doesn't believe it was her, so she's accusing us instead."

Mabel's head swiveled in shock. Her lifeless curls fell behind her back, a few loose strands defying gravity. "Raven?"

Ainsley cut in before anyone else could answer. "She didn't do it. Where were you two weeks ago?"

Nia tutted. "She hasn't been here in months. Who are you going to accuse next?"

Mabel swallowed. "Dani and I were frie—" The word was lost in a gargle.

"Dani didn't have friends," Nia said. "She had people she used when it was convenient."

"We got along, and I wouldn't have killed her. She was always sweet to me."

"Don't lie. She's dead now," Martina said accusingly.

"I know," she said under her breath. "But she wasn't all bad." Mabel folded one leg under her, placing her head on her knee.

"How long have you been back?" I asked.

"Only a few days." She grimaced. "If I had known, I would have come back straight away. I'm sorry I wasn't there for you all."

"I think you are all trying to use Raven as a way out." Ainsley addressed the room, bringing the discussion back to focus. "Did anyone suspect Raven before the confession?"

Silence.

I sat up. "I heard you threaten Dani on the day she died. Maybe you are so sure Raven didn't do it because she is covering for you?"

Rage lit Ainsley's eyes. "Why would she need to cover for me if I didn't do it?"

I glanced down at the bruise on her hand.

Ainsley followed my gaze, tucking her hand under her arm.

"Why would anyone lie about killing Dani?" Mabel asked, confused.

I stared at Ainsley, waiting for her to respond, but Martina answered instead. "There was a knife found under her bed. The guilt was probably catching up with her."

Bianca shuddered beside me.

"The police were here to do their job," Martina said. "You asked us to delete pictures and not say anything because you have something to hide. You and Dani were fighting for weeks. Are you going to tell us what that was about?"

"Fine." Ainsley shrugged. "If you don't want to admit anything to me, you can go to the police."

"Oh, good to know we have your permission." Nia stood up. "This isn't going anywhere, and I'm not going to sit here and be accused all night."

Ainsley stood too. "Search for Michael. I heard he's lost his mind. He might even be crazy enough to take you back."

Nia was an inch away from her in one quick movement. She pushed Ainsley hard, sending her flying to the ground. Ainsley scrambled back up and attempted to launch herself at Nia.

Mabel intercepted. "Please stop!" she cried. Fear laced her voice, and she held up her arms as though she were the one going to be hit. The rest of us remained in our seats.

"Please sit down." Mabel held on to Nia's sleeves. "I think we should talk openly and honestly while we are all here."

Nia wrangled her arm free and stormed out. Mabel turned to look at Ainsley, who shook out her shoulders and sank back into her stool.

"I know I have been gone a while and don't know what has happened, but we have to live together. We have all had problems with each other in the past, but maybe now we can all focus on rebuilding our relationships."

Ainsley had her head in her hands. "Mabel, it's likely someone here is directly responsible for Dani's murder or knows who it is, because it wasn't Raven. And I hate to break it to you, but no one here is interested in becoming friends."

Mabel frowned.

"Can we go now?" Martina swung her legs into the open space.

Ainsley rolled her eyes and left without a word. Martina followed behind her, already engrossed in her book.

Mabel sniffed. "It's like everything has fallen apart." Tears rolled down her cheeks. She cupped her face in her hands. "I'm sorry." She hiccupped. "I know you guys have probably already processed your grief. I shouldn't bring it all back up again for you." She sniffed again and tried to smile. "I should probably unpack, and I have so much to catch up on. I'll see you later, Sienna." She paused by Bianca.

Bianca wouldn't meet her gaze. She picked at her fingernails, jaw tensed.

"Bianca," I said. "Can I talk to you, please?"

She looked up, unseeing.

Bianca didn't answer, but relief washed through her face.

Mabel looked between us, her eyes still glossy with tears. She pressed her lips together and nodded, walking slowly out of the room.

"Actually, Sienna," Bianca said before I could open my mouth. "I'm going for a swim. Can it wait?"

"It's about Dani," I said.

Her face was harsh lines and teeth. "Everything." She over-enunciated the word. "Is about Dani. She is just as annoying dead as she was alive." She clamped down on her lip. "I'm sorry. I didn't mean—" She sighed, and her features softened, but anger still bubbled below the surface. "I don't want to talk about her." She stepped back, palms raised, shielding herself from even the mention of Dani. She walked away, and I couldn't help feeling for the first time that I saw it—the rage it took to push someone over the edge and kill.

TWENTY-THREE

There was nothing I could do to drown out the cries. They shadowed me as I moved across my room. My right hand, holding a dry-erase marker, twitched. My left grazed the notes that lined the walls. I was missing something. A different outlook lay in this room. But first, I needed to see past Dani's last gift—the newspaper article she had left for me on the day she died.

A picture of August took up half the page; the half-formed tattoo branded onto his neck taunted me.

Letters in the article were circled and underlined. It was a message from Dani, one I couldn't decipher. Not without looking at *his* face. So I returned to the walls, hoping they could drown out my mistakes from the past, but another image came hard and fast. White thinning hair. Two missing teeth that took nothing away from the bright smile that filled his cheeks with color. Blood seeping from his mouth.

I blinked. I couldn't do anything for him, but I could do it for Dani.

It took two hours to rearrange the murder wall, high-lighting suspects and their movements instead of an overall timeline. I allocated different parts of the room to each person on the list. I started with Ainsley, the last person I could be sure had seen Dani alive. She'd fought with Dani, but why?

I skimmed the wall. Dani knew something. A secret Raven and Ainsley couldn't risk her leaving with. One or both of them had gone back, stabbing and killing Dani. If that was the case, maybe Ainsley had taken the knife, and when she heard Raven had confessed, it was the perfect opportunity to blame everything on her.

Wrong. The whole thing felt wrong. I stepped back, crossing Ainsley's name off the list and moving to the next.

Bianca. I'd seen her, and she'd said it herself. She never left The Bells. I had placed the threatening sticky note under her name, wishing I had looked closer at the ones Jamie showed me. Sam's and Rachel's names were listed beside hers. There was no reason why all three of them couldn't have done it together. After today, I definitely believed Bianca was capable. The utility room, the kitchen, and the common room were the only three rooms that didn't require a key, and if the dorm room was unlocked that night, I needed to move beyond The Bells. Bianca could have given them a code, and when she thought the poison hadn't worked, she'd stabbed Dani. Bianca wasn't in any pictures, but Rachel and Sam were. Dani could have ruined their careers, but instead, she'd taunted them, even after she had received the threats.

Three knocks issued from the door. The dry-erase marker dropped to the floor, and a buzz rang through my head. I waited, expecting a click of the door or a voice. Instead, there were four more light knocks.

"Who is it?" I croaked. I unplugged the desk lamp and tightened a hand around the thin spine.

"It's me." It took me a moment to place the owner of the low whisper.

I edged closer to the door and unlocked it, still holding the lamp in my hands. I opened a small gap, just enough for half my face to show.

Ainsley leaned against the doorframe, arms folded, hair in a bonnet, and dressed casually in a sweater and jeans. She looked over her shoulder. "Aren't you going to let me in?"

"No."

She rolled her eyes. "Please. If I wanted to kill you, I wouldn't knock."

"What do you want?"

"To talk."

I pressed my palm against the back of the door and drew my face back.

Ainsley was quick. Her foot was already lodged in the gap before I could close it.

"I don't want to argue," she whispered, glancing behind her. "You were right." The words came out with effort. "Raven is trying to cover for me. But I didn't kill Dani."

I felt exposed as Ainsley stepped into the room.

"What were you planning to do with that?" She nodded to the lamp in my hand.

I dropped it, my heart clattering.

"You've been busy." She took in her name scrawled in

red. "The last one to see Dani alive," she read. "That would have been the killer, not me."

I expected Ainsley to take more interest in the room, but after walking around once, she sat at the edge of Dani's bed. "This is the first time I've been in here since..."

I picked up the lamp, ready to revert it into a weapon at any moment, and walked to sit in the desk chair on Dani's side of the room.

"Why is Raven trying to cover for you if you didn't kill Dani?"

"Because she thinks I did. We fought on the day she died, hence this." She raised her bruised hand.

"Why?"

"She was blackmailing me. The money wasn't the problem. But there was no way I would give her anything because people like Dani would always be back for more."

"What was she blackmailing you for?"

"I was in a relationship."

This was the last thing I expected. I didn't think there were people brave enough to be with Ainsley.

"With a teacher."

My brows shot up, and my mind raced back to classes with Professor Locke after Dani died. I'd thought Professor Locke was looking at me, but it was Ainsley.

"Professor Locke?"

She nodded.

I stilled. Ainsley wasn't just telling me about her relationship. She was telling me about a motive for murder. "What did you do to her that night?"

She looked down at her hand. "I came in here, and I told her I wasn't going to pay the money. She really thought I was going to. She had pictures of us. We were stupid. I didn't realize we were being followed." She shook her head. "I broke it off with Reggie over a month ago, but she didn't care. I was eighteen. We weren't doing anything illegal. But if anyone found out, he would lose his job, and my dad would kill me. I refused to ask my dad for the money. At first, Reggie wanted to pay, but then he said if we ignored her, she would give up. She had nothing to gain if it came out, you know? She told me she wanted the money by that day, and I had worked out she was leaving, so I had the party, thinking she would just leave without confronting me. I hoped she would move on once she saw I was serious about not paying. Then she sent me a video scheduling an email with the pictures to my dad. I asked her to cancel it, and she refused unless I paid up on that night." Ainsley was tense, her thumb caressing the bruise on her wrist.

"I hit her. She fought back. She got on top of me, but Raven grabbed her back, and they both fell to the ground." She glanced over to the space between the desk and the bed. If she was telling the truth, that was the last place she'd seen Dani alive. "I started to hit her over and over. It hurt so much."

Her thumb pressed down on her bruise. "But I was angry. Raven pulled me off her before I could do any serious damage. I think I hurt myself more than I did her. And that was the last time I saw her. She had some cuts on her face, and she was bloody, but she was alive. I went back to my room and changed. I didn't feel like going back to the party. I thought I had just made everything worse, so I stayed in my room for a while. Alone. When Martina came, I returned to the party, but Raven must have assumed I used this time to go back and kill Dani. For a while, I did think I did it. When I heard she was dead, I thought maybe I had hit her harder than I realized, or there was some internal damage, and I had killed her. Then I heard about the stabbing and the poisoning, and I knew it couldn't have been me, but Raven still had her doubts."

Ainsley wrung her hands. "My dad's going to be police commissioner. I couldn't tell the police, and I wasn't going to risk Reggie's job."

"What made you decide to tell me?"

"Because I know you're the last person with the right to judge me." She didn't even mean it as a retort. Her lips pressed into a line. "And I don't think you killed Dani."

"Wow," I breathed. "You could have fooled me."

Ainsley fought against a smirk. "It was fun until Raven got arrested."

"Why don't you think it was me?"

"I saw you leave, and I don't think you hated Dani. Not really."

"Who do you think could have done it?"

Ainsley leaned back. "Anyone that came into contact with her."

"Professor Locke?"

Ainsley looked at me in disgust. "He wouldn't do that. He was all for paying her off. And I should have listened."

"Did she send the email?"

"Yeah. Even dead, she still needed to get the last laugh." Ainsley leaned back onto the bare frame of Dani's bed. "Dad's more focused on winning the election. He wants it buried." She inhaled deeply, and her eyes gleamed. "What did Dani have on you?"

"Nothing."

Ainsley shook her head and waggled her index finger in the air. "I thought we were building trust. What did she say to you again?" Ainsley tilted her head, searching for a memory.

I felt my stomach tighten.

"Monroe? I heard her call you that on the day she died."

I didn't react to the name. But something inside twisted from the effort. I cleared my throat. "How did Professor Locke take it when you broke up with him?"

Ainsley shrugged. "He wanted me back and said we could be more careful, but I was finished. I hear he's with someone else now, so none of it matters."

"Who told you that?"

Ainsley laughed. "Who else?"

Dani. "Do you know who he's seeing now?"

"I have no idea, and I don't care. That part of my life is over now." Ainsley waved the topic away. "Are you going to answer my question? Monroe? It sounds familiar."

My skin crawled. "It's a common name."

Ainsley's lips spread into a smile that lingered longer than needed, and I could tell there was meaning behind it. She would not stop until she knew the truth. "Fine. Later then. We need a way to prove Raven is innocent."

I chewed on my cheek. "I broke into her room the day she was arrested."

Ainsley's eyes narrowed.

"This was when I thought you or Raven had something to do with Dani's death. I checked under the bed, and the knife wasn't there when I looked moments before the police did. Someone planted the knife."

Ainsley frowned. "Nia." She threw her hands out like she had cracked the case. "Who else could have been in the room?

"I don't know."

Ainsley rubbed her head. "What do you think we should do?"

"I think we need to speak to Bianca."

"She hates me. She's only going to tell you it was me."

"And I'll listen because I still don't know for sure it wasn't."

Ainsley rolled her eyes. "Did you listen to anything I just said?"

"What you've told me is that you have a motive for her murder, and no one was with you to back up your alibi."

Ainsley leaned forward, and her mouth started to shape to say what would likely be a string of insults.

"I believe you," I added.

"Good." She leaned back. "Why Bianca?"

"She was doping."

Ainsley's eyes widened.

"I found that in my hoodie," I said, pointing to the note on the wall. "Dani knew about her and two other members of the swim team. I think one of them started threatening Dani. Jamie has a pile of them."

"Okay. We need to get the rest. Raven would never have written those notes. This will help her case with the police. Maybe then they will look for the actual killers."

"You think it's more there's more than one?"

"Or one person who ran out of patience."

"One of the girls?"

"I think we would be stupid not to suspect everyone," she said, and a thought formed.

"Professor Locke was here the night of Dani's murder?"

If Ainsley was surprised, she didn't show it. "I met him that day in his car by Stedmond Park."

"He was fighting with Jamie."

At this, she did react, but not how I expected. She laughed. "That's got nothing to do with Dani's murder."

"What's happening between them?"

"I will speak to Reggie," she said, brushing away my question. "There's no way a teacher would have been missed at the party or managed to get into this room, but he might know something about what happened."

"Isn't it awkward between you in lessons?"

"I go in and out. Just because we're not together doesn't mean I want to fail class."

I waited for a quip about my failing, but it didn't come.

She stood up, and Dani's bed groaned in protest. "We are unlikely allies. I don't think the murderer will see it coming." She walked toward the door and stopped short. "Of course, I think it's only right that I maintain my normal attitude toward you in front of the others. We wouldn't want anyone becoming suspicious."

TWENTY-FOUR

I'd hoped it wouldn't come for me tonight. But the tug of sleep beckoned, taunting me with the life I'd had before. August and I huddled in front of Dad's camera in matching T-shirts. Mine was blue and reached past my knees. "She is my best friend" was printed on the front. "He is my best friend" was on August's pink T-shirt, which had been cropped and tight against his chest. Dad hadn't been happy that we had changed shirts, but blue was my favorite color, and August didn't want to take the picture unless I was smiling.

"Right." Dad had pressed the timer on the camera. "Nice smiles please?"

August and I had taken it as a challenge. Mom and Dad posed as we threw our heads back and bared all our teeth. They had noticed just as the camera flashed. Mom had cupped August's cheeks, Dad's mouth hung open, and my puffy face was pulled into a snarl. In some ways, the memories were worse than the nightmares because they had been real. The photographic proof hung in a prison cell somewhere. It left a yearning in the pit of my stomach. I could never go back to the life I had.

I got ready. My brother's laughter rang in my head, and the sweet smell of sugar and chocolate filled the air.

When I entered the kitchen, Mabel was making pancakes. I watched in amusement as Martina tried to draw a smiley face with chocolate sauce. The two eyes connected, and the smile had become and large blob of chocolate.

Mabel gestured for me to take a seat. "Do you still like yours with lemon squeezed on top?"

I nodded and raised a questioning brow to Martina as I sat at the table.

"Team building," Martina said. "Mabel wants to make up for lost time in case anyone else dies."

It was hard not to miss Mabel's flinch as she flipped a pancake. She'd lived here with Vivienne Marks. Her best friend, Alex, had died of an overdose last year, and now Dani.

Bianca entered the kitchen and did a double take at the sight of us. "Sorry, I didn't realiz—"

"Take a seat." Mabel guided Bianca to the empty seat on my left.

Bianca took it and offered an apologetic smile.

I wasn't going to mention Dani, but it was as though Bianca thought I would. She turned away from me, her body small and ready for a quick escape.

Mabel brought her over a plate and cutlery, and we all ate in silence.

"This is so fun," Mabel called over her shoulder, drizzling chocolate on a pancake then turning to face us. "I've been so overwhelmed thinking about how I'm going to catch up with everything, so it's good just to be able to relax with friends."

No one corrected her.

Ainsley poked her head in the kitchen, then the rest of her followed. Her braids were in a neat bun, her baby hairs were slicked down in a spiral design, and she was smartly dressed in a baby-blue shirt and black pencil skirt.

Mabel beamed. "Ainsley, you look so professional."

"I have my induction day for my new job."

Mabel placed two fresh pancakes on a plate and handed them to Ainsley.

She accepted them with a quiet "Thank you."

Mabel blinked. "Don't we have a class with Professor Locke today?"

"No, we've been given group work, so today is a study day." I was going to meet with Sweaty. Then Ainsley and I would interrogate the girls on the swim team.

Bianca squirmed beside me as she bit into her pancake. She was hiding something. And I couldn't wait to find out what.

"You've been paired with someone called Jorge Rodriguez," I said.

"Oh." Mabel's face fell. "Who's that?"

I shrugged.

"Count yourself lucky." Ainsley chewed on the last of her pancake. "I was paired with Raven."

Mabel twisted the button on her sleeve. "I still have to go in. I think Professor Locke wants to go over everything I've missed."

I kept my eyes on my pancake, careful not to let them drift to Ainsley at the mention of his name. She had trusted me with something. I couldn't return that favor. Part of me questioned if everything that had happened last night was a dream, but I thought I saw the hint of a smile on Ainsley's lips before she said, "Don't worry. You haven't been here for weeks, and you're not failing as badly as Sienna. andThanks for breakfast." She dumped her dishes in the sink then left.

She was late. Ainsley had changed, deciding an all-black ensemble was more appropriate for our current plans. We met at the pool to avoid questions about us leaving The Bells together. Most of the swim team, including Bianca, had already left. I gritted my teeth as she passed, remembering how Ainsley had insisted I wait for her before speaking to anyone.

I regretted it the moment Ainsley arrived. She peered at the pools through the glass panel in the door. "Where's Bianca?"

"Practice finished. You should have been here over twenty minutes ago. She left."

"And you didn't stop her?"

I took a deep breath and faced the glass. Three of them were left.

"Sam and Rachel are here. Let's talk to them. Just remember we're not the police, and it's best if people don't know we are asking these questions. Try not to do anything to offend anyone."

"We need to get rid of the spare. Which two are they?"

Ainsley gave no sign she was listening. She cupped around her eyes and pressed her face to the glass.

I pulled her back. "Are you trying to get them to notice us?

Ainsley looked down at the fabric of her sweater I had bunched up in my hand. I let go and pointed to the two figures at the pool's edge. "Sam's the one with blond hair, and Rachel is in the blue swimsuit. I think we shou—"

Ainsley threw open the doors. "Hey."

My blood froze. Ainsley was shaping her mouth to scream over to them again. Then her lips pulled into a smile. She had their attention. But we had no plan.

We walked to the pool. The water shimmered, and a mixture of disinfectants and chlorine clung to the warm air.

Ainsley folded her arms over her chest. "I need to speak to these two." She gestured between Rachel and Sam. "Alone."

Kezia, "the spare," stepped forward. "You can say whatever you need to say in front of me."

Ainsley closed the space between them.

I pulled back on her sleeve, earning another look of disgust. "Ainsley, please."

"*You're* Ainsley?" Kezia said.

"*You're* still here?" Ainsley retorted.

"What is this about?" Sam asked.

"Dani." I stared pointedly at Kezia, who seemed to deflate. Sam's and Rachel's eyes widened. They shared a look but said nothing.

"We think she may have been having issues with people on the swim team," I said. "And how she handled it might have put her in danger."

Sam bit down on her lip.

Kezia wiped the dripping water from her head. "Dani had issues with everyone on the team. What do you mean 'might have put her in danger'?"

I didn't answer. I looked between Sam and Rachel and saw the moment they realized what this was about.

Rachel inhaled sharply. Sam held her elbows more tightly to her sides.

Ainsley seemed to notice it too. "Were you at my party on the day Dani died?"

Kezia shook her head.

"Then we don't need to speak to you," she said.

"They won't want to—" Kezia looked over her shoulder, waiting for one of them to object.

"It's all right." Rachel paced a hand on her back. "We will catch up to you."

Kezia hesitated for a second before slinging a towel around her neck. With one last glare at Ainsley, she strode toward the changing rooms.

No one spoke before the slam of the door.

Sam threw out her hands. "What did Bianca tell y—"

"Wait," Rachel snarled through clenched teeth. "What did you want to speak to us about?" She lifted her head, feigning confusion, but they had already said enough.

Ainsley laughed, but there was no humor in her tone. "Did you kill Dani?"

I tensed. That was ultimately the answer we'd come here for, but this wasn't the method I'd thought we would use.

Rachel flushed, and her nostrils flared. "Of course I didn't."

Ainsley looked over to me, apparently done with her questioning.

I stepped forward. "We asked because we know about the doping."

Rachel closed her eyes and sighed.

A strangled cry escaped Sam. "You don't understand the pressure we are under. It's not just here. I compete regionally. My parents want me to compete at the World Aquatic Championships. I have been training and swimming all my life, only to lose to Dani. She treated this like a side project. She never deserved to win."

Ainsley rolled her eyes. "At least she didn't cheat, still lose, and then start crying about how life isn't fair."

Sam lowered her head.

"What do you want from us?" Rachel asked.

"I don't have any more money," Sam muttered.

"Shut up," Rachel demanded, her eyes bulging.

I had been interviewed by the police enough times to know this wasn't how an interrogation was supposed to go. Rachel was defensive and guarded. She wanted to see what we knew. Sam was upset, and having Ainsley here wasn't helping.

"Dani and I shared a room at The Bells. I know exactly what she was like." My throat tightened. "And how she could be when she knew a secret. I spoke to Jamie, and I know about the drugs. We're not here to fight or blackmail you. Coach won't find out from us."

Rachel relaxed, not a lot, but I was getting through to her.

Ainsley turned, but before she could say anything, I

continued. "I just want to hear from you and see if this could have anything to do with what happened to Dani."

Rachel's eyes narrowed. "I already said we didn't kill Dani. But I'm not mad she's gone."

Sam hunched over. "Please stop. If the coach found out, our careers would be ruined."

"They already know." Rachel scoffed. "It started with Bianca. Sam caught her using in the locker rooms."

"I didn't like it," Sam said. "I threatened to tell Coach, but Bianca said she was going to turn herself in the next day. One day became two, and two days became a week. When we confronted her, she freaked. She was the only person who came close to pushing Dani, and everyone wanted Dani off the team. She said if she could beat Dani and show Coach and everyone else we didn't need her, we would be better off."

Rachel shook her head. "We agreed. That's when we started. We didn't know he was with Dani when we bought from Jamie. We wouldn't have been so stupid."

Sam chimed in, "We train almost every day. Even in the off-season, there's always some competition my parents want me to do. It's hard for our bodies to keep up sometimes."

Ainsley tutted. "Stop making excuses for the fact that you weren't good enough."

Sam drew her head back. "It's not that I'm not good enough. It was her. Anyone other than Dani, I could have accepted it."

"Was Dani blackmailing you?" I asked.

Sam's nod was barely perceptible.

Rachel's brows drew in close. "And it's like she wanted

everyone to know it. When we were around, she'd always have jokes about drugs or cheats. Even if she hadn't told Coach, we didn't think it would be long until someone worked it out, and people like Dani never stopped. So we knew she had to do something to stop her."

Ainsley drew in a breath.

"She needed money, but we didn't know what for. We figured if she was so desperate, something or someone was probably a threat to her. If we could find out what it was, we wouldn't have to give in to her demands, and we could have something over her. So on the day she demanded the money, we followed her. We don't live on campus, so we waited around after practice. She went to Noytin."

Sam tensed.

"She went into a house, if you could call it that. She spent some time inside, then she came out with another one of your roommates in The Bells."

I shared a look with Ainsley. "Who?"

Rachel shrugged. "I don't know."

"Describe her," Ainsley commanded.

"Brown hair, up in a ponytail."

Martina.

"Martina?" Ainsley echoed my thoughts. "Did she have a book?"

My head fell forward. "Really?"

"No." Rachel's brows furrowed. "But she did have a baseball bat."

My mouth fell open.

"She didn't hit Dani, but she threatened her with it. After a while, Dani left."

"Whose house was it?" I asked.

Sam swallowed. "There were a few people. Not exactly a family home. We waited until that girl—Martina?—left, just so there were less people who might recognize us, then we knocked. We didn't know any of them, but I recognized one. Candice."

The name sounded familiar, and a memory rose to the surface. "She lived at The Bells last year?"

Sam nodded. "I see her sometimes at parties. She can get you anything. One of the guys in my apartment failed his driving test five times. Candice got him a license, and he never had to redo his test."

"She makes fake IDs," I said, a puzzle piece almost slotting into place. Dani was trying to leave. What better way than with a new identity? I just didn't see how Martina fit into this.

"Next time we saw Dani, we told her we were done, and if we were kicked off the team, we would tell Coach about her trips to Noytin. It was Sam's idea. I didn't think it would work, but she didn't ask for anything else. Not from us."

"What about Bianca?" I asked.

"She always got it the worst," Rachel said. "I don't know if it was just the guilt eating her up from cheating, but I think she still had an agreement going on with Dani."

"We've told you everything." Sam took an uneven step forward, and her voice shook. "You won't say anything, right? You promised?"

"I didn't." Ainsley began walking to the exit.

"Please." Sam's voice broke. "We haven't touched anything since Dani. I never will again."

Rachel didn't meet my eyes. Her arms hung limp by her side.

Dani ruined lives. She taunted and broke people. I knew what it was like to want a second chance. It wasn't something I was ready to give everyone, but I could start here. "I won't say anything."

I had no control over Ainsley, so that was a different conversation, but I added, "And I'll try to speak to her."

I heard it first. I only managed one inhalation of unchlorinated air before I saw it. Faint jeers and whistles carried in the wind from the pathway away from The Bells and toward a small crowd Ainsley was already part of. My heart pounded in time with my quick steps up the path, each rapid breath a struggle as Ainsley slipped between bodies, and I followed closely in the spaces left behind.

"What happened?" I asked breathlessly.

"Shh," Ainsley instructed, pulling someone's shoulder back so she could step through.

I forced my way in behind her until we were in the heart of the crowd. Voices boomed from all directions. Some were just boos and whistles. I could make out words like *finally*, *caught*, and *murderer*. My heart stilled. I looked up.

Graybone building.

I had never been to the Graybone student halls before, but it had always offered comfort because it usually meant a day of peace without Dani. Heads poked out the windows from the floors above—the sound of shushing rushed through the crowd.

A narrow head called from the fourth floor. "He was refusing to leave with the police, but now I think they are going to drag him out."

Someone from the fifth floor shouted, "Michael has been arrested."

I pressed my hands against my ears, blocking out the roar from the crowd, my muscles numb. "Michael?" I asked in disbelief.

"It's about time," Ainsley said.

The doors barreled open, and the crowd stood up on their toes, everyone trying to get a good view, but it wasn't Michael. Two boys walked backward, cell phones raised in the air.

The crowd fell silent then erupted.

An officer appeared first, guiding Michael toward a police car. His head hung low, and hands were cuffed. A mixture of jeers and cheers came from the crowd as he passed.

Ainsley tapped on the shoulder of a boy in the crowd. "Why are they arresting him?" she called over the crowd.

"We don't know. But everyone is assuming it has something to do with Dani."

Applause filled the space as Michael ducked his head, and the car door slammed behind him.

I watched open-mouthed as it drove away. Even with Michael gone, the crowd didn't disperse. Everyone had their theories and opinions.

"He just has this look about him," a voice said.

"He's been lashing out. The guilt was eating him up. I hadn't seen him in class for weeks until Wednesday. He had a meeting with Professor Locke after. I bet he convinced him to confess."

"Rumor has it he admitted to it in the library, and you know how Mary is. She gives the security cameras a run for their money."

"I'm going to the police station," Ainsley said, already shrugging herself through the crowd. "If this has something to do with Dani, then maybe Raven will be released."

I turned to follow, but the crowd seemed to quiet. A lightness swarmed my chest, and I knew it was because of him. It took every bit of my willpower not to look up. My cell phone grew heavy in my pocket with unanswered calls and unread messages. I realized I had stopped walking, and I wondered what life would be like if I told him everything. Would he accept me?

This crowd had swarmed here to laugh at things because of who Dani had turned Michael into. I looked up with steely determination. Tyrell raised a brow when our eyes met. His eyes held questions. Things I couldn't answer. My lips parted. For a moment, I thought I would say something, but my legs were already turning away, carrying me up the path against the flow of students rushing to see the show.

TWENTY-FIVE

I saw myself in her eyes. My brown irises were fixed on Martina's gray. Both held the unwavering determination to do what was right no matter the cost. I had lost a brother, and Martina had lost her sister. In some ways, we were the same, so I wondered if she felt it, the churning sensation as the body threatened to explode under the weight of guilt, increasing with every family call or look. The feeling of falling every time you questioned if you'd made the right choice.

I looked away, scared if she looked for long enough, she would recognize it in my eyes. My eyes roamed behind her to a shelf. Four rows of thick books were organized by varying shades. Red slowly transitioned into green, which darkened into blue and ended with a rich black.

"At least it's not drugs, right?" She laughed half-heartedly, tapping a bookmark against her finger.

"How are you feeling after finding out about Raven?"

"I'm considering breaking her out myself to make living

with Ainsley bearable again." She smiled. "I appreciate you checking in, but what did you want to speak to me about?"

I blinked, meeting her eyes again. The first time I'd seen Martina wasn't at The Bells. It was on TV during a public appeal for surrender. She and her family had begged Maria to turn herself in. I remembered how my stomach had hardened with jealousy. Her mom had her arm around her, supporting her words for her sister to turn herself in to the police. Her dad had cried, saying he didn't know how his daughter had turned out this way, and he'd apologized to everyone affected. The two families had hugged. Everyone blamed Maria, not her family. I'd turned off the TV before Mom could see. I could imagine what she would have said.

"Oh, she looks so innocent. Locking her up won't rehabilitate her."

"Maybe she would come home if they didn't just blame her and show her that they cared."

"It's about Dani," I said. "I'm just going to be honest because I think it's better if I talk to you than Ainsley."

"What's Ainsley got to do wit—"

"We heard that you threatened Dani with a baseball bat a week or so before her death."

Martina rolled her shoulders back. "Yeah, so?"

I wet my lips. It wasn't the response I'd expected. "Why were you two fighting?"

"We weren't fighting." She drew her head back and scoffed. "You think I had something to do with her death?"

"No. I just want to understand what her movements were before she died."

Martina flicked the bookmark between her fingers. "Do

you know *where* we were when I had the baseball bat? At Candice's house. She was trying to help my sister escape. Maria should be in prison because of me. I knew it would be hard for her to accept, and I don't regret it. I know it was the right thing to do, but now she hates me." Martina tapped on her chest. "Hates me so much, she wants me dead, and Dani knew that, just like she knew everything else. Like where Maria was."

Martina bounced on the balls of her feet. "Dani would always make comments about how the weekly code for The Bells might slip into the wrong hands or how she needed to meet up with an old friend, and I would spend each day looking over my shoulder, wondering if this was another one of Dani's games or if my sister was going to make sure whatever happened to Vivienne Marks happened to me. So instead of stealing my work, Dani said if I did her assignments for her, she wouldn't help Maria."

I swallowed. "Do you really think your sister would hurt you?"

"I don't know what she's capable of. I didn't touch Dani. She was the only person who could tell me where my sister was. What my sister did tore my family apart. I wouldn't do that to my parents again." She raised her palm to her forehead, taking in a deep breath. "We were best friends. It hurts that she feels this way about me." Tears slid down her cheek as she wrapped her hand around her elbow.

"I'm sorry." My mouth was dry, and my throat was tight. I thought of August. I felt sick. I needed to leave. Martina's feelings were suffocating, and mine were clawing their way to the surface.

"I'm sorry." Martina wiped at her eyes. "I didn't think I would still get so emotional about this."

I cleared my throat. "Did you threaten Dani with the bat because she was taunting you?"

"No." She shook her head. "Not just that. I threatened her because she had been helping Maria. There's no other way she could have survived this long. She lied about Maria's role in Vivienne's death, and she has been trying to make up for it. She was at Candice's to get a new identity, fake passport, and money. I can admit the baseball bat was a bit much, but I would never have used it. I just wanted to let her know I was serious. Sometimes, it feels like I can't breathe. I hardly ever leave campus because I know Maria's out there somewhere."

I opened my mouth to apologize then closed it. Despite everything I'd done, August had never hated me. He had forgiven me. It was me who couldn't forgive him for making me betray myself.

Martina rubbed at her neck. "Now Dani is gone. It's only a matter of time before the police get her."

I thought about August alone in the streets.

"I don't even recognize who she is anymore," Martina said. "I hate her."

I flinched, my clenched jaw tightening. The pit in my stomach burned the same way August's letters had. In the first few, he'd written about our childhood and his new life in prison. It was confusing. They didn't read as the monster he was supposed to be, so I'd stopped opening them.

"My parents spend their whole day hoping she doesn't turn up dead in a back alley somewhere. For me, at least that would give me peace of mind."

I got to my feet; my chest hitched. "I should go."

Martina looked up, the bookmark clenched in her fist. Her eyes had softened, but I recognized the look moments ago. Rage, anger, and hatred—all the things I didn't have for August.

And I was jealous.

TWENTY-SIX

The walls closed in, and I couldn't outrun them. My feet grew heavier with every step through the hallway until I admitted defeat, steadying myself against the wooden panels. The ringing in my ears seemed to bounce around them. I focused on my breathing and not how my vision blurred, the lightness in my head, the hollowness in my chest, or my brother's voice.

"Sienna." A hand fell on my shoulder. "Are you all right?"

I looked up, clearing my throat.

Bianca watched me, wide-eyed, a wrinkle in her brow.

"I'm fine." I shook my head, trying to clear the fog. I attempted to straighten but stumbled.

Bianca caught me, hooking her arm into mine. "I can get you some water to drink." She tightened her grip on my arm, bearing my weight, and led me into the kitchen. "Sit here," she said, pulling out a chair.

I fell into it, head in my hands, and sucked in the cool air. I heard the clink of glass and the water running, then

Bianca was in front of me, a pitying hand on my shoulder as she handed me the glass. I took it and drank.

Her curls shifted as she looked over her shoulder to the door. "Is there someone I can call for you?"

A rumble started in the back of my throat and escaped as wet laughter.

Bianca looked at me, dazed, then chanced another look at the door.

Who could I call to talk to about my family issues or the fact that now two people from Stedmond had been arrested, both likely to do with Dani's death? The more I questioned people about Dani, the worse she seemed to become.

I took another sip of water. "How did Dani do it?" When I closed my eyes, I could see her, how she would move around carefree like she hadn't stolen Michael from Nia, wasn't blackmailing Ainsley, and wasn't threatening Martina and Bianca. "Do you think she knew how everyone felt about her?"

Bianca didn't meet my eyes. "I don't think she cared." Her voice was low, barely audible. I strained to hear over the pounding in my head.

"I wanted to talk to you about her before."

Bianca looked to the door again, this time taking half a step back.

"I know about the notes you sent her."

She froze. Shallow breaths left her quivering lips.

"I spoke with Rachel and Sam today."

Her eyes widened, the whites showing around her whole iris. Tremors started in her hands, then her whole body shook.

I stood up, immediately regretting the action as the blood drained my head. I took her trembling hand, offering the same grace she'd given me, and we took our seats together.

"I shouldn't have done it." She shook her head. "She knew. Straight away, she knew. And it only made things worse." Tears lined her cheeks, and her breath hitched.

I squeezed her hand, and she turned her body toward me, our knees touching. "I started using. I was buying from this guy called Cole at the start of the year, but one time, when I went to collect, it was Jamie who showed up. I thought it was all over then, but Dani didn't say anything. She was still horrible, but nothing had really changed. Until the run-up to our conference championships." Bianca looked down at our clasped hands. "She cornered me before practice and said she'd let me win this one, so at least there was something to show for my doping. I won, and it was the worst thing I felt in my life. I was asha—"

"There you are."

We turned. Blood rushed to my ears.

Ainsley stood by the doorway. She strode into the room, hand on her hip.

Bianca pulled her hand away and placed her feet at the edge of the chair and her knees tucked beneath her chin.

"You started without me." Ainsley was opposite us now, directly in front of Bianca, who shrank under her gaze.

"She knows?" Bianca whispered.

"What about?" Ainsley placed her fists on the table. "The drugs, the notes, or killing Dani?"

Bianca flinched. I placed a hand on her shoulder, and she pulled away. "I didn't kill Dani."

"Your friends seemed to think you did."

I widened my eyes, but she waved me away.

"Rachel and Pam."

"Sam," I corrected.

Ainsley leaned forward. "Why would they think that?"

Bianca was a ball. Ainsley was ruining all her opening up. Bianca's lips were pressed into a line. I didn't think she was going to answer.

Then she looked up, eyes filled with tears. "Because she wouldn't stop. She kept pushing for more money. Then she told us it was over. We thought she was done, but only with them."

Something Rachel had said came back to me. *I think she still had an agreement going on with Dani. She always got it the worst.*

"What did she ask you to do?" I asked.

She pulled her sleeves over her wrists. "She would make me dress up and pretend to be her."

I blinked.

Ainsley laughed. "Had either of you looked in a mirror?"

Bianca owed her deep hue and curly hair to her black father. Any attempts to keep it straight were wasted as soon as she touched the water.

"It would always be baggy clothes, sweaters, joggers, and I'd normally go out at night. She'd text me the location, and I had to go. I'd keep my hood up and walk around."

I frowned. Ainsley and I shared a look.

"Was someone following her?" Ainsley asked.

Bianca nodded. "I only noticed it a few times. Someone behind, always wearing a hood and keeping a safe distance.

I never saw their face, but one time, when I got there, there was a note and flowers. I panicked at first, but then it gave me an idea. I knew someone was following Dani, and she was scared. I had sent the note when she threatened to tell the coach about the doping, and she knew it was me. So I sent the second, pretending to be whoever was following her. I said I knew she had been tricking me. If she tried it again, she'd regret it."

"What about the rest of the notes?" I asked.

"That was it." Bianca's brows furrowed. "I didn't write any more. I didn't have to. She didn't ask for anything else until the day she died."

Bianca only wrote two notes? That didn't make any sense. I saw the stack of threats.

"She sent me a text and told me to pack a bag and go to Rosemary Station at one a.m.," Bianca said. "That's where I was when Dani was killed."

I looked at Ainsley to see if she had realized what I had. Bianca was a distraction, probably for the stalker, so Dani could get to the Sherwood station. Right time, wrong station.

Ainsley huffed. "She was sending you out as bait for her stalker, beating you every day in training, and she knew the secret that could ruin your career. You finally stood up to her. You threatened to kill her, but instead of scaring her off, Dani laughed about it, taunted you, and constantly reminded you that she could ruin your life. No one saw you at the party. But you were definitely at The Bells, because how else could you have stabbed Dani?"

Bianca's chair scraped back. She had a look of horror on her face.

"You won't win any Oscars for that performance." Ainsley straightened, looking down at Bianca. "Admit it."

"Ainsley." I stood up.

Bianca shook her head. "I didn't do it."

"Was it one of your friends?"

Bianca gripped her wrist. "I don'—no."

I stepped between Ainsley and Bianca. "She said she didn't do it."

"Oh, and of course, the killer wouldn't lie to our faces."

"What happened at the police station?" I asked.

A vein in Ainsley's neck twitched. "They said Michael's arrest is unrelated to Dani's death. So Dani's killer is still out there." She looked pointedly past me, at Bianca.

"I know you're upset," I said. "But you can't—"

"Upset?" Ainsley pounded her fist into the table. "Raven is sitting in jail because of me, and you think I should talk to her a little more nicely because I might just be upset."

I raised my palm. "Let's just leave it for today."

Ainsley stormed out, her steps echoed in the hollow halls, and as soon as Bianca felt it was safe, she scurried away.

Doors slammed, and I exhaled, waiting for the pounding in my head to slow. I stumbled back to my room. My cell phone lit up. I declined Mom's call. I was already facedown on my bed when I realized my first mistake. I stood up, and the hairs at the back of my neck rose.

My heartbeat roaring in my ears, I looked down at my bedsheets creased in the shape of my body. Heat prickled in the back of my eyes as they darted around the room faster than my mind could fully process what I had seen. But I was sure of it. Little things screamed out to me. The pillow was on top of the duvet instead of tucked in below the way I'd left it in the morning. My books, crammed into the shelf, were now in a different order. I closed my eyes and took in a deep breath. Maybe I was tired. I hadn't been thinking straight. Bianca practically had to drag me into the kitchen.

Then my eyes caught the sticky notes. Some were misplaced or scattered on the floor. *The wind? No.*

Someone had been in here. Blood drained from my head. There was a new sticky note with unfamiliar writing in thick block letters. My eyes dragged over the words.

BE CAREFUL. YOU MIGHT BE NEXT.

I pulled books from my shelves, threw them down to my desk, and flicked through them until I saw August. Cramming the newspaper article into my pocket, I scanned the room, no longer looking for what had changed or been taken, but things I needed to leave.

I clumsily gathered essentials onto my bed. Clothes for a few days, bathroom products, laptop. I threw them into a bag. Then I held on to the rail at the foot of my bed as the room spun. *Be careful. You might be next.* The words wracked my brain. I held my breath, gulping down air to stay quiet. I needed to be anywhere but this room. The killer had managed to get in here twice. Once to kill Dani and now to threaten me. I knew all too well they were capable of making good on the threat, but there was nowhere to go, no one to call. I rushed to the door and pulled at the handle with clammy hands.

It didn't move.

Did someone lock me in? I held back a scream. My heart racing, I wiped my hands on my thighs and tried again.

Nothing. Dizziness enveloped me. I bit down on my lip and steadied myself, pressing my key pass to the door. I pulled the handle. My body almost gave out as the door swung back, slowly revealing the long, dim hallway, illuminating three other bedrooms with people who had good reason to want me to stop.

TWENTY-SEVEN

I shifted under the glare from the brass 801 pinned to the door. It saw through me, recognizing the arrogance in my presence, but I didn't have anywhere else to go. That was what I had said when Tyrell answered on the second ring. He buzzed me up in response with no questions.

Now that I was standing in front of his door, I realized how true it was. I had nowhere because once I told Tyrell the truth, he would turn his back on me too. I bit down on my lip, a tear sliding down my cheek. Tyrell didn't deserve this—someone too scared to love, unable to trust, broken. I could tell him the truth, and he would hate me, or I could remember him like this, always there for me even when I didn't deserve it.

My body decided for me, stepping back and tightening my grip on my bag. The door seemed to grow smaller, as if pleased with my decision. I had done it again, leaned on him, only to disappoint him.

Mom's voice was in my head now. *Us Monroes, we do anything for the ones we love.*

I took a deep breath. A painful tightness in my throat, I walked back to the elevator. Maybe it was time to go home.

"Sienna?" Tyrell's voice washed over me.

I stilled. I wiped at my tears but didn't turn, repeatedly pressing the elevator button in the hope that it would make the elevator come faster. I was tired, and I didn't have the strength to pretend.

"Sienna, where are you going?"

I kept my head down and held my breath. Even though my body shook with the effort, the tears didn't stop. I didn't speak. I couldn't.

He was beside me now. He placed a finger under my chin and slowly lifted my head until our eyes met. His features softened. "I'm glad you came."

The weight on my shoulders lifted as he took my bag. I opened my mouth to tell him it was a mistake, but he was already walking back to the room, my bag hanging over one arm and the other guiding me to his door.

"I'm sorry." My throat closed around the words. "I think I should go."

"Have you eaten?" he asked after he sat me down on his sofa and placed my bag on the coffee table.

I blinked up at him.

"I'll take that as a no." He rubbed his hands in response.

My eyes grew hot as he backed into the kitchenette. He opened and closed cupboards and lined the counter with ingredients.

I swallowed the lump in my throat when he brought out freshly toasted bread and a small pot. "While you wait, here's some garlic butter, your favorite."

I wanted to question how he could still be so nice after

everything I had done. Instead, I pointed to the TV as a robot saved a falling cat that was supposedly from planet Mars. "What is this?"

Tyrell chuckled as he returned to the kitchen. "We literally watched this two weeks ago. It's out already. I thought I'd take the chance to watch it without all the questions."

"I didn't ask you any questions about this movie."

"No, but you kept asking to leave."

I dipped my bread in the sauce and chewed, suppressing a smile.

He grinned. "And whether it was done five minutes into the movie."

"It must have been a long five minutes," I mumbled.

He opened the oven and put a filled tray inside. He set the timer. Each beep felt like it was counting down to the end of all of this. The easy talks. The teasing. Us.

The sofa dipped as Tyrell sat beside me, not touching, but I could still feel the heat from his body as he leaned over and took the remote. The TV went blank.

He smiled. "Since the movie didn't go down so well the first time."

I cringed.

"Sorry," Tyrell said. "We can just watch something else if you're not ready to talk about it."

"I'm not." My throat was thick. "But I don't think I will ever be ready." I took a deep breath and stared ahead at the blank screen, and not at Tyrell, who was focused on me. "Have you ever heard of Black Quietus?"

Tyrell shook his head.

"It's a gang. They are all over the country, including Kinwick, where I'm from."

Tyrell leaned in and listened.

"Kinwick is quiet, so whenever something happened, we would always know it was because of the Black Quietus. They groom people who are isolated and desperate for a chance to fit in and prove themselves. My brother, August, was one of them. It started with fun stuff. They'd shoplift together. I started to notice things in my brother's room, things I knew there was no way he had the money for. They'd get together to watch a game and chill. They make you feel as though you're a part of something, then they threaten to take it all away. He was going to lose all the friends he had." I shook my head. "The gang." I spat.

"Just to be around them, they would test you. Pets would go missing, fires would start, and if you wanted to join, they had to have something on you, something worse." I looked at Tyrell. "They would give you a target to kill." I swallowed hard. "For August, it was our neighbor. It wasn't just August. There were three of them.

"I had the flu, and my friends decided to video call me so we could play silly games and speak for the whole night. In the morning, when we woke up, August was back, and Mr. Griffin was dead. One of the boys had dropped his cell phone, and when the police caught him, August knew they would be coming for him next. He told Mom everything, how he tried to stop it, but it was too late. It was an accident, but it didn't matter, because they went there to kill him. But August wasn't the one who left anything behind, and the boys couldn't be trusted. They had reputations. August was good. No one had ever complained about him. Plus, how could he have been there when he spent the whole night with me?" I pressed my hands against my stomach, a bitter taste in my mouth. "Dad was away for work, and Mom was having dinner with the neighbors, so she said I had to say August was home taking care of me. I did. I lied to the police." My voice broke.

"Then I lied to my friends. I told them I forgot August was upstairs, but I had already told the police he was downstairs, helping me recover. They knew something was wrong, and soon enough, so did everyone else. All the neighbors turned against us and said we were as good as murderers. I never wanted to lie. But Mom gave me no choice."

Tyrell placed a hand on my knee.

"There wasn't enough evidence tying August to the crime, and even though Mom forced him not to say anything, I could tell it was eating him up. I still have dreams about Mr. Griffin. I couldn't imagine what it was doing to August. I wanted him to stand up for us. He knew what Mom was making me do. I had lost all my friends, and we could barely leave the house. Mom didn't want us to talk to anyone. We couldn't leave without her. I never slept. I don't think August did. He heard me leave, he watched from behind the curtain, and he knew what I was going to do."

I sniffed. "I betrayed my family. If I had told someone earlier about August, maybe no one would have died."

Tyrell squeezed my knee and closed the distance between us.

"He didn't say anything when the police took him away. Mom screamed. I'm selfish and disgusting. How could I do this to someone who loves me?" I rolled off the insults I knew so well.

"I know what's right and wrong, and I never want to love someone so much I lose myself." The words came out in a strangled cry. My whole body wracked.

Tyrell was there. He tucked my head under his chin, holding me close as tears stained his shirt.

"I'm sorry," I said into his throat.

The timer dinged, but Tyrell didn't let go.

I pulled back and wiped my cheeks. "The food is going to burn."

He leaned in. "It's not fair that you were put in that position, and I'm sorry that happened to you. Everyone who turned their backs on you is missing out on the most incredible person I've ever known. And I know this isn't about us, but with me, you can be selfish. I will always want you to put your happiness first."

It was what I needed to hear. A weight in my chest lifted, I parted my lips, then my stomach grumbled.

Tyrell smiled. "Okay, let me get the food."

I didn't realize how hungry I had been until I started eating. Then I was desperate for more as soon as I finished the creamy pasta bake.

"Do you want more?"

I hesitated, and Tyrell was already sweeping up my plate to serve seconds.

"Dani knew," I called to him. "She left me this." I pulled the newspaper article from my pocket and unfolded it, smoothing the creases. August's face didn't hurt to look at. I wanted to hate him and blame him for everything that had happened to us, but he wasn't a monster. He was scared. I let my eyes take in the article properly. Some of the words telling August's story were circled and unlined, not part of the print. *Dani.*

I picked up a pen from the table.

"What are you doing?" Tyrell placed the plate of food beside the article.

"I think Dani left a message for me in this. She circled some of the letters."

"Would it be too much to ask for it to be the name of her killer?"

I wrote out all the letters underlined. Two letters were in the headline.

August Monroe, the third suspect arrested in connection to the murder of a sixty-seven-year-old man.

T and *I*. I combed through the rest of the article. Some strokes were short and barely noticeable.

It was un. Your secret is safe with me.

"Un?"

Tyrell tapped on the page. "You missed an F."

It was fun. Your secret is safe with me.

TWENTY-EIGHT

BE CAREFUL. YOU MIGHT BE NEXT.

I jolted awake. My heart raced, and adrenaline shot through my body. It was dark. I reached over my shoulder for the switch to my lamp, and my stomach hardened as my hand collided with a wall.

Where am I? I didn't remember falling asleep. I should have known better than to risk it after the note.

I was in a full-sized bed. Soft layers of fresh citrus and musk created a warm feeling in my chest. I wasn't at The Bells. I was with Tyrell, but this wasn't like the times before. Now, he knew the truth. It felt freeing. Not only had a weight been lifted, but I knew myself better. Maybe I was even ready to talk to August again.

I rolled over, stretching out my arm, searching for Tyrell, and finding only empty space. The hairs on the back of my neck stood up. I scrambled out of bed and fumbled around the bedside table until I found my cell phone. I turned on the flashlight and moved around the room.

Tyrell was here, tucked in on the sofa. His upper body

was bundled under a towel, and his legs were cloaked in his jacket. My heart swelled. I pulled the duvet from his bed and laid it on top of him.

I wasn't ready to leave yet. But I had no choice.

He didn't stir as I got ready or as the door clicked softly behind me, and I couldn't get back in until he was awake. That thought unsettled me.

The lights turned on in the passage as I walked to the elevator. I clicked the button and waited. The air was still, and I couldn't fight the feeling that I was missing something. A thin strip of light was visible beneath Jamie's door. I thought back to the stack of notes threatening Dani.

Bianca could be lying, but why? Jamie hadn't said they were from her. He didn't know who had been writing them. Someone could have picked up where Bianca left off.

The elevator whirred, then the doors opened. I just needed to step in, one foot in front of the other, but curiosity lured me to Jamie's door, closer and closer, until I was in front of the silver 803. There was only one way to be certain.

I raised a fist to knock. My knuckles connected with the oak wood. I pulled my hand back as the door creaked open. I leaned forward, into the room where almost every surface held a part of Dani. Early sunlight crept through the blinds, reflecting off the trophy engraved with her name and her loopy handwriting, promising a tomorrow.

One corner of the duvet had been folded back, but I couldn't see Jamie. I allowed myself one step into the room. "Jamie?" I called in a hushed whisper.

A chirp of a cell phone by the bed was the only response.

A chill swept through the room—never a good sign. My brain agreed, firing messages to my legs to retreat. I looked back at the door, with every intention of taking the one step back to exit the room, to leave without having touched anything. But technically, the door had already been open. I hadn't broken in, and I'd only come for one thing—the notes.

Jamie had offered them to me the last time I was here, and I knew exactly where they were. It wasn't stealing. Before I could question myself, I was already leaning back against the door. "Hello?"

When no one replied, I moved back, squeezing my eyes shut until I heard the door click. At least I would have a warning if anyone tried to enter. I crossed the living area and fell to my knees. The row of shelves loomed in front of me. I wasn't sure which of the drawers Jamie had pulled the notes from, so I started at the top, sitting on my heels. The first drawer was filled with plugs and chargers. I moved to the second. My heart sped up. Notebooks and printed lecture slides filled the drawer. The notebooks were smaller than the ones that held the notes, and none had the gray circular design. My fingers halted at the edge of the drawer. A block-red notebook lay at the bottom. I had seen this notebook before.

No, I had owned it.

I opened the first page. My name was etched at the top, crossed out, and replaced with "Dani Bishop." My heart raced. I glanced back at the door—it hadn't moved—then flicked to the next page. The dates were from the start of the school year. Dani's doodles covered the edges of the pages and captured notes and assignments. Then they were replaced by harsher lines, barely-there dots, and unfinished crosses. Dates. Times. Locations.

Monday - Swimming practice at 6 am or 7 pm. Speaks to Sam after practice. Wait by the gym to incept.

Tuesday - Stayed at Graybone. Michael lives here? New black hoodie, white strings.

This continued, the dates getting closer and stopping right when Dani died.

Leaving one am from the Rosemary station. Follow from The Bells.

My heartbeat thrashed in my ears. My hands gripped the notebook. My eyes darted around the room. I wasn't alone. There was another presence here. Traces of Dani were scattered around the room. Jamie couldn't let her go. Not when she was alive. Not in death. I saw the room through a different lens. Dani's message was an unkept promise he was determined to make her keep. Jamie was the stalker. Trophies, shoes, clothes—he'd kept everything the same because he wouldn't accept the truth.

I placed the notebook beside me and moved to the third and final drawer, where the notes must have been. I held my breath and pulled. No notes. I could see the bottom of the drawer, but I still moved aside the creams and sprays just in case.

A sharp ring sliced through the air.

I straightened, my legs weak. I looked by the bed, where Jamie's cell phone buzzed, and blew out a breath. I was still alone. My heart thumped. My eyes locked on the bedside desk, and my legs advanced. Three phones lay on the wooden surface—one shielded in a white case and two in a clear plastic bag, a smartphone with a blue case, and an old black phone. It was the first one that caught my attention. I had seen it several times before, but not recently, because Dani had lost her cell phone before she died.

My heartbeat picked up. Jamie had trapped her. The puzzle pieces slotted into place.

Jamie had found out Dani was going, and he'd done everything he could to stop her. When it didn't seem like that was going to work, he'd poisoned our room. But she was still leaving, and time was running out, so he'd killed her.

Two of the notes were from Bianca, and the rest were from her stalker. From Jamie.

I remembered the look of horror on her face on the day she died, like someone had been watching her by the Stedmond Park exit—exactly where I'd found him. I stuffed the plastic packaging with her cell phone into my bag. I had more than what I'd come here for. The last thing I needed to get was the notes.

"What are you doing?"

I looked up. Realization slammed through me. He was back.

A primal scream built in my chest. Jamie's large frame blocked the doorway. I hadn't heard it unlock. His stare pinned on me as he kicked the door shut.

"What are you doing here?" He didn't budge from the doorway.

I went with the best answer I could give. The truth. Or at least part of it.

"I-I saw your door was left open, so I wanted to come back and look at the notes again." I walked away from the bed, hoping he didn't realize the cell phones were missing, and moved closer to the door. Closer to Jamie. "It wasn't there, so I tried to search the nightstand."

His gaze was intrusive. I couldn't exhale until it stopped.

He searched the room, eyes lingering for a moment on the bed.

I found the strength to keep my voice steady. "Where are they?"

"Safe," he said, not yet finished scanning the room. He turned to face the shelves where the stack of notes had been yesterday. My eyes followed, and that was when I saw it—the reason I wouldn't be allowed to leave.

Jamie's eyes widened at the red notebook on the floor, opened to the dates and timing of Dani's movements, including the day she'd died. I could have stayed calm and pretended I didn't know what they meant, but I impulsively took a sharp step back.

Jamie moved forward. "Why did you come here?"

I heard something in his voice I hadn't expected. Regret.

"You just wouldn't leave it alone."

I swallowed. "You killed her?"

He didn't speak. He sank back against the door. My only option of escape. His fists pulsed at his sides. Then his glossy eyes caught mine then held my gaze for a moment that seemed to last a lifetime. Eighteen years flashed across my eyes. Mom, August, Tyrell... Then everything was a blur as Jamie crossed the room in quick strides.

His voice tight, he said, "I'm sorry, Sienna."

My body went numb. He'd hurt Dani. Why was he apologizing to me?

I wanted to call someone—the police or Tyrell. It took a

moment for my body to catch up. My finger twitched at the cell phone in my pocket. There wasn't enough time. In seconds, Jamie's thick legs closed the distance between us. So, I did the one thing I could think of.

I screamed.

TWENTY-NINE

Jamie's shoulder charged into my abdomen, forcing air from my lungs. A sharp surge of pain coursed through me, and I landed on my side with a crack.

I spluttered for breath. But he was there. Pulling me flat and clamping a large hand over my mouth, the full weight of his body over my chest.

"Sienna," he breathed.

I felt it, hot on my skin, but I could barely hear him through the rush of blood in my ears.

"I'm not a murderer." He slowed his breaths and lifted his hands from my mouth. They hovered around my throat. A peace offering of sorts. "I don't want to hurt you."

I wasn't listening. There was a way out of this. I just needed to stay calm. My cell phone was still in my pocket, but there was no way to reach it with him pinning me down, and I couldn't fight back. He was too big. Too strong.

Now that my mouth was free, I fought the urge to scream again. I just needed to buy time. A framed picture of

Dani and Jamie was above me on the desk. Her green eyes gleamed.

"Why did you kill her?" My voice was raspy.

"I didn't kill her. She shouldn't have been there," Jamie said in a low voice, his eyes straying to the floor.

A lump rose in my throat. I was confused.

"I loved her." His voice shook. "I couldn't let her leave. With him." Anger laced his voice. "She would have regretted it. We were always supposed to end up together. We'd have fights and argue, but we always came back together."

"So why did you stab her?"

His hand clenched around my throat. "I didn't stab her."

I gasped, struggling for air. "Okay, okay." The words managed to escape.

Jamie's grip loosened.

The skin around my throat burned. "I know Dani wasn't the easiest person to love. I know you wouldn't want to hurt anyone. Just tell me what happened?"

He moved back, freeing my body as he slumped onto the floor. His hand scrubbed wildly across his face. "I didn't want her to go." His voice was tight. Tears laced his eyes.

I could breathe again but wasn't fast enough to reach the door. I tucked my legs in, breaking contact with his outstretched leg and creating a barrier to hide my cell phone once I slipped it out of my pocket.

He looked up, shaking his head, and blinked back tears. "At first, I just wanted to know what she was doing, how she had changed. I thought maybe if I knew, I could be better for her." He cleared his throat. "Everything was the same—her routines, her habits." He smiled.

"The only difference was Michael. I couldn't get through to her. She didn't understand. I'd call her and send her all kinds of messages, and she replied, so I knew she was still thinking of me. Then she stopped. I thought she was ignoring me. I didn't know she lost her cell phone until after."

"You took Dani's phone?" It seemed to burn through the bag at my waist.

He shook his head. "No. Someone left it for me. I was going to give it back to her. Maybe then she would trust me, but I was scared she would think I had taken it, and at least I knew she couldn't contact Michael. After, I kept it as something to remember her by."

"Who left it for you?"

He chewed his lip. "I don't know. It was outside my door when I came back one evening. Dani was there for me when my dad was sick. During all the hospital visits. She came to my little brother's recital. We were a family. She only started acting cold when we came here. Maybe we were drifting apart, but she knew she could always rely on me. I was always there for her. When she had problems with Vivi last year, she called me. She would always lean on me. I knew she would." He sniffed. "I got the code for Ainsley's party a few days before, and I thought if I gave Dani a chance to see how much I could support her like I did before, she would realize I was the one she could rely on."

My blood chilled.

"I went into the utility room and blocked the ventilation for the gas water heater. It happened to a family where I grew up. They got sick, and no one knew why. I thought I'd get her back. I just wanted to make sure she didn't leave, and if she was a little sick, I would take care of her. But someone stabbed her before I could help s—"

"But she died from the poison."

"No." He jerked his head. "She just needed air. Whoever stabbed her stopped her from getting the help she needed. I was outside, waiting. I would ha—"

"Jamie," I said softly.

He refused to meet my eyes, and his head shook in his hands.

I kept my eyes trained on him, brushing the length of my thigh until I felt it. "She was stabbed after she died. The police confirmed it was post-mortem." I closed my hand around my cell phone and pushed it. It slid up, almost at the end. "I'm sorry. I thought you knew."

His eyes met mine now. Stern and bloodshot, they held no surprise. "I didn't kill her."

"Okay." I nodded, my head throbbing. "Did you send the notes you showed me?"

He gulped. "Yes."

"And you put the one in my room?"

"No. I always left them for her at practice."

"Yesterd—"

My slither of hope clattered to the floor. The cell phone slid between us, the screen lit.

Jamie pounced, grasping my lifeline. "What were you going to do with this?"

"Jamie, it was an accident." Something rattled in my throat. The words were barely more than a whisper. "We can go to the police and explain."

236

He jerked his arm, and my phone crashed on the floor. Fragments flew across the room. His lips pulled back, baring teeth as he brought down his foot on the cracked screen. Then his eyes darted to me.

I could barely talk. My lips parted, begging my strained throat for one act of mercy. If anything happened, someone needed to know I was here. I inhaled sharply, ready to cry out. Then his palms, wet and warm, crashed against my teeth. The metallic taste of blood filled my mouth. My vision clouded, but I could still see his features, hard and determined.

Tears rolled from my eyes. I didn't think it was possible, but his grip tightened. I whimpered, trying to speak, to plead. But it was futile.

I clasped my hands around his, trying to pry his fingers away and ease my breathing. He held firm, grunting from the effort, eyes scanning the room. His stance left his chin exposed. I closed my right hand into a fist and thrust it into his jaw.

His body jerked back. Surprise clouded his eyes—then rage. His arms bulged as he hoisted me into the air by my neck. He bore my full weight with ease as I kicked out and struggled for breath. I'd underestimated his strength.

Then suddenly, my throat was free. But my body was hurled across the room, smacking into the kitchen counter. Something snapped in my left arm. I couldn't move. My body was wracked with pain.

This is it.

I'd thought my final thoughts would be about my family, who didn't know I was about to die, or Tyrell, who would never know how much he meant to me. But now that I was about to meet my fate, all I saw was Dani.

My eyes brimmed with tears. Everything moved quickly as Jamie stalked toward me. Dani's framed face smiled, a glint in her green eyes. No, not a glint, a reflection. I twisted, bearing my weight on my broken arm, and leaped to grab Dani's trophy from the mantel.

Hands wrapped around my wrist, but it was too late. I seized the trophy and swung wildly behind me. A dull thud rang out as the metal collided with Jamie's head. After another, he fell to the floor.

An erratic beat hammered in my head as I tried to make sense of the scene before me. Jamie lay at an awkward angle, unmoving. His straw-colored hair was matted with blood. My hands fluttered by my sides. I dropped the trophy. The room was spinning. Jamie was dead.

I squeezed my eyes shut. My breaths were quick and shallow. I prayed things would be different when I opened my eyes, but Jamie still lay lifeless.

I held back a scream. My heart threatened to explode. Then his index finger slowly rose.

Dead people don't move. I eased forward. Every bone in my body ached as I pressed two fingers to Jamie's throat. Dani flashed through my mind, cold and bloody. There was a strong pulse but too much blood.

Help. He needs help. I gazed at the remnants of my phone on the floor. My legs drove me past them and through the front door.

I pounded on Tyrell's door and pressed my ear to it. There was no movement inside. "Please, please. I need you," I said, but the words were no more than a whisper. I threw my leg back and kicked at the door. Moments later, it swung open.

Tyrell squinted, shielding his eyes from the light. "Hey, what do you think yo—Sienn—" His eyes widened. He held out his arms.

I stepped back. It wasn't me who needed the help. I gestured to Jamie's room, the tightness in my throat only allowing one word. "Ambulance."

Tyrell ran back into the room, and I slumped against the doorframe, the bag weighing me down. Tyrell reappeared with his phone pressed between his ear and shoulder.

"You are going to be fine, okay." He slid my bag off my shoulder and placed it by his front door, then he tried to guide me inside. I stumbled back to the place that only minutes ago, I'd believed would be my deathbed.

Jamie had said he didn't stab Dani. He had said a lot of things, but I believed this—and he needed to be alive to tell his story. I needed him to be alive because I was afraid of what my life would be like if he wasn't. Maybe no one would know the truth about what had happened to Dani. Mom would have two killers for children, and I would spend the rest of my life in prison.

I staggered after Tyrell as he entered Jamie's room and crouched beside him.

They were dark figures, ebbing and flowing. I moved with them, swaying, trying to balance the blood and pain wracking my body. My throat throbbed. I needed to speak, to warn Tyrell, because someone had turned off the lights. Shapes loomed over me then disappeared, leaving me alone in darkness.

THIRTY

I was trapped in my own body. The rhythmic beeps of the heart monitor and the drip of fluids drowned out the low voices in the room. My throat had been crushed, and pain seared through my body. I blinked. My dry eyes were the only part of my body that seemed to move as normal. My gaze fixed on Tyrell's familiar low fade. He scratched the back of his head, and I looked past him—into the eyes of the woman wearing blue scrubs, her hair scraped into a tight bun.

"Hi, Sienna." She looked up and sidestepped, her entire face coming into view. A broad smile revealed a set of blue braces. "I'm your nurse, Kim."

I opened my mouth, and only a raspy moan escaped.

"You have sustained some damage to your throat," she explained. "You also have a mild concussion and a broken left arm."

I looked down. My arm was bound in a cast and sling.

Tyrell moved to my side. "Both will heal back to normal."

Kim smiled. "We will see how you get on throughout the day, but we may want to keep you overnight to monitor your progress and ensure there are no issues with your breathing. You have a few people here who have been waiting a long time to see you." She raised a brow at Tyrell. "But please keep the talking to a minimum."

I winced as I swallowed what felt like a boulder in my throat.

"Is there anything I can get you?"

"No," I managed.

"Okay." Kim smiled. "I'll be back to check in on you soon."

"Hey." Tyrell stroked his brow. "I thought—" His arms tensed, and he drew in a breath. "I'm just really glad you're okay."

My cheeks warmed. My thoughts lodged in my throat. Only one word managed to escape. "Jamie?"

Tyrell's face darkened. "He's in the hospital too. He's going to be fine. An officer is interviewing him." Tyrell leaned in. "Did he kill Dani?"

I nodded and immediately regretted it. The weight of the room crashed down on my head.

Tyrell sighed. "And you decided to take him on all by yourself?"

"Didn't know." I croaked then added, "I won."

Tyrell laughed. "I'm not sure I'd call this winning. You're effectively trapped in this bed, so I can tell you all about the movies I love."

I stared at the big red emergency button, and Tyrell's laugh deepened.

Someone by the entrance cleared their throat, out of the perimeter of my pain tolerance.

Detective Collins stepped into view. "Hello, Sienna. I understand you're not ready to give a full interview yet, but I have some questions for you." His hand dipped into the inside pocket of his long black jacket, and he pulled out a notepad and pen. "Police were called to the incident scene, and they found some interesting things in Jamie's dorm room."

Everything was circumstantial. Nothing actually linked him to her death, but he had confessed to me. The notebook and sticky notes could prove he was stalking her. There could be more evidence on Dani's cell phone or Jamie's burner. My face fell. I recovered quickly, and Collins didn't seem to notice. The cell phones were in my bag, which was in Tyrell's room, not Jamie's. I parted my lips to tell Collins then pressed them together in a line. If I told him now, I may never know what was on Dani's cell phone.

"I would like to know your account of what happened early this morning."

Two words grated their way through my throat. "He confessed."

Collins leaned in to hear, and I broke out in a series of harsh coughs. My ribs closed in with the pressure.

"To Dani's murder," Tyrell added as Collins scribbled on his notepad.

I thought of the least amount of words to convey all I had learned. "Only poisoning. It was an accident. He didn't stab her."

Kim popped her head into the room, and Collins's brows furrowed. "Okay. I will have to interview you once you have recovered a bit more. Thank you, Sienna. I will speak to you soon."

A pair of legs hung over the sides of the visitor chair. My nap wasn't peaceful. Everything hurt, and the loud, inconsiderate munching I woke to didn't help. Ainsley leaned forward and helped herself to an apple from a fruit basket. Our eyes locked, and I considered closing them quickly or playing dead, but she was already dropping her feet to the floor.

"Took you long enough. Don't worry, as tempting as it is, I'm not here to finish the job."

I groaned.

"Tyrell brought you these." She gestured to the fruits she had been working her way through. "And said he would come back later when you've gotten some rest."

It felt as though getting any rest would be impossible.

"I hoped there would be a development on getting Raven out. I was angry, and I snapped. I tried knocking on your door after yesterday. I wanted to check that you were o—alive."

I bit down a smile. "You worried?"

"Yeah, when you didn't answer, I thought there had been another death and we'd be kicked out of The Bells. It's a nightmare finding accommodation at this time of year."

I laughed. The movement rattled something loose in my body, and I winced.

"So." Ainsley raised a brow. "Tyrell said Jamie poisoned Dani, but he didn't stab her?"

"Yeah."

"Just in time for the funeral."

"You're going?" I asked.

"Dani's dead. Of course, I'm going. If they are still looking for whoever stabbed her, I'm not going to raise suspicions by avoiding it." Ainsley threw what was left of her apple into the trashcan.

As far as the police were concerned, someone had already confessed to the stabbing.

Ainsley's jaw tensed. She seemed to read the thought on my face. "Raven didn't do it."

"I know," I croaked.

"And I can't give up on freeing her."

I know," I repeated.

"Bianca's feeling guilty. She's booked a van from the swimming team and offered to drive us all to the funeral. I want to speak to the people there. We can see if anyone is acting weird."

I sighed. The funeral didn't seem like the best time to play detective.

"Do you have any better ideas?"

Search through her phone. "No."

"How did you even know it was Jamie?"

"I didn't. I wanted the notes he wrote."

"He wrote them?"

"He was the stalker."

My heart stilled as the door swung open, and my throat clenched as Martina, Mabel, and Bianca shuffled inside.

Mabel's lips deepened into a frown. If I had the strength, I would have shifted under her gaze. I hadn't looked in a mirror, but from her face, I knew it wasn't good.

Mabel brought a finger to her lips. "I don't think we are all supposed to be in here." She winked, and I wondered whether this would be a legitimate reason to ring the emergency bell.

"We brought some grapes." Bianca placed the container of grapes on the table; the plastic cover had already been ripped open.

"If you think they look suspiciously like half-eaten ones from our fridge"—Martina leaned against the wall at the back of the room, slowing as Mabel shot her a look—"it's just a weird coincidence."

"Nia sends her condolences," Mabel said, slipping into the chair next to Ainsley.

Ainsley rolled her eyes. "No, she doesn't."

"You don't know that," Mabel hissed.

"Jamie did this?" Bianca sat at the end of the bed. Her voice was small.

"Yes."

Bianca's eyes widened.

"You're so brave for confronting him." Mabel leaned over Ainsley to place her hand gently on my sling, and her bright-blue eyes flickered with admiration. "Dani would have been so happy to know you all had her back."

"She didn't do it for Dani." Ainsley drew Mabel's hand back. She leaned back and pressed her lips into a line.

Silence. Normally, the type I would walk away from. But considering I had a concussion, a broken arm, and my head pounded every time I moved, there was no way to escape it. My whole body stung with pain as I leaned forward to take fruit.

Tyrell had bought mangos, my favorite, but Mabel's face

beamed as I hovered over the grapes, so I took one and ate it.

"Do you know if they will let you out for the funeral?" Bianca asked.

I gave my best attempt at a shrug.

Mabel shook her head. "I still can't believe it was Jamie. He was so in love with her."

"That should have been the first red flag," Ainsley muttered. "Well." She stood up. "This has been fun, but I'll leave you guys to it."

I silently pleaded with my eyes for her to take the rest of the girls with her. She recognized it, and amusement traced her lips as she shut the door behind her.

I thought things couldn't get any worse, then, twenty minutes later, Mom showed up.

"Ah, friends." Mom opened her arms wide, glancing over each member of the group only brought together by my almost death. "I was beginning to think you didn't have any of those."

I rolled my eyes so hard, I was afraid I might pass out.

"Hello, I'm Erica. What's your name?"

Mabel jumped up, cleared the seat for Mom, and extended a hand. "Mabel. It's lovely to meet you, Mrs. Bassey."

"Oh, please." Mom waved a hand. "I am Mrs. Monroe. But you can call me Erica."

Blood drained from my ears. No one else seemed to notice, but the name hung in the air, making it harder to breathe.

Martina and Bianca took turns introducing themselves.

"We will go now, Erica. It was lovely to meet you." This

time, Mabel wrapped her arms around Mom in a hug. The other two gave curt waves and pitying smiles as they left.

"Lovely friends."

My throat tightened, but correcting her wasn't worth the pain.

"And I met a Tyrell outside." Mom raised her brows with meaning.

"What did you say to him?" I snapped.

"He's a nice boy."

"Answer the question."

She ignored me, fixing an all-white bouquet. "Do you know how worried I was when I got the call you were in hospital? Why not let the police do their jobs?" She moaned, taking the seat Tyrell had sat in that morning. Now that Mom was in it, the chair felt all too close.

"Because police don't have real jobs."

Mom waved me off.

"They are just bored pathetic individuals who are looking to ruin families," I quoted from one of her many rants.

"I couldn't agree more. But you can't be putting yourself in these dangerous situations. Your brother was worried sick when I spoke to him. Maybe we can speak to him together tomorrow. He'll be so relieved to hear you're okay."

I tensed. I didn't know if Mom didn't notice or was pretending not to see.

"I'm not ready for that yet. And Jamie broke my cell phone."

Mom pulled something from her pocket. "It isn't as fancy as the one you had, but we had this lying around in the house." She dropped a cell phone onto the bed. Then she looked down at the name tag. "Sienna Bassey," she read in disgust. "Are you that ashamed of people knowing who you are?"

"We are in a hospital. Murderers aren't exactly popular here. I don't want people to know I am the sister of one."

Mom scoffed. "Your brother is a good man who made a mistake."

"Would you say the same thing about Jamie if I had died today?"

Mom bit down on her lip and cupped my cheeks. "Look at what he's done to your face."

I was becoming more anxious to look in a mirror with every visitor. "Crushed throat," I reminded her.

She drew her hands back.

It took over an hour for me to figure out that the only way to get Mom to stop being overbearing was to speak to Dad. Mom sat quietly in the corner, refusing to speak to him as we video called. Mom still hadn't forgiven him for not fighting harder for August. She busied herself on her cell phone as we caught up. I only cut the call when I got my last visitor of the night.

Khadijah bounded into the room, equipped with textbooks I wouldn't use and an uplifting smile I could never forget. She placed the books and a box of chocolates on the table. "I wanted to come sooner, but I had to wait until Mary could cover. I'm so sorry."

"She was probably hoping I'd die."

"Sienna," Mom and Khadijah both scolded me in unison.

After they had finished lecturing me about making

better decisions and catching up on schoolwork, I was grateful for their presence. They spoke about the planning for Khadijah's wedding, and I listened, offering minimal input, and wondered if Tyrell would come with me.

"Everyone will understand if you don't go to the funeral," Khadijah said, pulling me away from my thoughts.

"Yes," Mom agreed. "Your recovery is the most important thing."

I shook my head and fought off the need to wince. "I'm fine."

Mom and Khadijah shared a look.

"No need to double-team me. My head feels much clearer. I'll drink plenty of water, won't talk, and I didn't even use my left arm anyway."

Mom sighed. "Would you listen even if I told you no?"

The corners of Khadijah's eyes creased. "So, it's not just me she doesn't listen to."

"I need to tell you about the time she was four." Mom huffed. "I told her three pigeons couldn't fly her to Disneyland, but she…"

I zoned out. White noise and static filled my head. Even if Dani was already dead, someone had brutally stabbed her. That was still a crime—one Raven hadn't committed—and the culprit was still out there.

THIRTY-ONE

I should have known Dani wouldn't go quietly. Sheets of rain pelted the window, the type that damaged umbrellas and ruined outfits. Darkness shrouded The Bell. Jagged lines bolted through the low-hanging clouds, flashing through the room for a moment, then it was gone.

"It must be hard to be in here," Mabel said over the low rumble of thunder. She gently guided my arm through the sleeves of my dress and sniffed, her eyes brimming with tears. "It makes everything feel so real."

"Yeah," I said mindlessly, my eyes fixed on the floor. It glistened with blood before I blinked away the image of Dani's lifeless body. Her death no longer lined the walls. I couldn't stand the sticky notes of names and motives hanging over me. My body had roared in pain last night as I tore and snatched at the walls and rubbed the whiteboard clean until the room resembled the past, a time when Dani was still here.

But the words were imprinted in my brain. They called to me from the sticky note in a box under the bed.

BE CAREFUL. YOU MIGHT BE NEXT.

I flinched.

"Sorry," Mabel said as she zipped the back of my dress. The material tightened around my sore skin. She faced me, sling in hand, and my arm throbbed in response. "Ready?"

"Yeah." I gazed down at her matte-black boots instead of the strained look on her face, and I bit down on my lip as she fitted my arm in the sling.

"Do you need anything else?"

"No, I'm okay, thank you."

She smoothed down her black skater dress, and her smile wavered as she looked at Dani's bed. "I'll see you in the van."

I took my time getting into my jacket, allowing one side to hang off my shoulder. My throat was hoarse, and even the slightest movement resulted in a pounding in my head. But I couldn't miss the funeral.

Silence tainted the lobby. The gloom was palpable, but my heart still managed to pick up the way it always did around Tyrell. Unfortunately, he wasn't alone.

"Do you think that's appropriate?" Nia tutted, shaking her head at Ainsley.

Ainsley stepped back and opened her arms to show her gray outfit better. Her braids hung down her back. The tips faded into a silver that matched her six-inch heels. Her jacket, the only black clothing she was wearing, hung over her arm. "Black is for people who are in mourning. I think we have all established that I am not. I would have gone with a bright-yellow number, but Martina said it would be disrespectful." She shot daggers at Martina, who was busy staring out the window.

"The van's here," Martina said.

"You okay?" Tyrell asked.

"Yeah." I tightened the jacket around me, bracing myself for the cold.

Martina threw open the doors as Tyrell lifted the umbrella above us. The wind swept it aside. Rain sprayed and splattered at our ankles, snaking under hoods and into boots during the short jog to the van. Bianca grimaced from behind the wheel and opened the sliding van doors.

Five of the fourteen seats were already occupied by members of the swim team. Sam and Rachel didn't meet my gaze as I clambered in with Tyrell's help then took a seat in the second row.

Everyone settled in. Nia untangled her earphones, and Martina buried her head in a book. Three of the swim team members' heads shot up as Ainsley entered.

"Where's Mabel?" Bianca asked.

"Probably changing outfits," Ainsley said. "Apparently, this isn't a festive event."

"She's wearing black like everyone else. You don't have to come." Bianca added in a low voice, "It's insulting to people who actually cared for Dani."

Ainsley raised her chin. "Like you?"

Bianca pressed her lips into a line, and Ainsley strutted through the narrow aisle. "Rachel," she said in greeting. "Pam."

Sam didn't correct her. She just gazed out the window and kept her head low.

Bianca shut the door. A small pool of water had formed next to it, carried through the space in overlapping footsteps.

A silhouette moved behind the rapid beads of water on the window. Mabel's red hair peeked out from behind a raincoat. She leaned against her beat-down car. Another figure towered over her, arms jutting out. Then a finger pointed at her face. My heart stilled as the figure leaned in. I couldn't see Mabel's face, but she must have done something, because the figure retreated, taking long, sharp strides through the parking lot.

Mabel held her hands over her head and approached the van.

"We're leaving now," Bianca called over her shoulder as Mabel pulled open the doors.

"Is everything okay?" I asked after Mabel took a seat in front of us next to Nia.

She smiled nervously, her cheeks bright red. "Just feeling a little upset about Dani."

I didn't push. That could be true, but it was more than that. I could see it on her face.

Bianca started the van and drove off.

This wasn't the first funeral I had been to. At least this time, the whispers were about how I'd caught the killer, not how I'd tried to help one. My family had not been invited to Mr. Finch's funeral. All our neighbors had been, but Mom couldn't understand how that didn't extend to us.

That was the turning point—when glances turned to stares, whispers turned to shouts, and friends turned to strangers. I remembered the looks of disgust. August wasn't there to take the blame or to see their hurt, but we were. My legs bounced, and I exhaled as Tyrell's warm palm cupped my knee.

"You're okay," he said softly.

The funeral home was wet and cold. Hushed conversations of stories about Dani overpowered the creaky pews and an unfamiliar song in the background. I squeezed past the crowd of mourners and entered the bathroom and was happy to find it empty. I balled up tissue in my hand and wiped at the rain on my face. My mascara was running, and my hair had reverted to tight coils. Something in my neck twinged, and when I looked up in the mirror, I wasn't alone.

My heart stilled. A pair of green eyes bore into me. I blinked, confident the image would disappear, like all the times before, because there was no way Dani could be here.

"She's dead," I mouthed to myself as I turned. My brain gripped onto reality. Dani had a little sister who was the spitting image of her, from the thin lips to the intrusive stare trailing me as I leaned in to wash my hands. She stepped forward to wash her own hands then dried them on a paper towel in silence. It wasn't until my one good hand pushed against the door that she spoke.

"Sienna. The sister of the Black Quietus killer."

My heart thudded. My limbs shook, and just as I was about to step back into the room, she was behind me. We exited the bathroom. I swallowed, unsure how to answer. It was a statement, not a question, so I said nothing.

"I heard about what you did. I thought you hated Dani."

Again, not a question. Hairs rose on the back of my neck. It was the same sensation as when I'd spoken to Dani —like only one person understood the meaning of the conversation, and it wasn't me.

I shifted uncomfortably. "I didn't hate Dani."

She smiled. The expression didn't quite reach her eyes. "Fran. Dani's sister."

"Nice to meet you." The words rolled off my tongue.

"I hope you did a lot worse to Jamie." She nodded at my sling.

"I hit him with one of Dani's trophies."

She laughed. "She would have loved that." Her cheeks fell. "Just a shame there wasn't time to do anything to Raven."

My body went rigid, but I recovered quickly. "Did Dani ever say anything about Raven or anyone else that may have wanted to hurt her?" I didn't know what to expect or how much Fran knew about Dani. My scalp prickled as Fran drew her head back.

"I never expected the police to catch whoever did it. They told us the stabbing was brutal, so I assumed you ganged up and all stabbed her once for all the things she put you through."

I blinked. "What do you mean the things she put us through?"

Fran stepped back, considering. The weight of her gaze was uncomfortable. She seemed to shake a thought away before she spoke. "It was hard to keep up sometimes because I had never met any of you. She told me about your brother."

I drew a sharp breath. I looked around to make sure there was no one within earshot.

This seemed to amuse Fran. Her smile was identical to Dani's. "And some boy you were seeing in secret." Fran craned her neck to look at the group I'd arrived with.

Ainsley sat on a pew, observing her nails. Martina, next

to her, engaged in conversation with Mabel and Tyrell. He had removed his black blazer, which hung over his arms crossed against his chest.

"Is he here?" Fran asked.

"About the other girls," I prompted.

Her lips twisted. "Stedmond was never short on drama. Her whole swim team was buying drugs and cheating to try and beat her. I think I recognized a few here today. Someone selling drugs." Fran checked off the list with her fingers.

I tried to keep up, matching people based on what I already knew.

"One of you was with a teacher. That was a big one for her. Someone isn't a student. She didn't seem to care about that one."

I took a step forward. "What do you mean 'isn't a student'?"

"I don't know. Dani said they made a deal for her not to talk about it. There was some crazy girl who sent her notes, but Dani said that she was harmless. It was someone else she was worried about. She thought someone was following her, leaving her gifts and weird notes. She was desperate to get out. She lost her phone, so I couldn't speak to her in the weeks before her death."

Another piece of the puzzle, one that could clear Raven's name, was in my bag, sitting in Tyrell's room. I swallowed, my throat struggling to get the words out. "Why are you telling me this?"

"You caught my sister's killer." She shrugged. "I guess I feel like I owe you."

She walked away, and a voice called out, asking everyone to move to the graveside.

A sea of bright umbrellas clashed with the black. Clusters of friends, family, and whatever we could be considered framed the small rectangular hole in the ground. I took a deep breath, but it seemed the open air evaded me. At the instruction of the funeral director, silence fell.

Tyrell held an umbrella over our heads, and my free hand was clenched in my pocket. The clatter of rain wasn't enough to drown out the sobs and sniffs. I peered at the wreaths and long-stemmed flowers on her coffin, and rain ricocheted off the casket as it lowered into the ground. Just like that, she was gone.

Some of the visitors stayed by the graveside. Most people streamed back inside, shivering. A short man in a suit waved from the front of the room, and all eyes snapped to him.

I had never met Dani's parents. She had already been living at The Bells for a year when I moved in, but I recognized them from pictures. She shared the same angular jaw as her mother and her dad's narrow nose.

Dani's mom gripped her husband tightly, her lips quivering from the effort of holding back tears.

"Words cannot express the pain we feel today," her father said. "Dani touched everyone she met, filling lives with love, laughter, and her infectious smile. While our hearts ache with the loss of such an incredible daughter, we want to celebrate her life. In the short time she had, she lived it to the fullest. Never afraid to go after what she wanted or tell anyone what she thought."

A few people snorted a wet laugh.

"I knew Dani. I would lay awake wondering which teacher would call home to complain or what excuse she would have for picking a fight with Francesca, and now I yearn for those sleepless nights instead of the empty life I am living because she's gone." His voice broke, and he cleared his throat; his wife tightened her grip on his arm. Sobs turned to cries. "I don't want to dwell on the sadness of this moment. Let's remember Dani for the joy she brought to our lives, even if we didn't know it at the time. Rest in peace, my beautiful daughter. Until we meet again."

THIRTY-TWO

The cold bit through my skin, and goose bumps prickled against Tyrell's blazer as he placed it over my shoulders. I breathed in the soft smell of fresh citrus that always reminded me of him.

"Can't you drop us closer?" Ainsley called as Bianca pulled up to the parking lot outside the rec center.

"I have to return the key to the rec center," she replied in a small voice.

Ainsley rolled her eyes. She parted her lips, but whatever she was going to say was cut off by the van door sliding back. Seat belts unbuckled, and footsteps scuffled along the wet pavement.

I braced myself against Tyrell as I rose and exited the van.

"Not the worst day out I've had," Ainsley said, leading the way back to The Bells.

Martina, Mabel, and Nia followed. I hung back. My room had looked different in the daylight. As pitiful as it was, most of the shadows were chased away, voices could be heard, and I knew everyone was awake. The threat lay in the stillness. So far, whoever had broken into the room only did so in the dark.

A shiver ran through my neck, and Tyrell tightened his blazer around me. "I'll check in and pick this up tomorrow."

"I'm coming back with you. I'm not tired and still need my bag from your room."

"It's late. You need to rest. Mabel will help you. You can't even get out of these clothes by yourself."

"Oh, because that's something you haven't helped with before."

Tyrell chewed his cheek.

My lips quirked up, and my heart fluttered.

"It's different." He recovered, pushing at the small of my back. "I'll bring your bag over in the morning. Once you have had a good night's sleep."

"Are you forgetting someone out there threatened to kill me?"

He frowned. "I could stay with you instead."

"No, it's okay." I smiled. Either way, I wouldn't get the time with the cell phones I wanted. If Tyrell came to The Bells, he would force me to sleep, and now, I had another lead to follow.

"Let me walk you back."

I glanced over my shoulder. Mabel's red hair was still visible. "It's fine. The girls are there."

"Okay." He stepped forward, his hands rising to the nape of my neck.

My heart rattled then sank as he pulled the blazer closer around my shoulders. "Be safe. I'll see you tomorrow."

"First thing," I reminded him. "I'll send you the code to get in."

A weight settled in my chest, and my limbs felt heavy.

"Oh. You waited for me." Bianca reappeared. She shuddered as the heavy doors to the rec center closed behind her. "Thanks. After everything with the stalker, I hate walking alone so late." She stepped past me. "Let's go."

I glanced over my shoulder. Tyrell kicked at a stone on the pathway then strode with his hands in his pockets.

"I'm glad the rain's stopped," Bianca said. "Everything always seems so much worse when the weather is bad."

We threaded the path, and the girls' voices were audible ahead. I wasn't in the mood for small talk, and Bianca wasn't particularly good at it. My mind kept racing to Tyrell. He was always there for me. I wished I hadn't ruined things, and we could go back to whatever we were before. I stared at the pathway, fighting the urge to kick one of the stones on the path, when someone screamed.

My head shot up, searching for the source of the piercing cry. The girls were out of sight now, already past the doors for The Bells.

Bianca whimpered faintly.

I turned to find her paces behind.

She shook her head. "What if there's something wrong?"

I looked back to the entrance. The wind howled, and cars rumbled in the distance, but other than that, there was silence.

"It's okay." I tried to sound more confident than I was. "It's probably just Nia moaning about something."

I ran up the steps. Bianca jogged to keep up. I typed in the code. Everyone was still in the lobby.

"What happe—" I started, but the black-and-blue stands of hair flopped over Ainsley's back answered the question.

"They let you out?" Bianca said in disbelief.

Raven drew her head back. Ainsley's shoulders were still hunched. She wasn't as receptive to the hug as Raven.

"I don't know why, but they questioned me a bit more and figured out I couldn't have killed Dani."

"But your confession?" I asked.

Raven's eyes dropped to the floor.

"It doesn't matter now," Ainsley chimed in. "We are just glad you're back."

"It's been ages." Mabel threw her arms around her, squeezing tight.

"Where have you been?" Raven mumbled into Mabel's wild curls.

"Nowhere as bad as you," she said, and I noted this was the second time Mabel had avoided answering the question directly.

"I didn't think you were coming back," Nia mumbled as she walked toward her room. "I've already started to get rid of your stuff."

Raven took in a sharp breath. She muttered something to herself. Then her eyes narrowed on me. "What happened to you?"

"Jamie killed Dani," Ainsley said, "and then tried to kill Sienna." She waved the words away as though it were less important. "We have a lot to catch up on."

Raven's mouth hung open as Ainsley led her by her arms into the common room.

"Mabel," I called before she could follow. "Can you help me get out of this dress?" I raised my sling, and pain seared through my arm.

"Sure." She smiled brightly.

Bianca hovered for a moment. "Does this mean whoever stabbed her is still out there?"

In here, I thought.

"It means I might finally be able to tolerate living with Ainsley again," Martina said with a wavering smile.

"It was a beautiful funeral. Dani, you were so loved," Mabel said to the room as we entered. "I wish I hadn't been away for so long. I don't even remember the last thing I said to her."

I thought back to the night of the murder. *What was the last thing I said to Dani?*

I closed my eyes as she unclasped the sling. Pain radiated as I lowered my arm. Mabel moved behind me, her hands gently pressed against my back. She was kind and caring, but something was off. I swallowed. Ainsley had a terrible investigative technique, but there were benefits to being direct. People tended not to lie if they believed you already know the truth.

"How long haven't you been a student for?"

Mabel's hands shook on the zipper then dropped to her sides. I had expected anger or denial, but her blue eyes were wide, and her hands shook as I reached out with my good hand.

"How do you know?"

A breeze brushed the goose bumps on my exposed back. "Something Dani's sister said."

She nodded, pursing her lips.

"It's okay." I squeezed her hand. "What happened?"

"I couldn't afford to pay for another year. So I'm not technically a student. I've been working and saving so I can come back and graduate. Dani knew, but she just warned me to be careful."

Her glossy eyes flicked to mine.

"Careful?"

She nodded, her cheeks burning.

"Are you in some kind of trouble?"

"No," she said softly. "Not yet."

I waited for Mabel to elaborate, not wanting to press.

Her shoulders were hunched, and her breath hitched. She parted her lips then brought them together in a pained smile. Whatever she was about to say was gone.

"Do you know anything about what happened to Dani?"

She flinched before shaking her head. "She helped me. I promise I don't know anything about her murder. I'm sorry." Tears brimmed her pale lashes, and her eyes searched mine for confirmation that I believed her.

"Okay. Is there anything I can do to help?"

Mabel gulped. "There is nothing you can do. But thank you." She breathed. "I want you to know I'm not a bad person." Her voice ticked up at the end of the sentence, almost in question. She didn't meet my eyes. She glared at our clasped hands.

I didn't know why she didn't seem to believe it herself. Mabel was the only person in The Bells who cared for everyone, the only person truly upset that Dani was gone. I didn't know what it meant to be a good person, but I recognized when someone was bad, and Mabel was far from that.

I nodded, giving her the confirmation she needed. "I know."

THIRTY-THREE

Pain seared through my arm. I gritted my teeth, biting down on a strap as I attempted to tie my sling with my good hand. Then blood rushed to my ears. My heart raced as a series of knocks shook the door. I jolted, and the sling flittered to the floor. I squeezed my eyes shut and sighed, remembering Tyrell promised to be here first thing, but it wasn't Tyrell; it was Ainsley. She stepped into the room, leaving a trail of shea butter scent in the air. A scarf tied down the edges of her hair. She spun to face me. "Well done. We did it."

I blinked. "Did what exactly?"

"Freed Raven."

"*We* didn't do anything. We don't even know who stabbed Dani."

She walked to my desk and peered into my open makeup bag. "As someone who no longer despises you—"

I tried not to take offense.

"Maybe you should drop the whole searching-for-the-stabber thing."

"You don't want to know who stabbed her?"

She shrugged, opening a small tube of concealer, and made a small patch on the back of her hand. "Only to complain that they didn't let me do it myself."

"You know, if I didn't know any better, I'd say this change of heart is a little suspicious."

"No, it's not. I only wanted Raven back. I'm not going through the effort for Dani. Now we can let the police do their jobs." She gasped. "I can never find this in my color. How did you get it?"

"What about being worried for the safety of everyone in the house or not wanting to live with a murderer?" I asked, taking the deep-brown tube she was admiring.

She cocked her head.

I sighed. "You have to buy it online. They won't have the color for our skin tone in stores."

Ainsley took out the beauty blender. "Technically, the stabber isn't a murderer. Jamie is." She tapped the product onto the back of her hand until it blended with her smooth, dark skin. "Dani made enemies and then pushed them to their limits. I know my limits."

I held back a laugh.

"All I'm saying is that if I were you, I would reconsider if it's worth trying to figure this all out." She dropped the beauty blender and strode to the door. "And maybe redo your eyeliner." She pointed at my left eye. "That one's wonky." Then she shut the door behind her.

In that short conversation, I had been insulted, complimented, and effectively abandoned. I grabbed a wet wipe and rubbed my failed attempt at winged eyeliner. I couldn't understand how Ainsley was ready to move on from all this. Jamie may have been the reason Dani died, but it was an accident. In his own twisted way, he loved Dani. He couldn't physically harm her. There was no love lost with whoever had stabbed her. I remembered the slickness of the blood, burning as it seeped into my skin. Her cuts and slashes were feral, and whoever was capable of that was a person to be feared.

Three soft knocks issued from the door. "Sienna?"

My heart squeezed. I dropped my makeup, not quite finished. I still looked considerably better than I had the last few times Tyrell had seen me.

I opened the door, and he entered with my bag hung over one shoulder.

"Thank you." I refrained from snatching at it, desperate to rush through the cell phones. I sat cross-legged on the bed.

Tyrell picked my sling up from the floor and took the desk chair.

"I couldn't get it on," I said.

He placed the bag on the bed and helped me put on the sling, his touch light and gentle. I held my breath.

Once it was on, I propped my bag onto my lap. I unzipped it then rummaged through the contents until I saw it. Wrapped in a plastic bag was Dani's phone.

"Whose is that?"

Heat crept up my neck. "Um, Dani lost her phone two weeks before she died." I looked up as realization dawned on Tyrell's face. His brows rose, and I could almost see the word *police* on his lips. "Jamie said he didn't take it. It was left for him. I think it was by whoever stabbed Dani."

Tyrell scratched his brow. "We need to give it to the police."

I took Dani's phone and turned it on. "I will right after I —" The blank screen mocked me, flashing an image of an empty power bar.

"It's dead?" Tyrell's relief was audible.

I grabbed the wire protruding from my desk. "I think I have the same brand." I squealed with excitement as the wire clicked into Dani's phone.

"Do I want to know whose this is?" He nodded to the slim black cell phone on my lap.

"I think it's Jamie's." I pressed a button, and the screen lit up. Its battery was at fifteen percent, and I had no charger. This could be the only chance I would get.

Tyrell leaned over my shoulder. There was nothing immediately identifying the owner. No background pictures or screensavers. I went straight to the contacts— only twelve were saved on the phone, all named after locations. My eyes snagged at The Bells. I clicked, and my stomach churned. The first word I saw was my name.

Sienna is with Tyrell 2-4.

The person on the other end responded: *Dani is not in her room. The house is empty.*

Weeks. They had been watching us for weeks. Blood drained from my face. The air shifted, icy and cold. The warmth of Tyrell's breath prickled against the raised hairs on my neck. It was someone in The Bells. I scrolled through the messages. No one else was mentioned by name. There were three messages from The Bells asking Jamie to meet them.

Seventy-three Noytin Road. Now.

Please, stop it, Jamie had replied.

I scrolled. "On the day Dani died, Jamie asked them to stop. Only one message was sent after."

It doesn't matter now. She is leaving tonight. I will kill her myself.

Tyrell's breath hitched.

"Whoever it is, they are here." My voice was weak; the words were barely a whisper. Understanding rushed through me in waves of panic. I had been living with them, and if Dani hadn't died from the poison, she would have died at their hand.

Tyrell was up. "Let's get out of here. You can stay with me."

"Wait." I gripped the cell phone. "We have a direct line of communication to the would-be killer."

He raised a brow. "To give the police?"

But I was already typing, clicking the number six three times to get the letter *O*.

Tyrell's face scrunched, and he ran his hand across his face. "Sien—"

"Sent." I turned the cell phone so Tyrell could see my message.

Who is this?

My mind was reeling. Nia, Raven, Bianca, Mabel, Martina, and Ainsley—only one of them would have received my message, but I couldn't trust any of them. Tyrell took the phone from my hand and looked through the rest of the phone. I couldn't imagine what could be worse.

Tyrell clicked on a number saved as Graybone. "Empty." He continued to click. "Wait, look."

My back straightened.

Tyrell turned the phone to face me, and the first thing I noticed was the date—the day Dani died.

I can't do this anymore.

Too late. Even if you back out now, you're going to prison for a very long time.

That was it. The end of the conversation.

I looked up at Tyrell. "Do you think it was about the poison?"

He shrugged. "Could be the drugs."

I nodded. I didn't believe it, but I couldn't accept the alternative—that someone else knew Dani was being poisoned and had done nothing to stop it.

A chirp sliced through the room. Tyrell stilled. The sound had come from the cell phone in his hands.

I hadn't expected a fast reply. I'd considered the possibility that I wouldn't get one at all, but a new message flashed on the screen.

This is your last chance to stop Sienna.

My heartbeat thrashed in my ears. The walls closed in. Tyrell's gentle touch felt like a vise-like grip, keeping me trapped here for one of my housemates.

Why did you stab Dani?

The cell phone pinged seconds later.

I gave you opportunities to walk away from this.

I typed out my message as quickly as the phone keys would allow and sent it. The phone shook. The chat sent back a message.

We're sorry, you have reached a number that has been disconnected or is no longer in service.

Tyrell blew out a breath. "We should give this to the police."

I agreed, my throat too tight to vocalize it. I let Tyrell take the cell phone from my hand and drop it back into the plastic bag. Then Dani's phone's logo lit up the screen. It finally had enough charge enough to power on. Unfortunately, that was all it could do. It was locked, and after several attempts of any four digits I thought were remotely connected to Dani, it was blocked.

I set the phone down. There was nothing to be learned from it. Tyrell placed it in the plastic bag.

"The police should be able to get into it." His voice was soft.

Raven was being held by the police when the murder weapon was moved. I couldn't rule Ainsley out. Mabel wasn't here but had other places to stay on campus. It could be the perfect alibi. Bianca had countless motives and accomplices in Sam and Ashley. Martina was at the party, and she had never hidden her dislike for Dani.

I threw things onto the bed, and Tyrell neatly tucked them away in my bag.

I still had questions that wouldn't be answered on either cell phones or sitting in The Bells. Since Dani's death, Noytin Road had come up too many times to be ignored.

"Anything else?" Tyrell heaved the bag onto his back and slid the cell phones into his pocket.

I glanced around the room, and my eyes were drawn to the spot where I'd found her. "Can you give the phones to the police?"

Tyrell's brow furrowed. "We can do it together."

I shook my head, pressing my lips into a thin line. "I'm not ready to go back there."

Tyrell stepped toward me. "We should stay together."

"Someone needs to give them the phones, and Platinum is a lot safer than The Bells. I'll wait for you. I'll be fine." I opened the door and stepped out.

The Bells was deathly quiet. Lights flickered on as we walked through the hallway. Tyrell pursed his lips. He wanted to argue, but while we were in The Bells, it wasn't safe. He tried to change my mind on the walk to Platinum and suggested we could call the police to come to us. I shut down the idea, but it didn't stop him from trying again once we were behind the doors of 801.

I sat on his sofa, and he stood with his arms folded as he looked down at me. "Sienna, if anything happened to you."

"I'll be fine, I promise. The sooner the police have those cell phones, the sooner they can catch whoever it is."

Tyrell swallowed. "Don't let anyone in here."

"I know."

"And if you need anything, call me."

"I will." My arm pulsed in my sling.

Tyrell gripped the edge of the sofa and leaned over me. "I—" He hesitated then pulled back. "I won't be long." He strode to the door, and his hand hovered over the handle.

I smiled. "Thank you. You're the only one I can trust."

THIRTY-FOUR

Half an hour had passed before my body started to twitch. I paced the room. There was someone else, someone I had lived with, who knew my every move. I couldn't shake the feeling they knew I was there. I only had one card to play to be a step ahead. Seventy-three Noytin Road.

Other than The Bells, it was the only place connecting Dani, Jamie, and the other person responsible. It was also the same place Dani went to when she wanted to escape. Reruns of my favorite reality TV show chattered in the background. But I couldn't focus. Dani's voice was heavy in my head. I was close.

I took a piece of paper and scribbled down, *I'm fine. I will be back.* I couldn't text Tyrell. He would panic, and we were never good at saying goodbye. We were blurred lines and unspoken feelings, but I would do anything to protect him, and I didn't want him to be part of this.

I pressed my ear to the door, and when I heard no noise, I opened it.

"Oh," a voice drawled.

My jaw clenched, and I turned to the figure in the hallway.

Sweaty raised a brow and tucked his bicycle helmet under his arm. "So that's back on?"

I shifted, the panic easing. "None of your business."

"No, but Tyrell's a good guy. And you're a heartbreaker."

My chest tightened. "Aren't you going out?"

"Lisa's party. You coming? I haven't heard the story of how you fought Jamie off firsthand."

"No." I backed into the door. "I don't party."

"Fine. You can tell me next semester. Don't forget to do your slides over the holidays."

I tried to control the widening of my eyes.

"You totally forgot, didn't you?"

"I'll do it," I said through clenched teeth.

"Good." Sweaty clicked his door shut and walked toward the elevator.

I leaned against the door and released a breath. Maybe I should wait for Tyrell, but now the door was locked. The Bells wasn't safe, and I was ready to finish what was started.

The night breeze whipped around my ears, stripping away one of my senses. Overhead streetlights flickered, threatening to rob me of another. My pulse picked up. Rowdy students walked through campus. Their shouts and laughter were lost to the wind. I worried about the things I couldn't hear. Whoever had been watching me had been patient. I imagined eyes in the shadows and felt the weight of a glare. It was hard to know if any of it was real.

I glanced over my shoulder as headlights approached. The app on my cell phone said my cab was still three minutes away. I stepped back. The car looked similar to mine back home. The obvious difference was the lack of the word *murderer* spray-painted onto it. Heels clacked along the sidewalk, and shrieking girls bounded into the backseat of the car.

I waited, keeping my head low as I contemplated going back to The Bells. I could confront my housemates, but I didn't trust that any of them wouldn't hurt me. Dani's lifeless body flashed in my head as the screech of tires ran up the street. A cab stopped in front of me, and a middle-aged man leaned across the passenger side and rolled down the window.

I cupped my ears to hear him clearly.

"Sienna?"

I nodded, and he settled back into his seat. I slipped into the back, hands shaking as I fastened my seat belt.

"Noytin Road?" he asked, slow and uneven. He raised his gaze to the rearview mirror, and his eyes fell to my sling. "Are you sure?"

I nodded, shifting in my seat to bend out of view. The engine started, and I stared out the window, watching as front yards adorned with rows of flowers, security cameras, and gates became overgrown weeds littered with broken wood, remnants of what would have been a gate.

A long beep bellowed from in front, and a group of people rushed out onto the street, faces covered, all dressed in black.

The driver shook his head. "So many gangs here," he said under his breath.

I swallowed hard. We drove down two more streets before we stopped outside a graffiti-covered two-story house. The number seventy-three was spray-painted in white. One window on the bottom floor was covered with cardboard, and shards of glass remained on the outside. The second window hid the inside behind blinds. Any care for the house had been neglected long ago. Moss and ivy claimed it as their own. I double-checked the number in hopes that it was the wrong place.

"This is it," the driver confirmed.

"Thank you," I croaked and opened the side door.

"You be careful in this area," he called.

I managed to pull my lips into a smile then shut the door behind me.

My shadow dimmed as the cab headlights retreated. Weeds and twigs snagged at my ankles, and the tightness in my chest increased with every step I took up the path. I raised a fist, not allowing myself time to second-guess as I knocked on the door. A car alarm blared in the distance, but inside the house, it was silent. I would have thought there was nobody home if it weren't for the subtle movement of the blinds. A glow flashed behind a gap occupied by an eye. I stepped back, and the blinds snapped shut. I didn't see who was behind them, but they'd seen me, and now they were deciding on their next move.

I didn't have a plan or know how this place was linked to whoever had killed Dani. I pulled out my cell phone, and the door creaked back. The latch was still on. The space opened just enough for me to see half a face.

It was a woman who couldn't have been much older than me. A small piercing glinted on her nose. Strands of unnaturally black hair fell in her face. "Hello?"

"Hi. My name is Sienna."

Her brows seemed to rise in recognition.

"Is it all right if I come in? I have a few questions about a girl named Dani Bishop."

She stepped back, considering, then peered over my shoulder.

"It's just me."

The door slammed shut and reopened just as quickly, swinging back without the restriction of the latch. She stuck her head out, eyes darting across the isolated streets before gesturing for me to enter.

The floor creaked beneath me. I moved farther into the living area. The torn carpet revealed scuffed wood. Dust and damp coated the tattered and fading wallpaper. It was far from what I could consider a home. It looked as though she could flee at any moment. No personal items. There was a gold frame, but I couldn't see the picture. It had been turned to the side, away from the room. But it'd been moved only recently—I noted the fresh swipe that disturbed the dust.

She tied her hair into a messy bun, her eyes never leaving me. "It's a work in progress." She chuckled silently to herself. "Please take a seat." She gestured to three camping chairs.

I stepped over a blue sleeping bag and sank into one.

"Can I get you something to drink?"

"No," I answered quickly, too quickly, then added, "Thank you."

She shrugged and took a seat opposite me, her eyes falling to my sling. "What's wrong with your voice?"

My hand rose to my throat. "It's just a bit sore. Did you know Dani Bishop?"

"Yes, and I heard about what happened." She shook her head, her bun swaying, and now that the hair was out of her face, she looked familiar.

"Were the two of you friends?"

She laughed. "No. Dani didn't have friends. We fought nonstop and hated each other. But it doesn't matter what I thought about her. No one deserves to die like that."

"Yeah," I breathed, the thoughts of her lifeless body coming back to me. "I'm sorry, what's your name?"

She hesitated. "Candice."

Something clicked. This must have been the run-down house Sam and Ashley had followed Dani to. "Dani came here. You were supposed to help her leave."

Candice leaned back. "She's dead now. Why did you want to talk to me about her?"

"I shared a room with her, and one of the things I found among her things was this address." Heat crept to my cheeks. "I have been looking into what happened to Dani, and this place keeps coming up."

"Oh." She drew her head back, but there was no surprise in her tone.

"I just wondered how this was linked to Dani."

"This house is very convenient for hiding things. She knew she was always welcome here if she got in any trouble. And Dani was always in trouble."

Something seemed off.

"Didn't they catch the guy that did it? Jamie." She drew

out the name. "They were together while we were in school together. He was obsessed with her. It's hard to imagine he would do something like this to her."

"Yeah." I cupped my broken arm.

We fell into silence. Candice was in no hurry to break it. Her eyes darted from mine to the broken arm.

I wet my lips. "What was it like when you lived at The Bells?"

"Chaos. You've probably heard about Vivi. Most of the girls from my year at The Bells are in prison. I dropped out, but it's hard to find a job. I've had to look at other ways to support myself." She gazed around the room.

"Do you ever see Jamie here?"

"No."

"Maybe it's not about you. It could be someone who was here before you."

"There was no one here before me. Students have used this place for ages. Whenever we wanted to get away from campus, we'd party here, and when we got bored, maybe we would have the occasional study session." She gave a thin-lipped smile. The expression didn't reach her eyes.

It didn't look like anyone had been here to party in months. "Why did it stop?"

"Vivi died. This was Tessa's spot, and she's in prison." She looked over my shoulder at the driveway. "Sorry I couldn't be of more help. I try to stay out of anything that has to do with Stedmond. Do you need a ride back to campus?"

It was safer to go back the way I'd come, and there was no car parked in the driveway unless it was hidden beneath the overgrown plants and weeds. "No, thanks."

Candice crossed her arms. "I haven't been one hundred percent truthful."

I sat up straight, my stomach sinking. "About what?"

Before she could reply, a buzz rang from my pocket. I took out my phone. Tyrell's name lit up on the screen. I groaned. He must have gotten back from the police station by now and seen that I was gone.

"Pick it up," she demanded. "Don't mind me."

I answered, my throat tight. "Tyrell?"

"Where are you?" His voice was frantic.

"I'm okay. I'm—" I glanced up at Candice. Her brown eyes watched intently. "I'm sorry for leaving. I'm fine."

She had just been about to tell me something. I had been getting better at sensing dangerous situations, and right now, I knew I was in one.

"Where? Send me the address, and I'll come and pick you up."

"Okay," I said slowly.

Candice stood up, a smile plastered on her face. "I've got to make a quick call," she said, pointing to another room at the back of the house.

"The police are hopeful the phone will turn up something. So you need to lay low for now and keep safe. This will all be over soon."

"Um." The sound was all I managed before Tyrell breathed my name on the other end.

"I know, but I'm at Noytin Road with Candice. She lived at The Bells last year." I lowered my voice. "I can't put my finger on it, but something is off."

I heard the car screech. "Door number, Sienna. We can come back later tonight with the police."

I lifted the phone from my ear. The temperature had dropped. Everything lay still. "Seventy-three," I whispered. "Ty, I'm going to call you back."

I heard the start of his protests before I cut the call.

The camping chair almost toppled as I rose to my feet, then I slowly walked to the room Candice had gone through. The first thing that hit me was the cold. The chill seeped into my skin. I turned on the flashlight function on my phone. It was a kitchen with cracked countertops and missing tiles. Under the pile of dishes, the sink was stained. I moved the flashlight through the room, shadows twisting in the corners.

"Candice?"

I made my way to a door at the back. It led to the backyard. A large dumpster was the only thing visible over the weeds. There was no sign of movement. No sound. She was gone.

A slam shattered the silence. Not from the kitchen, but from the living room I had just left. I raced back, my heart thudding against my rib cage. There was someone there.

Their features were replicated; a younger version was framed in a photograph. From this angle, I could see the photo that Candice had turned to hide. Her hand draped over a young girl's shoulder. She had brown eyes, a high ponytail, and a tight-lipped smile.

"Martina?"

THIRTY-FIVE

"Sienna?" Martina's brows furrowed. One foot hovered over the doorframe. "What are you doing here?"

I blinked, trying to process. Martina's ponytail swayed as she surveyed the room behind me. If I was right, Martina had been here at least once before to threaten Dani with a bat. I couldn't read her expression as she stepped over the threshold, the door still ajar.

I moved back, maintaining the distance between us. "I was speaking to Candice about Dani."

"Candice?" She huffed, the sound sharp. "Candice doesn't live here. My sister does."

Something in my stomach shifted, and I recognized the expression on her face. Rage.

"Where is she?" she hissed. Her eyes bulged.

"Sh-she left. She went out the back." I gestured over my shoulder, and Martina marched toward the kitchen. A switch flicked, and a feeble beam lit the room.

"Maria!" she screeched. "Come out. I know you're in here."

My legs wouldn't move. I had spoken to Maria. The last wanted person in connection to the death of Vivienne Marks.

The door to the backyard flew open. Martina didn't scream this time, but I could hear the faint sound of leaves crunching and low calls. Then the door slammed shut, the lock rattling uselessly.

I thought about calling the police so Martina wouldn't have to. I didn't regret turning August in, but I wished someone else had to live with the guilt.

Martina stormed back into the living area, breathing heavily, nostrils flared, fingers flexed around a brown handle.

My mouth fell open. My knees went weak at the silver glint at the end of her sleeve—a knife.

"Maria," she called.

I took a step back. "Martina, calm down."

"Did you know she is the reason why Dani is dead?"

I couldn't form coherent thoughts. Everything pointed to someone from The Bells. Someone who needed access. I hadn't recognized Maria, but most people at Stedmond would.

She jutted the knife. "This stops today. Have you already called the police?"

"No." I raised my hand. The other developed its own heartbeat, trapped beneath the sling. "Maybe you should put the knife down before I do."

"You don't know what she has put my family though." Martina wasn't focusing on me. Her eyes darted around the room. Bloodthirsty. Manic.

I thought of August. "I understand more than you think."

"How did you know she was here?"

"I didn't even know it was her until you told me. Let's go back to The Bells, call the police."

"No one knows."

"Just me and you."

She turned, eyes fixed. "So you'll understand why I can't let you leave."

A coldness seized my core. My mouth fell open, but no words escaped me.

She stilled the knife in my direction. "Your cell phone."

"Let's call the police. This isn't the way to deal with your sister."

Martina closed her eyes, her smile widening. "I would never betray my sister."

I felt sick. The words twisted something in my stomach. My quivering lips released a shaky laugh. "Martina, please, you don't want t—"

"No, Sienna. I do. And you saw what I did to Dani. You were the one to find her, weren't you? Or I guess I was. I just didn't realize it." She laughed, stepping closer. One hand gripped the knife. The other was open palmed.

I took my cell phone from my pocket. Messages from Tyrell lit the screen before Martina snatched it.

"What did you do to my sister?"

"Nothing."

She tilted her head and paused. "Sit down." She flicked the knife toward the camping chair. "I warned you," she said, slipping my cell phone into her back pocket. "You just wouldn't stop."

I didn't move. The door was a few paces behind me. With my broken arm, I could never overpower her, but I could run. I just needed to buy time.

"Did Dani threaten to turn your sister in?" It was the only thing that made sense. Dani had known where Maria was, and I should have known it wasn't like Dani to help anyone. "She was blackmailing you."

"She was poison. Jamie did the world a favor."

I took a fraction of a step backward and shuddered. Dani's corpse crept into my mind. Skin stained red, flesh ripped.

"I wanted to do it myself."

Another step back. "You didn't plan this with Jamie?"

"He wanted to hurt Dani for his own reasons. I didn't question him, and he didn't ask about me. Sienna?"

I froze.

"Do you think I'm stupid?"

My heart thrashed.

"Just out of curiosity." Martina stalked forward. "Where are you planning to run? You came here by cab, and you don't have a cell phone. This place isn't safe for someone like you, all alone." She pressed the flat side of the knife against my sling. Pain shot through my arm.

She held my shoulder, finger threading down to grasp the sling's material. "Let's take this off."

She slashed through the material and tugged at it. She jerked it free, glee in her face. My arm dropped motionlessly at my side, my body convulsing in agony.

"Move." She shoved me, away from the door, holding the knife high and pointing it toward the camping chair. I sucked in a breath as pain pulsed. My arm was on fire, but I sat, tears streaming down my face, a hand cradled around my limp arm. Martina moved to the TV stand. There was no TV, just a cluster of cables. She pulled at them, not bothering to untangle them as she dragged them toward me. I hunched over to contain the pain. But Martina was behind me, pulling back. I screamed as my arms were twisted behind my back. I wrestled, swinging wildly with the one arm I had. Until I couldn't. The strike came from behind. My ears rang, and my vision blurred as hot tears streaked down my face.

I heard the knife clatter to the floor, but I couldn't fight back. Everything hurt as Martina bound my wrists behind my back, grunting from the effort as my arm popped. There was another sound, something outside the house. Martina heard it too. She moved quickly, turning off the lamp and blowing out candles. Then she raised the knife to my throat and a finger to her lips.

A weak beam of light came through the blinds. Headlights. I heard a car. Maria could have gone to get a car, or maybe someone else knew she was here. I didn't want to allow myself to believe the alternative. *Tyrell.* I bit down on my lip, and a sense of hope rose in my chest. Tyrell was coming to help.

The headlights shut off, and we plunged into darkness. Two dim candles burned, just enough to make out Martina's movements in the silence. She paused. Her head was at an angle, as if she were listening for something.

The faint sounds of a conversation outside the house made their way through the ringing in my head. Martina moved behind the front door, knife ready for an ambush.

The conversation was growing louder, or the ringing in

my head had quietened. There were at least two people. Footsteps approached, cushioned by the leaves and twigs.

I thought Tyrell would have come alone, but maybe he'd brought the police.

The footsteps got closer—my only hope. I waited, and so did Martina, ready to attack anyone who opened the door. I wouldn't let her hurt Tyrell, but I needed to time it right. Everything stilled. No steps. No breathing. Then the door swung back.

"Behind the door," I screamed. It took all my energy, but the sound of a car engine drowned it out. Strips of light came through the blinds once again. Headlights illuminated the room enough to reveal the rage in not only Martina's eyes, but also Maria's.

THIRTY-SIX

Hope raced away with the retreating headlights. Maria rushed into the room, closing the door behind her, and fixed two locks before facing the room.

Martina's face lit up, embracing her sister. Maria bore a thinner frame than her younger sister, but it was comical that I hadn't seen the resemblance sooner.

I tried to steady my shaky breaths. It was all I could focus on. The rush of cold air came hard and fast, along with the realization that no one was coming to help. And now there were two of them.

"There was a boy out there looking for her." Maria peered through the blinds.

Martina pulled her back and adjusted the blinds to block out any light. "Probably her boyfriend, Tyrell."

"He's cute," Maria said.

My stomach clenched.

Martina crossed the room. She leaned over and tightened the bonds around my wrist. "What did you say to him?" she asked over her shoulder, disappearing into the kitchen.

"I told him she was here and that we spoke for a while. She asked some questions about Dani, then got a cab and left."

Martina was back. A wicked grin formed on her face, and a rusted can hung from her two fingers. "Good. Now we have to get rid of her and find somewhere for you to go. I'll have to come with you this time."

"No." Maria's face fell. "I won't let you ruin your life for me. You go back to school."

Martina shook her head. "I can't. It's only a matter of time before they figure out I had something to do with—" She stopped, her face reshaped in the darkness.

I stilled, trying to read her expression. I killed the rising hope in my chest. No one was coming to help.

"Let's go," Martina whispered. But she didn't move toward the door. She took off the lid of the can and spilled its contents onto the floor.

"It's gasoline," Martina said calmly.

I always thought her calmness was one of her best attributes, but now all I saw was how this equipped her with the ability to get away with murder. I had no doubt she was going to kill me, and she wouldn't even lose sleep over it.

Maria had turned her back. She produced a duffel bag and began packing, placing the picture of the sisters within her rolled-up clothes.

"Normally, I like to plan." Martina swung the can in my direction, and gasoline soaked my clothes. She grinned down at me. "But you have been a problem for some time. You know my sister had nothing to do with Vivienne Marks dying. Dani lied to the police about what happened. The only reason she has to live her life on the run is because of Dani. Can you imagine how sick I felt knowing I had to live in The Bells with her? How angry I was when she found out where Maria was staying? She didn't even want money. It was never about blackmail. She just wanted to watch us squirm."

Martina dragged a camping chair toward me and sat opposite me. "It took me weeks to figure out how I would get rid of Dani. Lucky for me, I wasn't the only person who wanted Dani dead. You wouldn't believe how happy I was to see Jamie trying to 'fix'"—she used her fingers to air quote—"our water heater."

"You knew?" The word burned through my throat.

"Yes, the rest of you were a sacrifice I was willing to make. Of course, at the time, I didn't realize how incompetent Jamie was."

There was a thud as Maria dropped her bag onto the floor. She had finished packing. There was no longer a reason for them to stay. Or to keep me alive.

But Martina wasn't finished talking. "He was so scared I was going to call the police. He kept wanting to change his mind, and I was hoping the poison would kill her quicker." There was an arrogance in her voice now. "I knew she was leaving on that day. I couldn't risk her threatening my sister's safety. When I walked in." She raised her hand and glared at the knife. "I went into a rage. I couldn't stop. With every blow to her body, I was setting Maria free." Her eyes met mine. "What a sight."

I shook my head, desperate for the image not to come. It didn't. Something clattered in the kitchen. My head turned.

Martina and Maria paused. Their eyes widened. I knew better than to scream. Martina still sat in front of me, knife in hand.

"Are you sure you saw him leave?" Martina kept her voice level.

Maria launched the bag over her shoulder. "Positive." She placed a hat low on her head. "Should I meet you at the usual place?"

Martina nodded. "I'll go back to The Bells to get my things."

Maria moved to the front door.

"Wait." I knew the voice was mine, but I had never heard myself sound so desperate. "If you had nothing to do with Vivienne dying, why don't you just turn yourself in? You haven't killed anyone. You still have a chance. When Martina stabbed Dani, she knew exactly what she was doing. If you leave me here, it won't matter to the police if you are innocent anymore. And if the police don't catch you, as soon as you become too much of a burden, she will turn on you."

Another splash of gasoline landed in my hair.

Martina laughed. "I know what you're doing." Martina's voice was undeterred. "It's too late for that."

Cool liquid dripped from my head, and my blood chilled as Martina brought out a set of matches.

"I never gave my sister up. My mother was the one stupid enough to go to the police. How do you think she has been able to stay hidden for all these months? Who do you think warned her?"

"And how do you think the two of you will survive? You can't go back to Stedmond. It's too late." I swallowed the lump in my throat, ready to throw out the only thing I had left. "I gave the police Jamie's cell phone. It still has the conversations between the two of you."

Martina gritted her teeth, but determination still filled her eyes.

"And it's only a matter of time until Jamie gives you up."

She stared at a matchstick, considering. Then she turned and nodded at Maria to leave.

Maria tightened her grip on the bag. "Nice to meet you."

I gritted my teeth.

"I would love to stay." Martina struck the match. The flame lit her fiendish features. "But according to you, the police should be here for me any minute now."

Maria had opened the door, and the chilling breeze swept in. I closed my eyes, preparing for death for the second time in my life. Then someone screamed.

Martina's head shot up. She turned to follow her sister's scream. It was a warning, which she realized too late.

Tyrell tackled her, her body jerked, and she fell off the chair. My heart plummeted, and something roared in my head. My relief at Tyrell's arrival was short-lived as Martina smacked against the floor. The lit match fell with her.

I yanked and twisted against my restraints. The wires securing my wrists didn't budge.

Tyrell's eyes widened at the flames, which quickly spread through the room then snapped to me. He was up, rushing toward me and pulling at the wires.

Martina lay on the floor, winded. She leaned forward slowly, struggling to rise and coughing violently as smoke filled the room.

"Martina?" Maria stood at the front door, separated from her sister by the growing wall of fire.

Martina scurried to her feet, struggling to get any words out. She waved her sister away.

Maria gave her an unsure look. "Go out the back. I'll be waiting for you," she called before the intensity increased, and she disappeared behind the flames.

I was no longer bound to the chair. Wires clattered to the floor.

"Come on." Tyrell held me up, leading me toward the kitchen.

The door was covered in flames.

"We can run through," Tyrell said.

"No." I coughed, shaking my head. "You go. I'm covered in gasoline."

"Okay." Tyrell scanned the room. Thick smoke bore down on us, and the fire blazed, blocking the front door and the kitchen entrance. Black smoke obscured the only option we had left.

Tyrell covered my body with his. "Upstairs," he cried over the crackling flames, his grip firm as we kept our heads low and aimed for the staircase, keeping our backs to the wall. The handrail was already covered in flames.

We stormed up the stairs. The smoke thickened, and the heat became more powerful. My body almost gave out once we reached the top. Tyrell let go.

"Find a window and jump," he instructed, turning to go back down the stairs.

I opened my mouth to call after him, but I could only cough and wheeze. I waited, and moments later, Tyrell reappeared, clambering up the steps with Martina in one arm.

The living room was engulfed in flames. Tyrell followed as I burst into one of the upstairs rooms. It was an empty bedroom. One solitary stool was placed under the window. My heart leaped as I stumbled toward it. Blue and red lights flashed somewhere outside, and the sound of sirens fought to be heard over the roaring flames. I threw myself against the window, using my right hand to push it open.

Cold air rushed through the room. I tried to peer below, but the dim lights were not enough to penetrate the darkness.

Tyrell grunted. I turned. Martina was trying to break free and run back into the flames.

"Stop." Tyrell pulled her back then pressed her against the wall beside the open window. "You'll die."

She bared her teeth. "Why would you want to help me?"

My arm throbbed by my side, almost echoing her question.

The staircase was now up in flames. The only escape was through the window. People were below. I could hear the sounds of the voices calling out. We just needed to land safely.

Tyrell let go of Martina. She turned to run, but I thrust my leg forward. The blow landed on her stomach, sending her tumbling through the window and into the unknown.

"You kicked her?" Tyrell's voice was frantic. He peered below.

There were no screams of pain from Martina, just a soft grunt as she landed. I leaned back, hoping there was more than Martina to cushion our fall. Neighbors hung out their windows, shining light on the surface below, and I blew out a breath as a giant dumpster was illuminated. Martina desperately tried to climb out. Her brown hair and panic-stricken face became clearer in the light.

"Did you know that dumpster was there to break her fall?" Tyrell asked breathlessly.

"Sure." I stepped back into the room, bracing myself for the fall, my right arm hugging my left, I silently prayed I couldn't damage my arm any more than I already had.

I leaped, whirled slowly through the air, then clattered into the trash below.

"Jump," I called up, my throat burning from the effort.

The house was beginning to collapse on itself. The fence to the backyard had been bulldozed over, and firefighters approached, screaming instructions.

Tyrell braced himself.

I curled into a ball in the corner. Martina had one leg over the dumpster, then an arm appeared and pulled her out.

The metal tin shook as Tyrell landed in the center. More arms reached in, and the firefighters pulled us out. I bit back a cry. My body was in so much pain, I didn't have the strength to lift my head as water sprayed into the building.

Sweat poured from my forehead. I could still feel the heat radiating from the house as the firefighters led us across the street. Someone placed a foil wrapper around my shoulders and water in my hand. I tried to sip, but my throat closed in.

"Move over here," a stern voice called out to onlookers, which included Detective Collins.

My heart stilled. I tried to break out of the firefighter's grip. My head pounding, I searched the area. *Martina should still be here.* I twisted out of the hold, my feet gave way, and I tumbled to the ground. Firm hands caught me before I could hit the ground.

I blinked. She was there.

Martina leaned against a police car, unharmed and expressionless. Shelley patted the side of her body. She stared blankly at the house.

Shelley ran her hands along the length of her legs, and I stilled as Martina's eyes snapped to mine. She didn't move. She said nothing. She didn't have to. I could see the contempt in her eyes, then Collins walked toward me, blocking Martina from view.

"It wasn't just her," I croaked. "Her sister, Maria Lanzo."

Collins nodded. "We know. Officers are on the lookout."

I swallowed. "She stabbed Dani."

"Yes, Jamie has been talking," Collins said. "I hear we have you to thank for the cell phones. We can interview you both once you have been seen to. Can I trust you not to get into any more dangerous situations during that time?"

I flushed and nodded.

The paramedics checked us over. No lasting damage had been done, but my arm needed proper care at the hospital. They helped me into the van. The doors began to close as Tyrell approached.

"Wait." His face lit up as he saw me. "You're okay?" He climbed into the back of the van.

"Yeah. I didn't exactly follow the doctor's advice not to put any strain on it."

Tyrell smiled. "No. But it's twice now you've caught the killer."

"It's twice that you came to save me." I matched his smile. "I was scared you wouldn't come back." I fought the tears welling up. "Thank you."

THIRTY-SEVEN

I closed and locked my dorm room door with my good hand. The other throbbed, confined to a sling, reminding me she was real. Not the Martina we knew, but the monster who'd attacked Dani. It was the only thing anyone was capable of talking about—how it wasn't like her. At least Jamie was known for breaking the law. Martina was one of the most intelligent students at Stedmond. Her head always in a book, and she was the type of honorable person who would turn her own sister in to the police.

I didn't correct them. The school was fickle, and as students left for the holidays, I knew something else would be the topic of conversation when we returned.

"Oh." I paused. Nia was already in the hallway. Clothes peeked out her soft-shelled black suitcase painted over in blue-and-pink butterflies. "Tyrell said you were thinking of staying."

Nia tried to stuff a skirt into the small gap in her overwhelmed case. "I didn't want to go back home because everyone will probably ask about Michael, but I figured that was still better than staying here."

It was hard to work out if she was referring to the living or the dead.

"Have you heard anything more about his arrest?"

Nia huffed. "Nothing I'd be stupid enough to believe."

My heart picked up. "What does that mean?"

Nia squeezed the two sides of her suitcase together and tugged until the zipper reached the end. "Aren't you supposed to be leaving now?"

I wasn't. I was waiting for Tyrell, but I knew when I was being dismissed.

Nia blew out a shaky breath as I continued down the hall and turned into the common room.

Raven and Ainsley sat on the sofas. "Hey," they said as they turned, an unfamiliar warm greeting. Ainsley had hardly insulted me since we'd found out about Martina.

"How does it feel to roam Stedmond without anyone thinking you did it?" Raven asked.

I left my suitcase by the entrance and sat by Ainsley. Everyone had moved on so quickly. People who had accused me not too long ago asked for the details of the night Martina was arrested. "I could ask you the same thing."

Ainsley grinned. "At least some good has come from this. I finally don't have to share a room."

I pursed my lips. There was always a long waiting list for accommodation on campus, even for places prone to murder, but I wasn't going to be the one to tell Ainsley when we were getting along so well.

"I can't believe I spent the past few months sharing a room with a murderer."

"That's not the shocking part," I said. "I can't believe Martina was sharing the room with you and decided to kill Dani."

Ainsley bit back a smile. "You know, I always knew she was weird. The way she would always be sitting there quietly, just reading."

I rolled my eyes. "Of course, you would think she was dangerous because she liked to read a book."

"Between the two of us, only one is failing a class. I'm not the one with a fear of books."

I laughed. Somehow, it was nice to be a victim of Ainsley's sharp tongue again.

"Have the police said anything about Maria?" Ainsley asked.

My stomach clenched. There had been an update from Detective Collins. Nothing good.

"They said they have everyone on the lookout for her, and they don't think she could have gotten far or left the city."

Ainsley scoffed. "Is that supposed to make us feel safe?"

I clenched my fist and shrugged. I hoped now that Maria didn't have Martina's help, it was only a matter of time before she was caught. She had seen my face and knew I was directly responsible for her sister going to prison. Safe was the last thing I felt.

Raven leaned back into the sofa. "The crazy really does run in that family."

I winced. My body jerked before I could control its movement. I couldn't be more like my brother if I tried, but this was just proof that his actions would always be linked to me.

"I'm going now," Nia called from the hall, followed by the clicking of heels and dragging of a suitcase.

The girls mumbled unenthusiastic replies. There was only one clear shout of "Bye," then Bianca entered the room, shoulders high. Martina's arrest had improved her confidence. "We are the only ones left now."

"Where are all your things?" I asked.

"I'm staying for the break." Bianca's face darkened, and she sat. "I want to practice more in the pool."

Her loss at the fundraiser was more embarrassing than she was willing to admit, and since then, Ainsley hadn't said a word about the doping. That didn't mean she wouldn't. But it gave Bianca time to work on herself.

"Are you staying too?" Bianca unclasped her hands and looked up.

"No. I'm waiting for Tyrell. He's going to drop me at the station."

Bianca chewed her lip. "So, it's just me?"

"No," Ainsley said. "I got the job. And if you're staying, at least I have some form of company."

Bianca half smiled, as if unsure whether this was a compliment, then her brow furrowed. "Mabel's gone again. But her things are still here."

Raven sighed. "That means we won't see her again for months."

Bianca shook her head. "I'm not sure. She left her car."

"That doesn't mean anything with Mabel," Raven said. "There was a time she left, and she didn't even take her phone. She'll be back eventually."

"If she's not back soon, at least it gives us the chance to have that rust bucket towed," Ainsley said.

Bianca frowned.

Something was wrong. I parted my lips to ask what it was, but my cell phone rang. My heart fluttered as I answered the call. Tyrell was outside.

I said my goodbyes, tension easing as I walked out of The Bells. The longer a person stayed, the more of themselves they seemed to lose.

"Hey." Tyrell was waiting at the bottom of the steps. He smiled and reached out to take my suitcase.

"Hey," I said.

"Are you the last one?"

"No. Ainsley and Bianca are staying. And I think Raven leaves tonight."

"Ah. I missed Nia."

Nia and Tyrell had a budding friendship. As it turned out, Nia could be nice to people she liked.

"Did she tell you anything about Michael?"

"Yeah." Tyrell dragged the suitcase, and I fell into step beside him. "She said there's a rumor that Michael's arrest was drug related."

I paused. "Wait. Really?"

Tyrell shrugged. "Nia doesn't believe it. She said he'd never touched the stuff."

"But it makes sense. The police did say it had nothing to do with Dani's death."

Tyrell narrowed his eyes. "It's not even been a week since you caught two killers. Please don't tell me you want to investigate this too?"

I rubbed the back of my neck. "I'm just curious."

"During this break, I need you to be curious about normal things, like all the reality TV you're into and maybe how we can see each other." His words became mumbled. "I wouldn't mind driving down, and maybe we could go out to eat or something."

My heart swelled, and I chewed my lip. "I don't know. I should really be spending my holiday studying. I'm still behind in class. I might even have to take you up on the offer of being my tutor."

He sighed. "You are never going to let this go, are you?"

I shook my head playfully. "I would love to see you over the break." A lump in my throat formed as I thought about Tyrell. I swallowed. "I know I've always been." I paused and wet my lips. "Well, I have been—"

"Distant?" He offered with a wry smile. "Hard to read?"

"Let me finish before you interrupt a good moment."

He grinned then mimed zipping his lips.

"I know it's weird now, and this whole Dani situation didn't help, but I want us to." I sighed. "I haven't been open with you because I don't know if I will ever be able to believe that you won't hurt me. But one day, I would like to. I just don't know ho—" I shrugged, unable to finish.

"How about we start over? No secrets. Clean slate." He smiled.

I took a deep breath. "I'm Sienna. My brother is a convicted killer, and I tried to help him get away with it. I almost died twice in the past few weeks, and spending a prolonged period of time with me seems to result in the urge to commit murder or the actual act of being murdered. I hope this doesn't put you off me, because even though we just met, I really like you."

Tyrell beamed. "I'm Tyrell. My brother is a tour guide, and sometimes I help prank the customers. I almost died once in the past week trying to help someone special. Spending a prolonged period of time with me results in the urge to solve murders." He raised his brow. "Or to share my irrational fear of holes."

Now it was my turn to raise a brow.

"It's a long story." Tyrell laughed. "And even though we just met, I think you should know I really like you too."

MABEL

A secret could only be hidden for so long until it broke a person from the inside. Reality distorted, and you began to wonder if the perception people have of you was still the real you or if the all-consuming truth was all that was left.

I peered through the open window. Smoke billowed in the reflection. Low music filled the room, and I counted the columns of windows in the opposite apartment.

On the first floor, the TV flashed with a popular family quiz show. Children watched, pointing excitedly and jumping at the screen. On the second, a couple sat down for a late-night dinner, candles lit, laughter on their faces. On the third, a woman had a towel wrapped around her head. She jutted out her chin and walked at an awkward angle as though her green face mask were obstructing her view. From the fourth floor upward, it was black. Curtains, blinds, and screens concealed the insides, as though they knew the closer you got to the top, the more they should keep out.

I peered down from the eighth floor. Sweat filled my palms. My body trembled. I couldn't shake the sensation of falling. Droplets of rain splashed on the windowsill then dripped onto the floor.

"Close the window." Wren snapped a finger as he blew out smoke. "Any more rain, and we'll drown in here."

The girl by his side laughed. She wasn't any of the ones I had seen before. I didn't know if she went to Stedmond, but the fewer people who saw my face in here, the better.

I pressed my face to the glass. Cool water splashed my cheeks.

"You can go now, sweetheart," Wren said.

The girl groaned. I saw her outline rise in the reflection. Then feet slapped against the floor, and a door shut.

"Close it," Wren instructed. "I've put it out."

I turned. We were alone now. The last whisps of smoke were disappearing in the air.

Wren jumped off the sofa. "You're probably going to have to cover Stedmond now since Jamie decided to get arrested." He pulled a bag from under the glass table. "Your look definitely works better on the streets. Police just look at me and assume I'm a criminal."

He *was* a criminal. But so was I.

He threw a battered gym bag in my direction. "That's all of Jamie's stuff I managed to get. Oh, wait." He lunged forward, snatching at the bag, and pulled out small plastic wrapping with circular pills. "Normally, I up the prices so our clients cover it. But if Jamie is doing life, I might as well get something out of it." He smiled.

I felt sick.

"Anything else that's missing, we can blame on the stash found on Michael."

"Michael?" I stepped back, my feet splashing in the small pool of water.

Wren didn't answer. He tutted and turned to grab a kitchen cloth. He threw it at me, and I let it fall to the floor before I cleaned the wet patch with my feet.

I had never done drugs. I hated them. My best friend, Alex, had died of an overdose. I knew the effects they had. They ruined lives, but I was the one who supplied. He'd died because of me. Alex wasn't here to forgive me, but that was fine. I would never forgive myself.

"This is for the boss." Wren placed cash rolled up in an elastic band on the table.

I took it. This was the last time. It felt heavy. It burned my skin.

"Do you know where to go?"

I nodded.

The drop-offs were never direct, never at the same place or time twice in a row, and he was never there.

Stedmond was different at night. Footsteps echoed in the wide hallways. The absence of students and their chatter stripped away a layer of warmth. My heart thumped. I wanted to change my life. I needed to get away from Stedmond, drugs, and *him*. I changed my mind with each step, trying to find the right words to articulate my feelings, but they evaded me. And I was there.

Dim light escaped through the letters of Professor Locke engraved on the outside of the door. I raised my shaking hand and brought it down on the hollow wood.

"Come in."

I held my breath and pushed the door back.

Professor Locke sat behind his desk, the top button of his shirt unbuttoned. His usually tamed hair was unruly, and stubble was forming at the bottom of his chin. His eyes narrowed. "Mabel? Is everything okay?"

I closed the door behind me. "The drop-off was fine."

Professor Locke thrust out an open palm and nodded to the seat opposite him.

I took out my cell phone and gave it to him. He held the button to switch it off and placed it in his desk drawer as I took my seat, leaning back and glancing at the door. "What did you want to speak to me about?"

I swallowed. *Be honest. Direct.* "Do you know anything about Michael's arrest?"

He lifted his chin. "I know it means you're safe." He met my eyes in an intense glare. "That's all I care about." His voice was soft. It didn't match his stern features.

"Why did they find the drugs on him?" I knew the answer but wanted to believe it wasn't true. If he lied to me right now, I would go against my better judgment and believe him.

"Because I put them there," he said coldly, without regard for the life he had ruined.

I met his gaze, thick brows framing his dark pools of black.

Professor Locke placed his hand on his chest. "Michael

was blackmailing me, and he threatened to go to the police."

"He knew about the drugs?" My voice shook. I hated the selfishness in my worry.

"No." He sighed. "He knew about something else, but now he has bigger things to worry about."

I shook my head. "He's innocent."

"Would you rather it was me?"

I gasped.

He raised his eyebrows. It wasn't a rhetorical question.

"No." I shook my head. "Of course not. But we're killing people."

"They are killing themselves."

I released a shaky breath. I needed to end this. If I didn't do anything, more people would die.

"Mabel." He reached out a hand. "Do you think I would ever let them catch you?"

"It's not about that." I withdrew my hand, and it shook mercilessly under the desk. "I don't want to hurt anyone else."

"You'd be hurting me."

I looked up. He was always so calm and passive.

"I need you."

I let the words wash over me. He had never opened up before, never seemed vulnerable. But it didn't change anything.

"No." It was difficult, but I held his gaze. Something dark flashed across his eyes. It was gone in an instant, and I questioned if I had really seen it.

"Where was your conscience when Becky Minister got

high and fell from the roof? Or when Daniel Barnes almost froze to death? He couldn't get into his house because of the drugs you sold him."

Something twisted in my chest. My gaze fell to the floor.

"I made it possible for you to still attend Stedmond and make enough money to return next year. I never made you do anything you didn't want to do. I didn't ask you to sell drugs to your own friends."

"I don't do that anymore."

"But you did. Do you think Alex stopped using just because you refused to sell to him?" He released a humorless laugh. "Do you think all this stops because you want out? Do you believe there is a way out?"

I swallowed. "I will go to the police." I hadn't realized how much I meant it until it was out. I had no other option.

He considered my words, nodding in amusement. "And tell them what?"

The pain in my chest expanded. Professor Locke was always careful. I had never seen him handle anything himself. There was nothing that could lead back to him— just me.

He smiled. "I see you understand."

"We never mattered to you."

He slumped back into his chair. His eyes drifted to the ceiling.

"Did you even care when Jamie got arrested?"

He brought his face back down in a sudden movement. His eyes were steady. Determined. "If Jamie had listened to my instructions, he would never have been caught. He would still have some value if he didn't get cold feet."

"You knew?" The sickening realization hit me. I shot up.

The chair skidded, metal legs screeching across the hard stone floor. "You just let her die?" I shook my head and moved toward the door. My hand closed around the handle. Then the chill in his voice sliced through me.

"Mabel. You know I can't let you do that."

To be continued in *Secrets to Kill For*.

**Two students missing. Everyone's hiding secrets.
And it isn't long before someone turns up dead…**

ABOUT THE AUTHOR

Simbi Feyisara started writing from a young age, uploading incomplete (sorry!) romance stories online. Things took a turn when she committed her first murder—fictionally, of course—and she hasn't looked back since. When she isn't writing twisty YA thrillers, she is procrastinating, usually with tea and biscuits.

SIMBIFEYISARA.COM

www.ingramcontent.com/pod-product-compliance
Lightning Source LLC
Chambersburg PA
CBHW011552190726
48287CB00010B/2857